Clara Louise Burnham

A West Point Wooing

And other stories

Clara Louise Burnham

A West Point Wooing
And other stories

ISBN/EAN: 9783744751032

Printed in Europe, USA, Canada, Australia, Japan

Cover: Foto ©Andreas Hilbeck / pixelio.de

More available books at **www.hansebooks.com**

A WEST POINT WOOING

And Other Stories

BY

CLARA LOUISE BURNHAM

BOSTON AND NEW YORK
HOUGHTON, MIFFLIN AND COMPANY
The Riverside Press, Cambridge
1899

CONTENTS

A West Point Wooing and *The Cadet Captain's Experiment* are reprinted from "The Ladies' World" by permission of the publishers.

A WEST POINT WOOING

NEAR a window in the library at West Point a young woman was sitting. She held in her hands a book, but her eyes often wandered from the page to the smooth green lawn without, or absently sought the faces in the large paintings which line the dignified room.

In truth the life of a girl at West Point is so far more interesting to her than any effort of the fictionist, little wonder that the spell of the latter is feeble to hold her. She cannot spare time from the engrossing heroes and heroines in her actual surroundings to those who have not the pleasure of her acquaintance.

Of course there are stars of varying magnitude in the picturesque orbit of the post, and this brown-haired young woman in the library was a bright particular star of the present summer. Even many of the plebes — those downtrodden, wing-clipped butts of every upper classman's ugly or merry humors — knew her face and name. Two of them were in the library now, a forlorn Damon and Pythias, companions whose friendly bond was born of their common misery.

Damon, feigning to be absorbed in the cartoon of a comic paper, addressed his companion softly : —

"There is that Miss Elliott, over by the window."

The eyes of Pythias moved circumspectly thither and he started a little, but not enough to imperil the military bearing which had been dearly gained by many encounters with a versatile and fluent yearling corporal.

"I know her," he returned, and his heart began to beat until there was risk to his beautiful new buttons, despised of maidens, though never so shiny.

The sentiment which caused such commotion and made his face crimson was one which can scarcely be appreciated by one who does not know the daily petty miseries of a plebe at our military academy. When after weeks of daily rigors and heartfelt thanks that no one near and dear to him is by to witness his humiliations, he suddenly sees a face connected with home, the associations called up are overwhelming. That remote, happy time when he was a gay, careless individual, respectfully entreated, comes up before him, and the face, though once belonging to the most indifferent acquaintance, now becomes excitingly dear, and he is filled with an eager desire to be recognized.

The longing Pythias felt at present to strain Miss Elliott to his bell-buttoned breast would have remained just as strong if she had suddenly turned into old Jerry, his father's janitor. His uppermost thought was not for her blue eyes and the crisp freshness of her duck suit; it was that she had broken gingerbread with him at his mother's table.

"I am going to speak to her," he added.

"Don't!" responded Damon, in a whisper as explosive as he dared make it, at the same time grasping his reckless friend's arm. Damon had arrived at stolid heights, or depths, of philosophy, wherein he had decided that a glance or a word outside of grooves prescribed for the "beasts" and "things" which composed his class was not worth the candle.

Pythias was of more elastic material; but eager as he was, he cast a glance around the spacious room before shaking off his monitor's hand.

Damon anxiously perceived his valorous intentions.

"Wayne's spoony on her," he breathed; but Pythias was too far gone to hear reason. Even the name of Wayne, the adored, the worshiped, the unapproachable cadet-adjutant, failed to awe him. He had fallen under another spell, — the thought of home. He was a boy again, and this was only Sally Elliott, once the dearest friend of his sister Winifred. Not speak to her? *Well!*

For Damon with his neutral policy, it was an awesome sight to behold his companion cross the library with a free stride, and present himself before a belle of such importance that it was hard

even to decide whether she was an officer-girl or a
cadet-girl, so assiduous in her case were the attentions of both these antagonistic rivals.

"Miss Sally!" exclaimed Pythias, gazing down
eagerly on the blue ribbon of her sailor hat.

The young woman looked up, the mild surprise
and doubt in her eyes giving place in a moment to
recognition.

"You?" she said, offering her hand heartily.
"I'm glad to see you. I knew you were to enter
this summer. Sit down," she continued, in the
hushed voice due the place, but speaking cordially.
"How are you getting along? What do you think
of the Point?"

"Great place," returned the young fellow, accepting the chair, and bending only at the hips, as
he leaned toward her. "Never received so much
attention in my life."

Her eyes sparkled appreciatively as she scrutinized him.

"I have been thinking about you. Winifred
wrote me to hunt you up when I came. I was
asking Mr. Paxton about you yesterday."

At the mention of the tactical officer, Pythias
shook his head admiringly.

"Do you know Mr. Paxton? He is the spooniest tac. we have," he returned, and Miss Elliott
knew he was referring to the elegance of the lieutenant's appearance, and not to the susceptibility of
his heart.

"I see you have your uniform. Lots better than the shell jacket, is n't it?" she went on.

Pythias experienced a mild glow as she looked him over. One year from now her gaze should be unmixed with compassion.

"I asked Mr. Wayne about you, too," she continued, "but he could n't remember."

"Of course not," returned Pythias. "But I am Mr. Wayne's washerwoman."

"Indeed!" returned Miss Elliott, approving the smile with which this announcement was made. "He has the right stuff in him; he 'll do," she thought.

"Yes," went on the cadet, "I wash his gloves; clean his buckles, too. In fact, I get a good many buckles lent me, first and last."

Pythias looked so good-natured as he spoke that Miss Elliott nodded at him confidentially.

"I believe you have come here to stay," she said encouragingly, "and we are all going to be proud of you."

These friendly words, and the kind, familiar face, warmed the cockles of the lonely plebe's heart. In the fullness of his rare pleasure, he thought of Damon, and turned toward him with the intention of beckoning him over and introducing him.

A wild gaze of horror met his genial look. Each hair on Damon's head was evidently trying to rise. His face was as pale as the long tanning of the summer sun would permit. With one convulsive jerk of his hand, he summoned Pythias back, then feigned to be again absorbed in the papers on the table before him. Anon his eyes furtively rose to the library entrance, where was the apparition which had so discomposed him.

Geoffrey Wayne, the cadet-adjutant, had come in. He was dressed for parade, and the light glittered on his gold chevrons and radiated from his white, polished trousers, as he paused a second to adjust his sword-knot, his plumed hat in hand.

Damon trembled. He considered it quite among the possibilities for a violent explosion to shake the library from its foundation to its golden dome, if Wayne should discover a groveling worm of the dust like a plebe conversing with the girl he had distinguished by his own dazzling attentions.

Pythias, wondering at his friend's agitation, turned back to his companion.

"It was so fortunate I happened to meet you here, Miss Sally," he said. "There are so few places where I am allowed to go. I hope you will let me see you again. It does me more good than I can tell you. Just excuse me a minute, I have a friend over there" —

For Damon had again caught his eye and motioned so wildly that Pythias rose perforce, and moved in his direction.

Only just in time, according to Damon's judgment; for now the young adjutant's irreproachable figure came into the room. Pythias perceived

the lighting of the upper classman's fine brown
eyes, — sole expression of pleasure of the dignified
and impassive face at perceiving the form by the
window.

"'I thought you would never leave her," growled
Damon through stiff lips, when Wayne had safely
passed them. "I saw him come in, and if his knot
had n't got twisted he 'd have caught you."

"Caught me!" repeated Pythias indignantly,
unable to recollect all at once his helpless plebe
condition. "Nonsense! I am going back to say
good-by to her."

"You blooming idiot!" returned Damon, seizing
his companion by the arm with a force of mind
and body which ultimately carried him through
the academy's course with flying colors. "Your
head 's turned. Come out of this place. She 'll
understand."

She did understand, and she sent a pleasant nod
to Pythias across Wayne's broad shoulder, as the
former waved his cap to her in his forced departure.

"I 've been having a very pleasant chat with
your washerwoman," she said, when Wayne had
seated himself and was looking into her eyes with
an expression which he did not even wish to be
mistakable.

"Been to the laundry, eh? Well, Paxton is
certainly full of resource when it comes to entertaining a young lady!"

"I have just been assured that Mr. Paxton is the spooniest tac. you have, so I find I am quite right in admiring him," said Miss Elliott sedately.

"Oh, there's no doubt of that," returned the cadet.

"Your washerwoman is a man, as it happens."

"Oh, got Chinamen in, have they?"

"Geoffrey Wayne, you don't know what I'm talking about."

"That is nothing new. Two years' experience has adjusted my brain to that."

"I am talking about the plebe who washes your gloves," announced Miss Elliott, with dignity.

The adjutant raised his eyebrows.

"What makes you?" he asked lightly.

"Because I like him. I've always liked him. Why, I have held him in my lap lots of times."

Wayne looked a second, then remarked:—

"Odd taste, that."

"And I want you to befriend him."

"You want me to hold him in my lap?"

Miss Elliott was evidently engrossed in reminiscence.

"When he was a few months old," her voice lowered even from its subdued murmur, "I distinctly remember that once I dropped him on the floor; but I was only six."

Wayne shook his head.

"I'm afraid that I should do the same thing, even at my advanced age."

"I dare say he polished the very finery that you have on," pursued the girl, regarding the distorted reflection of her face in the adjutant's shining breast buckle.

"Been whining to you, has he?" asked the cadet-officer quietly, examining his sword-hilt.

"Not a bit of it," returned the other indignantly. "He is the jolliest boy in the world. Whine! I guess not."

"I have been trying to find you to talk about to-night's german," said Wayne, with evident impatience of her subject, "and there goes the first call now;" he went on to enlarge upon this common interest, and Pythias was forgotten.

Miss Elliott saw her plebe again the next morning. Guard mounting was over, and the band was giving the customary morning concert under the elms. The laughing, chatting, and flirting, that had been quenched by the roll of the inexorable drum at the dance the night before, was going gayly forward from the point where it left off.

In contrast to the groups of talkative youths and maidens distributed all about, stood a small squad of motionless plebes in dress uniform and painfully braced. They were offering themselves in competition, each hoping to be chosen for the color guard, the duty of watching the flag all day carrying with it certain privileges, and being bestowed upon the cadet whose person and accoutrements should be found by the adjutant to be the most nearly faultless.

As Geoffrey Wayne in the gray and crimson, white and gold glory of his dress uniform approached the waiting line, Sally Elliott stood near, regarding them. Beside her was Pythias, whom she had sent for to sit with her during guard mount. He was in a sympathetic tremor, his eyes fixed on Damon, who was a member of the squad, and whose toilet Pythias had zealously superintended, jumping about him at the last with a whisk broom and a bit of chamois leather, "painting the lily" by every means in his power.

"Your friend looks quite uncomfortable," observed Miss Elliott, as she scrutinized that member of the stiff-backed line.

"Not half so much so as he feels," returned Pythias. "But I don't see how even Mr. Wayne can find any fault with him. It would take a magnifying glass to find a speck of dust on him."

The adjutant, the official severity of his countenance unsoftened by Miss Elliott's proximity, approached the first victim of his inspection.

The band was playing a Sousa march, to whose strains Sally had danced the last two-step with Wayne the night before. She smiled at the contrast between the face of her partner then and the expression he now bent upon the luckless cadet, who was even denied the privilege of trembling beneath it.

As if a string had been pulled, the rifle of the competing plebe flew from one hand to the other, and with a jerk was offered to the adjutant.

Miss Elliott's low laugh bubbled forth.

" *I* should call that snatching," she remarked, commenting on the cadet-officer's mode of accepting the firearm. " Is it military to snatch?"

Pythias was too preoccupied to hear her. He endeavored to look impassive, but his eyes glistened. Damon stood second in the line. Wayne muttered something to the first plebe as he tossed back the rifle, then moved to the next.

Damon at his approach became galvanized into motion. His gun leaped from one hand to the other in approved style.

"My, what a Jove-like frown Mr. Wayne wears!" remarked Sally. She was watching intently, in sympathy with the interest of Pythias. She saw the cadet-officer take the rifle, gaze down its barrel, and unfix the bayonet. He drew his white-gloved finger along the socket, then presented it under Damon's nose with threatening energy and a frowning stare which the plebe received with a beating heart, but without the quiver of an eyelash.

" Oh, it's not clean!" cried the girl regretfully.

" Miss Sally," said Pythias, in quiet desperation, "that gun has been unscrewed and each separate part soaked in alcohol before it was rubbed."

"Well, it is a shame!" she returned warmly, watching the adjutant with disapproval as he continued down the line, looking each competitor over closely, and drawing his white-gloved fingers around triggers and over gun barrels, displaying the result to their immobile owners.

"You seem interested, Miss Elliott."

It was Lieutenant Paxton who spoke, the young cavalry officer whose military perfections had won the encomium from Pythias. The latter effaced himself as Miss Elliott turned to speak to the newcomer, and as he went he cogitated. Mr. Wayne's severity had been so impartial Pythias did not wholly despair of his friend's success after all.

"Yes, I am interested, Mr. Paxton," replied Miss Elliott. "I was just thinking that Mr. Wayne needed some one to recite Watts's hymns to him: ' 'T is dogs delight to bark and bite,' and ' Birds in their little nests agree,' and such moral stanzas. He looks at those poor cadets as if his angry passions had risen permanently."

Mr. Paxton smiled with rather strained indifference. He did not like to have Sally Elliott interested in Geoffrey Wayne even sufficiently to deplore his manner ; but this, of course, he did not confess even to himself, for not many years had elapsed since he too wore the cadet gray under these old elms.

"Is it a part of an adjutant's duty to look so savage?" pursued the clear voice.

"A part of his pleasure, perhaps," returned her companion. "Wayne makes a good adjutant," he continued, remarking the quizzical expression on the girl's face as she still regarded her friend's discharge of his official duty.

"I wish you would come up here in September, when the officers get their innings, Miss Elliott," went on the lieutenant, as he returned the salute of a passing cadet.

"I'm sure I should like to," she answered, turning to him frankly. "I doubt if there is a month in the year when West Point has not some special charm."

"I mean to ask your mother if she won't promise me to bring you to one of our hops this fall."

"Alas! it would be useless. My holidays do not last so long."

"Isn't life one perpetual holiday for you? I judged it was."

"Indeed, no!" The natural vivacity of the bright face deepened till the blue eyes danced. "I should not enjoy myself as I have here if it were. You may be sure I need all the strength, nervous force, and resource that can be stored up in a vacation, for I am a kindergartner."

"Indeed? I should like to see you at your labors."

"Come by all means and visit us, but wear your uniform. Your brass buttons would enrapture the whole school. One of the favorite songs of the children begins: —

> " ' A sword and a gun,
>   A gay prancing steed,
>   The brave soldier boy,
>   What more can he need!' "

Geoffrey Wayne approaching, his labors over, caught sight of this pair laughing together, and allowed himself to be seized upon by a couple of maidens who had been biding their time until he should be free.

"You see, Miss Elliott," said Paxton, "I'm afraid if we don't get you for an officers' hop this fall we never shall — that is, not in my time. I was credibly informed last night" — the lieutenant lowered his voice, and his face became grave and respectful — "that you are engaged to Mr. Wayne."

The wondering eyes regarding him remained no less mischievous.

" ' *Credibly* informed'? Dear me, Mr. Paxton, you frighten me. In these dangerously advanced days, when nobody knows when she may be hypnotized, or her astral body be lured off in an uncanny manner, one can never tell what may not have happened in some moment of unconsciousness."

"I see you don't wish to admit it, if the report is true," said the lieutenant stiffly. "Forgive me."

Sally smiled demurely.

"I have nothing to forgive, indeed, and I wish — I do wish I could come to your hop, Mr. Paxton."

She gave him an expressive gaze, then half turned her head and caught one of the glances which Wayne was continuing to throw in her direction. He received her look as a summons, and, lifting his cap, held it off his much-brushed crisp hair in an attitude of provisional departure, while the maidens chattered last words which fell on deaf ears.

Lieutenant Paxton, seeing the cadet impending, drifted away, and Sally smiled an acknowledgment of his adieu, then turned to meet Wayne. As he drew near she puckered her white brow into the darkest frown it would assume, and stared at him, forcing her lips into a severe line.

"What is this?" inquired the adjutant, holding out his hand in spite of her forbidding attitude.

For answer she drew her bare finger across his shining buckle, then thrust it toward his face with an energy which surprised him into a most unmilitary start.

"There; do you think that's pretty?" she inquired, dimpling. "That is what you have been

doing for the last twenty minutes. Where are
those poor plebes to be interred?"

"I wish you would n't talk shop to me," said the
adjutant plaintively.

"I do it for your good. A West Point training
makes young men so muscular you can surely get
away from me if you don't like it."

"No, I can't get away from you," remarked
Wayne, as if stating a fact oft repeated. "What
are you going to do next?"

"It is growing warm here," said the girl, sti-
fling a yawn. "I think I will go back to the
hotel."

"Yes; let us go and sit on the piazza."

"Oh! did you think you were coming with
me?"

The adjutant regarded her with as much indignation as was compatible with a strictly society
expression.

"Seeing you will be here but a week longer, I
most decidedly am coming," he returned.

"I think I shall talk quite a little more about
that squad of plebes," she remarked, as they started
to walk toward the hedge.

Eloquent silence on the part of her companion.

"That second one in the line — the stiffest dummy
of them all — is Damon to my plebe's Pythias. His
gun " —

"He was the best of the lot," interrupted the
adjutant curtly.

"Did you recommend him?" asked Miss Elliott eagerly.

"Yes."

She smiled upon him delightedly, and Geoffrey, thanking his lucky stars, drank in the sweetness of her approval, enjoying the radiance while it lasted, and then successfully changing the subject.

A couple of evenings afterward there was a concert in camp. The half-moon made mysterious the elm shadows, and into a retired nook of which he had experience the adjutant ushered his lady.

Pretty Sally had, since Mr. Paxton's announcement, had more than one bad quarter of an hour. The conviction stole upon her at inconvenient times and seasons that she was not treating Geoffrey well. The summer had been so gay, so happy! Was it, after all, going to leave a bitter taste behind it? She had first met Wayne in his yearling camp. He had visited her a number of times during his furlough, and now this summer, when he was at the height of his popularity, it had caused her some secret elation to have him the chief and frankest admirer of her little court. Over and over again she met her recent self-accusation with the assertion that she had been honest with him. "In words, yes," answered conscience, "but had not vanity incited the actions, which speak louder than words?"

Sally leaned back against her tree trunk, and the band began to play Schubert's "Serenade."

The sighing melody waved and flowed through the drooping elm branches with the softly breathing summer wind. Wayne, leaning on his elbow in the grass, looked up at the white curve of his companion's cheek.

"You were a good girl to wear my favorite gown," he said.

"A lot of good it did," she answered, in a practical tone. "You have put me in a corner where you can't see it."

"I can feel it," he answered contentedly, upon which Miss Elliott gently but firmly drew the thin fabric away from his clinging fingers.

"Hush! I want to hear the music," she said, and the violins drowned her companion's smiling sigh.

They had not paused, on their way, to inspect the programme, and so when midway of the evening the cornet, after a short preluding flourish, began a sweet and sustained melody, accompanied by the other instruments, Wayne's hands met in brief applause.

"Bravo!" he exclaimed. "I requested that."

"What is it?" asked Miss Elliott.

He sank back again on his elbow, his dark head almost touching her arm, and looked up into her face.

"'You are the darling of my heart,'" he said.

She was glad to reflect that the moonlight tends to make one look pale, as she silently regarded him.

"Don't you know you are the darling of my heart?" he asked.

"Please don't be funny," she returned briskly.

"But don't you? I 'm surprised at your neglect of the English classics." Then in an easy voice he sang softly with the cornet : —

> "' She is the darling of my heart,
> And she lives in our alley.' "

"Oh, 'Sally in our Alley,' " said Miss Elliott reflectively. "I knew it was familiar."

"Sally!" Wayne suddenly but with great gentleness imprisoned the moon-white hand lying near him on his favorite gown. "I am going to ask you again, dear."

"Why do you?" came the answer, with startled glibness.

"For several reasons. Partly because you are going away so soon, partly because you are going to cut to-morrow night's hop to go on Paxton's drive, and partly because it will be the third time, and the third time never fails. No, you need n't try to draw your hand away. I am going to hold it."

"Why?" exclaimed Miss Elliott again, being too much bewildered by this reckless firmness on the part of a hitherto respectful individual to do more than repeat her feeble question.

"For several reasons," returned Wayne, also repeating himself. "Partly because a West Point training makes a man so muscular that I am able

to, and partly because whoever becomes the ultimate
owner of it — if he knew all, he would surely feel
that I had earned this much.   Then beside " —

"Oh, Geoffrey! " there was a piteous little tremble
in the girl's voice as she uttered her interruption.
Heart and conscience were making a strange mixed
tumult within her.   "I have always been honest
with you, have n't I ? "

"Yes," was the dry answer, "I can say unhesitatingly that honesty is your forte; but," slowly
kissing her hand, a feat which the place, the music,
and her gentleness made easy, " I love you."

"Let us be sensible," said Miss Elliott hastily,
in a tone which strove to imply all sorts of practical
and prosaic ideas.   "You live such a narrow life
up here you don't know what you do want.   In a
few months you will be out ; you will see the world.
You will meet other girls " —

"*Girls !* " exclaimed the cadet, with justifiable
protest.   "In the name of reason, have n't I met
girls enough ? "

"Well, then, no matter about them.   If you
would drop my hand I could talk better."

"There is room for improvement, I admit ; but
I need your hand unless you are going to give me
some hope to work on this winter.   Say something
kind to me, Sally, can't you ? "

"This is the merest infatuation, Geoffrey," returned Miss Elliott decidedly, "such as a young
man often feels for an older woman."

" Pshaw ! " exclaimed the adjutant in much
scorn. "Are you going to ring in that chestnut
again ? What are those few hours by which you
got a start of me ? "

" I had a year and two months the start of you,
Mr. Wayne," said the girl, as coolly as though she
were not fearing to be overborne by his will. "A
small matter perhaps in some cases, but in ours
an added reason against — against what you wish.
I have no money," she went on, "never shall have.
If it were not that I am the happy possessor of an
aunt who likes to give me an occasional treat, I
should n't be here now. A second lieutenant needs
a wife who can help him."

"And a wife who can love him — love him
enough to trust him," said Geoffrey, trying to see
her face clearly in the dim light. " You don't care
for me — yet. Here, take your hand ; " he dropped
it gently on her knee.

" I do care for you," she said.

" As a sister, no doubt. Another chestnut,
Sally."

" No, more as a mother," returned Miss Elliott,
with much dignity, and then started at the laugh
which fell from her companion's lips, jarring upon
the music. "You are very rude to laugh," she
said, with spirit. "My feeling for you *is* mater-
nal, and I care for you very much."

" Awfully good of you, Sally, and you 're a jolly
little mother ; but, you see, I have one already.—

a perfectly satisfactory one, too. It's something else I need."

So they parted, still agreeing to disagree, when Miss Elliott left the post and went back to her home in Brooklyn and the kindergarten circle.

Geoffrey Wayne, being of determined stuff, kept his high standing throughout the difficult struggle of that last winter, and graduating, was assigned to the corps of engineers. His post being within easy reach of Brooklyn, he managed occasionally to see Sally Elliott, and that young woman was frequently disconcerted, at the moment of patronizing the lieutenant's prospects, to find that underneath his equable demeanor lurked a repressed fire which still burned for her alone, in spite of the persistent and deliberate dampening process which had seemed to her the only proof of true friendship possible from her to him since that evening when the West Point band, by special request, performed " Sally in our Alley."

Lieutenant Paxton, moreover, did not forget her bright eyes. Many a Saturday night did he come down to New York for the sake of a Sunday call upon Miss Elliott, and speedily discovering that she was not pledged to his rival, those visits increased in regularity and length until Geoffrey Wayne heard about them.

" You must remember, Sally," he said quietly one day to his obdurate lady-love, " that promotion comes faster in the engineers than in the cavalry."

She flushed slightly, meeting his straightforward look, and had nothing to say.

"Since you are avowedly mercenary, I want to remind you that it is well you are going to marry me instead of Paxton."

Her lip curled. "What an invaluable servant of the government you will be," she remarked. "It is impossible for you to understand when you are beaten."

Wayne felt himself change color, her tone was so cold. "Then is it to be Paxton?" he asked.

"I will tell you when it is to be anybody."

He studied the carpet awhile before he spoke again. "I don't want to quarrel with you," he said, "to-day of all days. You know I wrote you that my mother was very ill? Well, she is here; her nurse brought her. Will you go to see her?"

"Indeed I will," returned the girl, all sympathy at once.

Geoffrey took advantage of her sudden cordiality to get possession of both her hands. "Don't let Paxton come to see you so much," he said, and her eyes fell before his strong gaze. "It is n't fair to him."

He was gone before she could frame the crushing reply he deserved; and indeed, after meditating awhile, she went straight to her desk and wrote the cavalry officer a note of excuse for not seeing him the following Sunday, when, as he had informed her, he was intending to come.

Then she betook herself to the hospital to visit Mrs. Wayne. It was their first meeting, and somewhat embarrassing, inasmuch as she found Geoffrey's mother astonishingly well posted about her. The sick woman's attitude toward her was that of an affectionate old friend, and when the girl left she had promised to return the next day.

But Sally, from Mrs. Wayne's first cordial greeting, entertained a conviction that the elder lady's manifest approval of her sprang from a knowledge of her firmness with regard to Geoffrey. She expected that this mutual understanding would remain a tacit one, and therefore was surprised one day when the invalid opened the subject.

Sally had made some deft change in the sufferer's pillows, to the increase of her comfort.

"I don't wonder Geoffrey loves you, my dear," said the sick woman.

The girl sat down beside the bed, silent under the kindly scrutiny of the large eyes.

"He says you have not promised to marry him."

"No," returned Sally, in a rather choked voice.

"But why not? Don't you care for him?"

The girl shook her head hurriedly. "It is no matter whether I care for him, Mrs. Wayne. It would be the most inappropriate, unwise thing for Geoffrey." And Sally launched into a detailed account of her serious objections.

To her amazement, the sick woman appeared as

unmoved as her son by these weighty arguments. When the girl had finished, steadied by her own logic, she met the wistful eyes still bent upon her.

" Dear child, these things are trifles if you love my boy even enough to let him love you; and to learn that you do not would add the last misery to the bitterness of death. I know, though I have not yet had courage to tell Geoffrey so, that I shall not live long. I must break it to him soon. Let him have this great consolation. Promise me that you will marry him before I die."

Sally's startled color rose, and her lips trembled.

" Don't make me feel that I am leaving him alone, rejected by the woman he loves so devotedly, and with no one to befriend him in the temptations of life. Oh, Sally, my daughter!" The voice died away, the eyes half closed, and a greater pallor overspread the pinched face.

" Mrs. Wayne!" exclaimed the girl, terrified, starting up and seizing a glass of water. " Yes, yes, I promise!"

A feeble pressure of the hand replied to her.

As Miss Elliott was leaving the hospital a few minutes later, she encountered Geoffrey entering.

" Don't go up now!" she ejaculated, and he exclaimed at the agitation in her face.

" Your mother had a sinking spell. It frightened me. She is better, but — perhaps you had better not see her." The girl's white face was suddenly scarlet.

" My dear little Sally," breathed the troubled young man. "How good you are.   You will never know how I appreciate it."

Day succeeded day, and the vision of a hurried marriage beside a deathbed, at first constantly before Miss Elliott's mental vision, faded slowly away.

Mrs. Wayne grew strong enough to travel, and returned to her family in the South.   Geoffrey was held more and more closely by the demands of the graduate course of study he was taking, and when he succeeded in making a hurried trip to Brooklyn his reception was only the customary one. Nothing but the light in his eyes and a new elasticity in his manner betrayed that he knew of the decisive interview between his mother and Sally, for the latter's docility had proved short-lived. Mrs. Wayne might outlive them all, she said to her mother, and she continued to hold her lover at the old distance.

Mrs. Elliott sighed resignedly.   Geoffrey, as he had taken pains to ascertain, had her good wishes.

" But how he can be patient to keep up such a long game of hide-and-seek is beyond my comprehension," she remarked once to her daughter.   Indeed, she said as much to Wayne himself one day when they were *tête-à-tête.*

" I 'm biding my time, Mrs. Elliott," he answered, smiling.   "By autumn my affairs will permit me to carry the fort by storm, and, little as your daughter suspects it from my meekness, I am going to marry her and carry her off in triumph and show her to my mother and the rest at home."

"I don't see how you will succeed," returned Mrs. Elliott. "Sally does n't seem to think of marrying."

Spring wore away into summer, and the fervid heat of a July sun was reflecting from Brooklyn pavements and parching its streets, before the Elliotts decided upon flitting to cooler regions.

Whether Geoffrey Wayne remained away as a discretionary measure, or whether business kept him, Sally did not know, but she had not seen him of late, and had heard from him but seldom.

As she started one day on a modest shopping tour to purchase the articles needed by her mother and herself before leaving the city, her thoughts returned to him obstinately, despite repeated efforts to divert and control them. She pictured scenes on the parade ground, on the piazzas, and upon the wooded walks and drives about his post, in which the summer girl figured conspicuously. There were always such a lot of them. No wonder he preferred their flattery to her cavalier attitude. It was probable that he was forgetting her, and that was quite right — the event she had always prophesied and wished for.

When her errands were done she felt that she could not return home at once, and, taking an electric car, she rode for a couple of hours before

she considered her thoughts sufficiently ordered to
admit of meeting her mother with her customary
insouciant manner. As she left the car, to her surprise she caught sight of Wayne himself. He was
advancing with his familiar military air, and upon
his face was a noticeable gravity. She saw him a
moment before he recognized her, and before they
met she was well fortified to make it clear that the
field was entirely open to the summer girl, and to
prove triumphantly that his devotion to herself
had never been seriously regarded.

He hurried forward at sight of her. "This is
fortunate, Sally," he said, and his face showed
haggard lines. "I have a telegram calling me
home. My mother is sinking very fast."

The girl gave an exclamation of sympathy.

"The telegram ends, 'Be married before you
come.'"

Sally's heart leaped and beat fast. "But that
does n't hold," she began feebly, with a dim idea
of letting him off.

"I have been to your house three times, and
could not find you. I must go by the nine o'clock
train to-night, so I took it for granted that you
would consent. I have the license. What time
would you prefer to have the minister come?"

Sally gasped. Geoffrey had never looked so
tall and commanding.

He consulted his watch. "It is now four
o'clock," he said.

" Really," she stammered, "really, there does n't seem to be much choice." Then, as Wayne's white, troubled face was waiting, " Half past seven," she finished.

He left her, and on the way home it seemed to her she was in a dream. But her mother's excited face brought her to a sense of the practical side of the situation. Their stout maid-of-all-work was afflicted with a mysterious malady, described by herself as shortness of breath, and having had an attack that morning, Mrs. Elliott had excused her for the whole day.

Sally gave her mother a reassuring hug.

" What a mercy it is," said the latter, half hysterically, " that we had asked your cousin Dick to come to dinner. I was regretting it a little while ago, since it proves we must be our own cooks; but if it were n't for him, there would n't be a guest at your wedding, Sally. Why, my dear, it is all the strangest, most unexpected " —

" And the warmest time," Sally finished for her, " that we ever knew."

Forthwith she plunged into the kitchen and cooked the dinner, with her mother's help.

Mr. Richard Elliott, who had ridden up in bicycle knickerbockers to aid his aunt in some business problem, was a most amazed man to find himself a guest at a wedding.

" Don't worry, Dick, you will do very well," said Sally reassuringly. " You shall give me away."

When the meal was over, the bride, whose continuous *sang-froid* amazed her companions, donned an apron over the street dress she had not had time to discard, and proceeded to make lemonade, the only available refreshment in the house.

"Oh, Sally! how different this is from my expectations. Not a cake at your wedding!" groaned Mrs. Elliott.

"Well," returned the girl, smiling demurely at a lemon, "the question is, whether it is better to have a wedding without a cake or a cake without a wedding?" Then, meeting her mother's loving, puzzled expression, "Don't leave Dick alone any longer, dear, and Geoffrey will be coming now."

Mrs. Elliott obediently disappeared, and when Sally's labors were finished she followed her. Covered by the voluminous apron the bride entered the parlor, bearing a large bowl of ice and lemonade. Three men started to their feet as she entered, and to her horror she discovered that the minister, a stranger to her, had already arrived.

Mrs. Elliott hesitated in her embarrassment. "My — my daughter, Mr. Ford."

The minister advanced to the girl. "Is this — Miss Sarah?" he asked doubtfully.

Sally, being relieved by Geoffrey of her burden, shook hands with the stranger and acknowledged her identity.

She knew that her cousin Dick was secretly

impatient to return to the little family he had left
to oblige his aunt, so, looking about upon the company, she suggested that, as they were all there,
the wedding might as well take place. There-
upon, to Mrs. Elliott's intense relief, she removed
her apron, Geoffrey returned to her side, and they
were married.

After the ceremony the bride served the lemonade with her own hands, then said good-by to the
minister and her cousin, and ran upstairs to put
on her staying-at-home gown. When she came
down arrayed in some besprigged white stuff,
Geoffrey was waiting at the foot of the stairs.

" Will-o'-the-wisp no longer," he said wonderingly, as he slowly took her in his arms and kissed
her willing lips. " To think that you belong to
me ! "

They went out of doors and sat upon the piazza
until it was time for him to go to his train, scarcely
speaking as they clung together, so awesome was
the shadow of death which lay athwart the sunshine of their love.

Geoffrey's mother lived but a few days after he
reached her, and one week after the funeral he
sought the seaside resort where Mrs. Elliott and
her daughter were staying.

He arrived one day just before dinner, and
during the meal a girl guest at a table near the
one where he and Sally were sitting called the
attention of a friend to the couple.

"I am sure that is a bride and groom," she said confidentially.

"Why, no, it is n't," answered the second maiden. "Have n't you noticed that Mrs. Wayne before? She has been here as long as we have. I suppose that must be her husband just arrived."

The first speaker sighed. "Well, I hope my husband will look at me just like that," she remarked appreciatively. "His wife has the happiest eyes I ever saw, and no wonder."

PURSUER OR PURSUED?

THEY were standing in the museum on the ground floor of the old Academic Building at West Point, when it was discovered that the conversation, they hardly knew how, had veered from shells to sentiment, from war to love. There were Colonel Mackenzie, a professor in the academy; Lieutenant Cary, a tactical officer, and with them two ladies, mother and daughter, guests at the hotel for the gay graduation season. Colonel Mackenzie, assisted by the lieutenant, had been showing the ladies about the post; and, wandering in through the gymnasium to the museum, the professor paused beside a Gatling gun to emphasize his remarks upon a subject so foreign to the surroundings.

"You may convince yourself of it simply by observation," he announced, the kind eyes under his heavy brows twinkling but earnest. "In affairs of love it is the woman who chooses. Every nice girl has a lot of admirers. They gather about her like bees about a flower. She chooses one. Whiz! The other bees go off somewhere else. Plenty of flowers, — eh, Miss Bruce?" asked the colonel cheerfully, smiling at the younger lady, who caught his eye as her own roved from one to another of the warlike objects by which she was surrounded.

"Oh, yes," she replied, apparently quite unembarrassed by the fact of listening to the colonel's views in company with the young officer who stood by, seriously thoughtful. "Flowers are especially plenty in West Point just now."

"There are plenty of bees, too," added Mrs. Bruce, raising her eyeglass to inspect a hideous effigied warrior who stood near her, full panoplied for the fray. "Busy bees of all sorts. Not a drone in the hive, I suppose, Mr. Cary?"

The young man stirred from his thoughtful attitude. "It is not a healthful place for drones. Do you care to see the section-room upstairs, Mrs. Bruce?"

"Oh, yes; where the poor fellows recite," returned the lady, in that tone of commiseration usually adopted by women who ever have had, or ever expect to have, a relative among the cadets. Mrs. Bruce belonged to the latter class, and was full of hope and fear concerning her only son. "Yes, indeed, I want to see where you teach the young idea how to shoot."

"Oh, that is done outside on the plain," remarked Colonel Mackenzie, twinkling again at Miss Bruce.

They ascended the old stairs and entered one of the recitation rooms.

" I 've had that young man standing up here to recite, with his little fingers at the seams of his trousers," observed Colonel Mackenzie, with a wave of his hand toward his subordinate.

The lieutenant smiled. " And I dare say stood up here yourself in the same attitude for the same purpose," he remarked.

" How odd ! " said Miss Bruce, regarding the professor's stout military figure and gray hair.

" Oh, yes. Other things in this fast country of ours are ever changing, but West Point goes on forever the same for the best of reasons ; it could not be improved upon," said Colonel Mackenzie, with devout sincerity. " Come up a little higher ; I think you will like to see the drawings."

When the latter exhibition had been duly examined and admired, the quartette descended to the ground floor and came out again into the sunshine. The officers escorted the ladies to the hotel, and at the door Mrs. Bruce voiced her thanks for their attention. " I am sure the morning has been a liberal education, Colonel Mackenzie. You have not only shown us the mechanics of light and sound, but have explained to us the workings of our own emotions as we have never known them."

" Ah, you are laughing at me, madam. You will not admit that you are convinced."

" And mamma is not more easily silenced than other women," remarked Miss Bruce, " so I advise you not to argue with her."

"Never mind. Wait till I write my novel. I'll do it yet," said Colonel Mackenzie, with a firm nod. "The woman chooses the man, and not the man the woman. I will show that it's so."

"Why, of course," returned Mrs. Bruce, half laughing. "If a girl receives proposals from several men she chooses the one who pleases her best."

"That is not what I mean," was the uncompromising reply. "A girl worth having does not receive proposals from several men."

"Wait, wait, colonel. You do not know what sensitive feelings you may be trampling upon."

"No, I am entirely impersonal. Theories are impersonal, you know. A girl worth having usually receives a proposal from a man because she has already chosen him. Watch and see. Just observe and see. Good-by." The colonel's face beamed with smiling good nature as he lifted his cap.

Cary removed his. "Will you be ready by half past three?" he said to the younger lady. "Your daughter, Mrs. Bruce, wishes to make acquaintance with some of the wild flowers about here. I can at least promise her some very pretty laurel."

"A nice way for a young soldier to win his laurels!" remarked the colonel.

They made their adieux once more, and the lieutenant parted from his senior outside the hedge, and took his way down the road past the

Academic Building.   He was hailed by a young man who had run down the steps of the rear entrance to the library, and now crossed the street.

"Well, I've made up my mind," announced the newcomer, as he fell into step with his friend, the red stripe upon his army blue making gay contrast to Cary's yellow decoration.

"About what, Thornton?"

"Going across the water."

"You have decided to go?"

"Yes, and I only wish you could come too," said the artillery officer, clapping a hand on the other's shoulder.   "What's up?   I fancied you were looking rather glum a minute ago."

"Oh, not at all; I was thinking of — of love. That is all."

Thornton laughed.   "And quite enough, apparently," he said.   There was a strong friendship between the two men.   Cary had been a third-class man in the academy when Thornton was as dismally homesick a "plebe" as ever walked, thumbs out, across the plain.   Cary, contrary to the usual custom, had befriended him on one or two occasions when the slight kindness had sunk deep into the sore heart of the seventeen-year-old boy, making him the older man's friend for life. They happened to be thrown together in this West Point detail, and to Thornton's gratification even to have quarters in the same house, so that opportunities for cultivating their intimacy were plenty.

It was, however, no tribute to this intimacy that Cary declared so frankly now the delicate subject of his thought. He was a man of a logical, studious turn of mind, much given to analysis, and Thornton knew, as his friend stared gravely before him, that he would have owned the cause of his pre-occupation quite as willingly to any other listener.

"I should advise you to think about something else, then," said Thornton lightly, "something more in your line."

"It is a very important subject, and one that ought to be in my line, — in the line of all men," returned Cary seriously.

"And quite time for you, I should say," remarked the other. "You will never see thirty again."

"That is what I was thinking of. A man should be married by the time he is thirty."

"Provided he has at least one bar in his shoulder-strap," added the second lieutenant dolorously, "otherwise it is a questionable experiment."

"Well, I have the bar, and I have made some lucky investments," said Cary equably, "yet I am not married nor likely to be, and at last I understand why. I have not been chosen."

His companion stared into the serious countenance. "What? You have not been *what?*"

"Chosen. Colonel Mackenzie has been propounding theories this morning which are new to me, and I am inclined to think he is right. He says the man does not choose the woman, but *vice versa*."

" He must have had a peculiar experience, then. Did Mrs. Mackenzie propose to him ? "

Cary received the flippant question with gravity. " I don't know ; but if she did, you must admit she acted wisely. Theirs is one of the most harmonious homes I ever entered."

By this time the two officers had reached Thornton's quarters, and ascending the steps they seated themselves in chairs on the piazza, amid a bower of honeysuckle which clambered over the porch and to the second story of the house.

" Is n't it something new for the professor to be dabbling in the mysteries of the tender passion ? " asked Thornton, rocking back in his chair.

" It is a subject worthy the attention and best thought of a scholarly mind like his. The working of the emotions, the action of the positive and negative currents in the sensibilities of men and women are, I dare say, discoverable like other scientific facts. I have great confidence in conclusions arrived at by a man like Colonel Mackenzie."

" All right, Cary," said his friend, breaking a spray of honeysuckle. " I won't regret any longer that you cannot go abroad with me. You won't find a place on the footstool where such a variety of maidens can have an opportunity to look you over and examine your good points as right here at the post. If I come back the last of August and find you still unchosen, I shall set you down as a pretty bad lot." His companion's contagious chuckle provoked Cary to a smile, as he twisted his mustache and looked into space.

"Almost noon," he said, suddenly rising. "I must do some writing before luncheon, for I am going to walk with Miss Bruce before parade."

"At her invitation, I trust. Don't tell me you forgot the coyness becoming your sex and invited her."

"I had n't heard Colonel Mackenzie's theories then. But in any case it is entirely compatible with his ideas that I should ask a young lady to go to walk with me, — yes, even to journey through life with me, — but she must lead me up to it, you see. She must lead me up to it," — an emphatic gesture accompanying the repetition.

"So she shall, my dear fellow, so she shall," said Thornton soothingly, repressing his smiles as he, too, rose, and they passed into the house.

It happened that he did not sit beside his friend at lunch, and the next time they met was in the afternoon at parade. Thornton strolled along the path fronting the plain amid an incessant din of talk and laughter. The long row of packed seats was reinforced at this crowded season by myriad camp-stools, and all were filled by the gayly dressed spectators. He stopped now and then to speak to an acquaintance, and paused finally before Mrs. Bruce, who sat upon a camp-stool under a majestic elm, and, in order to bow to Thornton, looked around the arm of her daughter, whom she was holding in her lap.

" Is that the best you can do? " asked the young man, raising his hat. " I think I can get you some sort of a chair."

" Oh, if you only could, Mr. Thornton," said the young lady plaintively. " I know I am awfully heavy, and mamma will make me sit here."

" It looks as if every chair in the place were already in use," said Mrs. Bruce, glancing down the double and triple lines of gay summer costumes with the swaying rainbow tints of hats and parasols; " but if you can get us one, Mr. Thornton, you will be an angel."

" I will try, anyhow; only I protest against becoming an angel in consequence of such slight exertion. Here goes. If I fail in my quest, that will alter matters. You may know that I have perished of mortification and am attending dress parade in another sphere."

With this the young officer crossed the street under the heads of a spirited pair of horses and entered the yard of an opposite house. It was the home of a professor whose wife happened to be Thornton's relative, and as the latter was intimate in the family he made bold now, in their absence, to run up the steps and prefer his request to a servant. Meanwhile his beneficiaries were applauding his efforts.

"I do like a young man with his wits about him," remarked Mrs. Bruce severely. "I should have supposed Mr. Cary would have made his appearance in time to have been of some use to us. What did he say to you when you parted this afternoon?"

"That he would see me at parade," returned Miss Bruce shortly. She looked down at the stars of laurel which lay in a large cluster on her breast.

"And so he will, no doubt, by the time Mr. Thornton gets us comfortably settled," replied her mother, "and then be too absent-minded and distrait to realize that he has omitted anything he ought to have done."

"My, Aunt Frances! How hard you are on the poor man," exclaimed the large fair young woman who was their next neighbor. "I think Mr. Cary is just splendid. Fanny introduced him to me this afternoon before they started on their walk. I only wish I had arrived sooner. I am quite envious of her because she is so well acquainted here."

"You won't be a stranger long, Belle," remarked her cousin, with a little smile. "I know your energy in a good cause."

"I know I have n't any military laurels," retorted the fair girl discontentedly.

"Oh, take them. I am heartily tired of hearing jokes made on these poor things," and Miss

Bruce drew out the long pin that confined the laurel, and began fastening it at her cousin's belt.

"My dear, I won't," ejaculated the other. "I was only joking; I won't take your flowers."

"Yes, you will," said Miss Bruce firmly. "I am not joking. I don't want them."

So the laurel was adorning Miss Laflin, and Miss Bruce's cheeks were flushed from the slight dispute, and the feeling which on her side lay behind it, when Lieutenant Cary came walking down the path. He moved quickly, and looked anxiously among the crowd until his glance lighted upon the party he sought. He showed his handsome teeth as he lifted his cap, and met Miss Bruce's bright eyes.

"How time slips away!" he said. "I had no idea it was so near the hour for parade, and now the seats are full. By the way," becoming conscious that Mrs. Bruce's camp-stool was carrying double, "why, that is too bad. Were you late, too? Were n't there chairs enough?"

"Oh yes, plenty," replied Miss Bruce, "but I always prefer to sit in mamma's lap to anywhere else, and you like to have me, don't you, mamma?"

"Well, you 're not exactly a transparency, my dear." Cary looked at them a little perplexed. There was a ring in the young girl's voice that had not been there an hour ago.

"Are n't you going to speak to me, Mr. Cary?" asked Miss Laflin with an arch smile.

"Oh, how do you do? I did n't see you," and the officer shook hands with the young woman punctiliously. He was a soldier certain to perform his duty when the latter was made clear to him. He observed now that Miss Laflin wore a generous bunch of the mountain laurel, and looking quickly at Miss Bruce, saw that she was undecorated by blossom of any kind. It displeased him that the young lady should have given away the flowers they gathered together.

At this moment a cadet hurrying down the path toward barracks paused suddenly and took the hand Miss Bruce held out to him with her sweetest smile.

"Pshaw! Can't you get a chair?" he exclaimed, as he lifted his cap to the ladies.

"Yes, in a minute," she returned.

"I am looking forward to to-night."

"So am I."

"Good-by, — I 'm late," and the young officer strode on his way.

Cary smiled. "That is the most important man on the post to-day," he remarked.

"Oh, who is it?" asked Miss Laflin.

"The adjutant, Lenox. He has been a good adjutant, too," added Cary, responding to the salutes of two cadets who caught his eye as they hurried toward the rendezvous.

"You are going to the ball with him, then, Fanny," said Miss Laflin.

"Yes," admitted her cousin languidly; her sudden vivacity seemed to have departed with the passing of the handsome cadet officer.

"Ah, there comes that good Mr. Thornton," exclaimed Mrs. Bruce with satisfaction. "Yes, he is really bringing a chair."

Cary looked with interest to see his friend springing across the street, a light chair in his hand.

"Good!" he said heartily, with entire freedom from envy of the gratitude and praise immediately showered upon Thornton. "That is first-rate."

"Ah!" sighed Mrs. Bruce, as her daughter rose and took possession of the new seat, "you do weigh something, Fanny."

"Then I think you should be ashamed of all the fibs you told half an hour ago; Mr. Thornton, let me introduce you to my cousin, Miss Laflin. She only arrived to-day, and is very unsophisticated in the ways of the post."

"But I am a very apt scholar, Mr. Thornton. I am principally interested in having my cousin point out to me the cadet who is to be my partner to-night."

"As well search for a needle in a haymow, as you will see," remarked Miss Bruce sententiously.

"I think he might have called upon me this afternoon."

"That is because you do not know the myriad engagements of these fortunate young men," said Thornton.

" Oh, but she is n't going with a first-class man," explained Miss Bruce.

" Not going with a first-class man?" inquired Miss Laflin, agitating her pink parasol excitedly. " With whom, then?"

" A yearling," responded her cousin briefly.

" Sounds like a calf! I won't go with him," said the other decidedly.

" Yes, you will, and be very glad to get him."

" Cut the infant and go with me, Miss Laflin," suggested Thornton.

" She can't. Her card is all made out. You ungrateful creature! If you knew all the trouble I had having to arrange everything for you at the last minute!"

" But you are going with the adjutant," objected Miss Laflin, much aggrieved.

" Well, when your yearling is a first-class man, you come back here. Perhaps he will be the adjutant then. Be very sweet to him to-night and you may reap the reward," laughed Miss Bruce mischievously. " There comes the band. Now watch mamma, Mr. Thornton; you will see her begin to look pensive from the moment the first set, or squad, or whatever you call it, appears at the sally-port. She is always examining the battalion to find a cadet whom she fancies Gerald will resemble *if* he gets into the academy. You know my brother is to try this month. He insists, however, that we shall leave when he comes. He says he is not going to let us have the satisfaction of seeing him squad-drilled. It would n't be much satisfaction to mamma. I know exactly what she would do. She would go up to the corporal of Gerald's squad and say, 'Dear, good, kind Mr. Cadet, please watch my boy, and don't let him work after he grows pale!' They do grow pale sometimes. I saw that last summer."

"Hush, Fanny," said her mother. "You make me miserable. There come Mr. Lenox and the sergeant-major," as the cadet officers appeared in full panoply of crimson sashes, plumed hats, shining swords, and white gloves.

Lenox raised his hand, the trumpets sounded the adjutant's call, and then the band burst into a martial measure to whose strains the battalion marched out upon the plain.

Lieutenant Cary did not care particularly to witness parade at the best of times; and just now he felt a vague discontent and discomfort, the cause of which did not appear. Miss Bruce and Thornton were viewing the scene with pleasure, the latter smiling at the young girl's comments. Cary would have preferred to be the one to receive these. It did not console him at all that Miss Laflin lifted her blonde head from time to time to ask him artless questions. She had a little impediment in her speech, and this, in connection with the fact that the brasses were blaring loudly, and that Cary had no interest in what she was saying, made it difficult for him to hear and answer her, and irritated him more than was reasonable in one whose firm principle it was that hunger for information should always be satisfied.

He watched indifferently the long lines of cadets as they executed the movements which brought them to " parade rest," and tried to smile at Miss Laflin's strictures on the drum-major's dress hat as that functionary preceded the band up and down the plain.   The march they played was the one that Cary was partial to in his best estate of body and mind; but now, when Miss Laflin praised it, and hummed a little as she tapped her foot to the marked rhythm, he wished impatiently that the U. S. M. A. Band would learn a new tune.

The drum-major convoyed his gay company back to their place.   The trumpets sounded the retreat, and the sunset gun elicited a little shriek from Cary's fair neighbor.

" You ought to have *told* me they were going to shoot," she said, casting up her eyes reproachfully.

" Hush ! " exclaimed Miss Bruce, putting her gloved hand in her cousin's lap.   " Watch Mr. Lenox.   Just think !   This is the last time he will have to say, ' Sir, the parade is formed.'   After to-morrow he will be nothing but an ordinary army officer."

" Miss Bruce," said Thornton, " you have been goading me into frenzy for the last fifteen minutes. Beware ! I hate Lenox with a fearful hatred."

"Oh, how can you hate anybody who walks like that?" said Miss Bruce pensively, her eyes fixed upon the immaculate form of the straight cadet officer, who, for the moment of his advance toward the commandant, was the cynosure of all eyes.

"I suppose," grumbled Thornton, "if I should tell you that I was the adjutant of my class I should be of some importance."

Miss Bruce did not reply at once. She was attentively watching the cadet, who, saluting with his bright sword, pronounced his stereotyped phrase and then marched to his place, facing the battalions.

"Were you the adjutant?" she asked then, lifting her eyes and regarding the lieutenant approvingly.

"No; but Cary was adjutant of his class, so you see he can rise in your estimation at once."

Miss Bruce looked back languidly toward the hundreds of gray and white figures who were executing the manual of arms with faultless precision and unanimity of movement.

"Oh, but that was so long ago," she said indifferently.

Thornton thought this remark and the tone of it rather insolent. He cast a glance at Cary, who was regarding Miss Bruce's coiffure with a reflective and studious air, which the young officer found amusing. He bit his mustache, and smiled.

"I need n't worry about Cary," he mused. "He is, no doubt, trying to deduce from that speech some idea of Miss Bruce's up-bringing, and the succession of motives which led to her making it."

Thornton was not far wrong in the latter guess. Simultaneously with the booming of the sunset gun there had come to Cary a flash of comprehension of the young lady's altered manner toward himself. He recalled the uncomfortable position in which he had found her and her mother when he put in his tardy appearance at parade, and understood that in their minds their discomfort and his tardiness were closely related. He had made himself Miss Bruce's cavalier for the afternoon, and they had both enjoyed their ramble through the wild and lovely paths up the hill beyond the South Gate; but had his obligations not ceased when he bade her good-by on the hotel piazza? Evidently she thought not. She was offended with him, and, Cary decided, unjustly so.

"She is a pretty, spoiled girl, who has been taught by the attention she has received to be exacting. I shall not aid in the spoiling process," he declared mentally.

Suddenly Colonel Mackenzie's simile occurred to him. According to theory, it was his place now to leave that flower represented by Miss Fanny Bruce and fly away to another whose sweetness might be for him. Just here fell the young

woman's slighting remark, which should have left
the bee no vestige of a doubt as to the advisability
of his immediate departure. Instead of deciding
him to leave, however, it raised in his mind only
the query as to the probable difference in age between Miss Bruce and himself, and the consequent
calculation absorbed him so fully that when Miss
Laflin exclaimed upon the perfection of the cadets' drill, and asked him how long it took to ac-
quire such quickness and precision, he looked quite
through her upraised blue eyes, and answered that
he could n't be sure, but he should think about ten
years.

"Oh, I know you are a perfectly awful tease,
Mr. Cary," returned the young lady, with a twirl
of her pink parasol. " I shall never ask you another question."

This was a consummation so ardently desired by
the lieutenant that it arrested his stammered apo-
logies. There was a general silence now also, as,
the graduating class advancing in line, the commandant addressed to them a few words of con-
gratulation, after which the band again burst forth,
and the battalion began the return to barracks.
The novel sight and sounds so delighted Miss
Laflin that she uttered enraptured little shrieks.
Cary did not like women whose outlets for emotion were little shrieks.

Miss Bruce turned to him suddenly, evidently
for the moment self-forgetful, and gave him her

bright smile. "This is the time when I cannot sit still," she said. "I want to follow them."

"It is rather thrilling," he responded, eager to preserve that cordial expression, "and there is always some impressiveness connected with the last performance of anything."

"Yes, I do not like to believe those first-class men are wholly glad it is the last time."

Cary smiled. "Don't ask me any questions about it then, Miss Bruce."

• "Were you, *you* the adjutant, glad never to come out here again on this beautiful plain, in all that crimson and gold and gray and white, and be admired by the common herd of civilians?"

The lieutenant laughed. "That is a very tempting way of putting it. You see, I did not know what an interesting object I was; so you must forgive me if I say that that June was the happiest month of my life."

"Oh dear, what bad taste!" Miss Bruce turned away, and Cary said to himself that she had remembered his delinquency.

He walked back to the hotel by her mother's side, and Thornton followed with the two girls. Mrs. Bruce had evidently forgotten her annoyance, if she ever felt any, and talked with absorbed interest of her boy's chances for getting into the- institution which she both feared and admired.

The graduation ball that evening was, as usual, a large and gay affair. Dancing was enjoyed under difficulties, owing to the number present, but the scene was a brilliant one to the chaperons and officers who lined the walls and watched the promenading or whirling couples.

"What a lot of pretty girls!" said Mrs. Bruce to Cary, who stood beside her.

"Yes, and we unfortunates may only look at them," returned Cary with a smile, as Miss Bruce, in white and gold, passed on the arm of the tall cadet adjutant. "This is the night when the cadets are in their glory, and the officers simply of no account at all."

"What trim, upright, attractive fellows they are," said Mrs. Bruce, scanning the military gray and white figures admiringly, and looking after her daughter with an agreeable certainty that no girl present outshone her.

"The cadets? Yes," said Thornton, who stood on her other side, "and what a nice place West Point would be without them!"

Mrs. Bruce laughed. "I have noticed they get in the way of you young officers sometimes. Poor things! I should not think you would grudge them the little freedom they have at this time of year. Good evening, Colonel Mackenzie," as the genial professor approached.

"How do you do, Mrs. Bruce. Ah, Cary, Thornton," said the colonel, greeting the lieutenants.

"Well, this is paradise for these young people, eh?" and the speaker cast his glance over the restless mass of humanity, two individuals of which were his own daughters.

"Yes, indeed; quite an object lesson, colonel," returned the lady. "Unlimited flowers, unlimited bees."

"Yes; oh, yes," said the officer, laughing at this reference to his impromptu figure of speech; "and depend upon it, madam, there is choosing going on."

Thornton, who was looking interested but mystified, suddenly remembered what he had heard of the professor's theories, and smiled at Cary.

"Choosing going on, and we're not in it," he remarked *sotto voce*.

"I should hope there was very little choosing taking place in this company," remarked Mrs. Bruce dryly. "These cadets are very ornamental, but, like all ornaments, a matter of luxury."

"Well said, Mrs. Bruce," said Thornton. "Come up to one of our hops next winter."

"She'll see nothing ornamental there, I suppose you mean," said Cary, and just then his eye was caught by Miss Laflin, who beamed upon him with an impressive bow as she approached with her partner. She was dressed in white, and looked blooming. Her plump arms and neck gleamed in the gaslight, and her face was flushed from heat and exertion.

"I am going to sit with you, Aunt Frances, until the next dance," she said, with a parting bow to her partner. "Oh, thank you, Mr. Cary," as the lieutenant placed a chair for her. "It is so warm and crowded."

"But I hope you are enjoying yourself," he returned.

"Oh, yes; I dare say these boys do not bore me more than I bore them."

It passed through Mr. Cary's mind that the young lady must be rather a heavy-weight as a dancer, so his next remark was a trifle uncandid.

"Thornton and I are looking on at the gayety enviously."

"And some of us girls are looking at you covetously," responded Miss Laflin, using her eyes effectively.

"It is very kind of you to soothe our feelings," said the lieutenant, after a moment's pause.

"How gay it must be here all summer. Three hops a week, one of the cadets told me. Surely you dance at those?"

"Occasionally; those of us who remain here. Many of the officers spend their vacations elsewhere, you know."

"Ah? Are you going away this summer, Mr. Cary?"

"No. I get my vacation at another time of the year."

"Oh, I wish I could stay through June. We might do so only that Gerald does n't wish his mother to witness his sufferings. Every man I have danced with so far seems to expect to have a hand in drilling the plebes. I have warned them that a cousin of mine is coming, and that they are to be gentle with him."

Cary smiled significantly. "If you really wish well to your cousin, Miss Laflin, let me advise you not to say much about him to the cadets."

"Why?" asked the girl wonderingly.

"Oh, well, you 'll be apt to overreach yourself, that is all. Better not herald him in any way."

"I only told them that he was perfectly lovely, and I would n't have him hazed for the world."

The officer laughed lazily. "Poor fellow," he remarked, pulling his mustache.

"Oh, dear! I hope I have n't done any harm, any mischief," raising her eyes appealingly; but Cary was not called upon to answer, for at this juncture Miss Laflin's recent partner approached with the cadet whose name stood next on her card, and she rose and took the young fellow's offered arm.

"You must be thinking up something very comforting to say to me when I come back," she said over her fair shoulder to Cary as she moved away.

Her departure was a slight relief to him. He found himself once more at liberty to search the room for the small, dark, well-carried head, whose whereabouts he had known every moment up to the time of Miss Laflin's appearance. He could not find it for some time, although he looked carefully about here and there.

" I don't see Fanny," said Mrs. Bruce, who had been talking busily to Thornton. " Where is she, Mr. Cary? You are tall enough to see over the heads of all these people."

He continued his search avowedly now. " There — there she is, just going out of doors," he said, espying the white and yellow gown as it disappeared through the open doorway, escorted by a cadet captain.

" The foolish child. She is very imprudent. It is not at all warm to-night out of doors."

It certainly was, indoors. To Cary it seemed that the temperature had risen suddenly thirty degrees. He was astounded to find that it had made his heart leap to see Miss Bruce leaving the hall; and there could be no doubt that he was glowing, uncomfortable, annoyed, displeased.

" Of all the astonishing things I ever knew in my life this is the most astonishing," he said to himself, frowning, and furtively laying his hand upon his heart to inspect its unusual pumping. " What does this mean? What is Miss Bruce to me? " he inquired, pursuing his investigations. He had met the girl last summer, and had come to know her rather well, for she was then a guest in Colonel Mackenzie's family, where Cary was a favorite visitor. He knew her to be pretty, and graceful, and spirited, but he had not been conscious of more admiration for her than he had felt for a dozen other girls he had known. She had been more gracious to him in those days than at any time this year. When had this amazing change in himself begun?

He looked around the hall. He saw several couples leave the room to breathe the coolness of the summer night, but no flutter of another gauzy skirt caused a responsive flutter within him.

"Well, now, this is very interesting," he mused. "I am positively uncomfortable because Miss Bruce is out there on the walk. When she comes back, not until, this party will seem to have some point and brilliancy. I feel murderously inclined toward Beach (her partner). I want more than I ever wanted anything to go out of that door and follow them; to know if possible what they are saying to one another. Well, have I come to this!"

He evidently had come to some wholly novel state of mind, for at this moment Miss Bruce reappeared with her cavalier in the open door, and again Cary experienced that strange tightening in the chest, followed by a sensation as though his heart were trying to get out.

"This is marvelous," he said to himself, and, an idea suddenly striking him, the color rose in his face. "It can mean only one thing if Colonel

Mackenzie is right. How wonderful that would be. What can she see in an old back number like me?"

It was toward midnight when Cary had his first opportunity of the evening to speak to Miss Bruce. There were no signs of fatigue in her bright eyes as she approached her mother and consequently himself. Lenox, her escort of the evening, was beside her in that state of evident satisfaction which befits a young man in the last stages of honorable cadetship, especially when he has secured the partner he most desires for his graduation ball.

"Mr. Lenox, I do not wish my daughter to walk out in the air again to-night," said Mrs. Bruce emphatically, and Cary took advantage of the young fellow's reply to speak to the girl at whom he looked with new eyes.

"This is proving a rather exasperating evening to me, Miss Bruce," he said in a low tone.

She raised her gloved hand to the back of her head as if to adjust her hair, a movement common to many women in moments of self-consciousness; but her tone was wholly indifferent as she spoke:

"You do not miss much in not dancing to-night, really. It is too crowded."

"I wonder if you will not save one dance for me at the next hop."

"We may not be here. Our movements are quite undecided." She lifted her fan of white feathers. Last night Cary could have taken it from her hand and fanned her; but now the commonplace action took the dimensions of a liberty in his eyes. The big cavalry officer was having unprecedented difficulty in concealing his own white feather.

"But if you are here," he persisted, "may I dance with you?"

She met the gray eyes that gazed at her with such disproportionate earnestness. "I have so little to do with it," she said coolly. "A girl really does n't know whom she will find on her card, you know."

It was a rebuff, of course; but it was the memory, tenaciously clung to, of his companion's pleasant friendliness during their walk in the afternoon that pressed him forward now. "Do you not wish to dance with me?" he asked seriously, and the unexpected bluntness brought a tide of color to Miss Bruce's face.

"What a question!" she said with an uneasy laugh. "What do you expect a girl to answer to that?"

"Why, I should like it very much if you would tell me the truth."

"I have been too well brought up for it to be possible for me to take either horn of the dilemma you so kindly offer me. Yes, Mr. Lenox, I am ready," and with a little bow, her face looking more brilliant than when she had approached, she moved away.

Cary stood rather rigidly watching her and her partner as they drifted into the waltz which had begun. The adjutant of that particular First class of the United States Military Academy was an especially good dancer, and the couple wound their way through the throng with the suppleness of ribbon.

It would imply a long stride toward the Marcus Aurelian standard for any young bachelor officer at West Point to lay his hand on his heart and aver that he felt complete cordiality toward a cadet of the First class; but John Egbert Cary of the ——th cavalry was unconsciously a promising disciple of that uncompromising philosopher. He looked now quite through the slender-waisted, gray-coated figure of the adjutant and saw only the young woman the latter was guiding so cleverly. Cary was greatly stirred, and his instinctive effort to analyze this case was futile. His wounded self-love should have been soothed by the looks which Miss Laflin did not fail to cast upon him each time she and one of her yearlings passed in his neighborhood.

"She looks like a good-natured girl," he thought vaguely, as she paused once more near her aunt, and her partner left her with a bow.

"It is so warm," she remarked to the lieutenant; "but I believe I have said that before once or twice."

"It becomes truer with each dance, I suppose," returned Cary. "Shan't I fan you?" taking her fan.

"I wish you would take me out-doors," she said with her usual directness; "I am stifled."

Cary hesitated ungallantly. "Your aunt will object. She "—

"I do not propose to ask her," returned the girl decidedly, and the lieutenant had no alternative but to offer his arm. They made their way with difficulty to the door and descended the short flight of steps to the broad stone flagging. Miss Laflin breathed a deep sigh of relief and satisfaction as they sauntered southward under the great elms.

"This is ever so much nicer than being there in that crush. I hope you did not dislike leaving. I wonder that you have been willing to stand about so long."

"I like to watch dancing," said Cary simply. He thought he was telling the truth; but the taste was certainly a suddenly acquired one. "Your cousin seems to be enjoying herself exceedingly."

"Oh, yes, it is different with Fanny. She has a great many friends here. It is not easy for me to make friends. I am very peculiar about that. I take dislikes more often than I take fancies to people."

"Indeed? I should n't have thought it," replied her companion, since some comment on this calamitous state of things was evidently expected.

"Why should n't you have thought it?" asked the girl, charmed to have given a personal turn to the conversation.

Cary sighed patiently. "Because if I were guessing I should guess you to be so good-tempered!"

Miss Laflin gave a delighted little laugh. "Well, so I am; but not sufficiently so to like everybody, and if I do not like a person I cannot help showing it." She leaned a little more heavily on her companion's arm. "Don't you think it is libelous to say that women are always fascinated by brass buttons, Mr. Cary?"

"Quite so," returned the lieutenant passively. "There goes the music, Miss Laflin," and he stood still, for they had passed the hospital; "shall I take you back?"

"No, indeed. I am but just getting cool."

"But I can see your partner in my mind's eye, gazing and rushing frantically in all directions."

"What does he care? He does not know me, nor I him," said the girl decidedly. "I have refused to dance the german."

"Do you want me murdered over there in camp some night this summer by a pack of irate yearlings?"

But Miss Laflin was a large body who was not to be moved as yet in the direction of Mess Hall. "Indeed, I would do a good deal to keep you from being murdered, Lieutenant Cary," she replied in an unmistakably sentimental tone, "but don't ask me to go in yet. This is so perfectly charming."

Cary moved on perforce, and his thoughts, which had been lingering with Miss Bruce, became fixed with decided sensations of chafing and uneasiness upon his fair companion, who continued with complacent satisfaction : —

" Are you fond of walking ? "

" Very. It is my favorite pastime here," was the unguarded response.

" Oh, I am so glad ; I just love it," said Miss Laflin effusively. " You must show me some of the beauties of the place. Take me to-morrow, won't you, to find that pretty laurel such as my cousin had ; and then Flirtation Walk. Why," looking up innocently in his face, " do they call it that, Mr. Cary ? "

" Good-night," exclaimed a voice, and a figure walked swiftly past them.

" Oh, that is Thornton," said Cary hastily. " He is going home, and I must not be long after him. Our quarters are adjoining and I — I don't like to disturb him after he gets settled for the night."

" But what has that to do with our walk ? " asked Miss Laflin plaintively.

" Nothing, of course. I — I shall be pleased. What time would suit you to go ? "

It was half an hour later that Cary ran up the stairs leading to his rooms. Thornton called to him from the darkness of an opposite apartment, " Got through star-gazing ? "

" Yes," came the answer in a depressed tone. " I might not be, only there are no stars to gaze at.

It is raining. What was your hurry when you passed me out there ?"

"Thought you might be getting chosen ; so, as Uncle Remus hath it, I 'split de wind.' "

Cary came in and threw himself on the foot of his friend's bed. "I shall never be chosen, I 'm afraid," he said, with frank downheartedness. "Women do not like me. It is perfectly evident."

"Oh, go 'way, old fellow. I need glasses, and you don't ; but I can see more with my eyes than you with yours. You should have seen the rear elevation of Miss Laflin's head as she gazed up into your face a little while ago."

"That girl," said Cary, straightening up, and speaking in a lowered, confidential tone, "that girl, Thornton, is n't right in her head."

The second lieutenant burst into a loud laugh.

"I mean it for a fact," averred the other.

Thornton rolled over in bed.

"Hold your noise. You 'll disturb the people downstairs. There 's nothing to laugh at, I tell you. She is off. I am sure of it."

"I know. I understand. She has been making a dead set at you all the evening. Just what you have been yearning and panting and sighing for for thirty years, and now look at your black ingratitude ! "

"You don't understand," returned Cary testily, "and, what is more, you have n't the ability to."

"No, I don't believe I have," gurgled Thornton, as his friend closed the door behind him with an expenditure of nervous energy unbefitting a philosopher.

Cary found his thoughts unpleasant companions that night, and he awoke next morning in a dissatisfied frame of mind. He attended the graduating exercises, and looked on at the whole in a gloomy and cynical spirit. It was nearly ten years since he had sat among his class under similar circumstances. How full of hope and happiness he had been then! It seemed to him now that he had been getting ready to live ever since. It was of no use to harbor false and vague expectations any longer.

"This is life," he thought. "I am living now as truly as I ever shall," and he found himself gazing at Miss Bruce's handsome and expressive face, lighted with interest in the ceremonies that were taking place.

He could not regard her, however, without running the risk of appearing to gaze at Miss Laflin, who was seated beside her. That young woman, perfectly dressed, even distinguished in her appearance, gave him a shudder by the eagerness of her recognition. He had the walk with her in prospect for the afternoon. He even scowled as his eye fell upon Colonel Mackenzie's benevolent countenance. He wished he had never heard that gentleman's precious theories.

Miss Laflin was not to be envied her cavalier that day, yet as Cary was habitually silent and grave she did not apparently feel any lack. The necessity for exertion in the locality he had maliciously chosen for their ramble absorbed her energies, and as they returned, rich in flowery spoils, the lieutenant became less taciturn in proportion to their approach to the hotel. She parted from him in undiminished spirits, but, he devoutly believed, so fatigued that she would not propose another walk among the highlands. When she had disappeared within the house Cary did not leave the hotel at once. He knew it to be an hour when the piazzas were not popular, and at all times of day he liked the view up the river, and never wearied of watching the varied craft that plied up and down. He strode toward the back of the building, straight to the piazza rail. He knew those hills and their varying expressions as he knew his friends' faces. They were more soothing to him now than any friend's face could be.

A little motion made him turn, and he saw that there was a woman sitting in the corner of the piazza. Her head and shoulders were concealed by a black and white parasol which Cary knew well. He had held it over her on several occasions. He denounced the fate which had made him choose to come to the spot now, and determined to withdraw without disturbing the solitary figure. Turning on his heel, he took two of his long steps, but was arrested at the third because the girl under the parasol said, "Oh."

"Good afternoon, Miss Bruce." Cary lifted his cap and paused because she met his eyes and looked glad to see him. "Rather sunny for reading, is n't it?"

"Not under my parasol, and I do dislike to waste time in the house in this weather, don't you?"

"Yes. You could find more shade on Trophy Point."

"I suppose so."

"And more cadets," continued the lieutenant rather uncivilly.

Still she smiled upon him. "My friends are all gone, you know," she said sweetly. "What a good time they are probably having at this moment!"

"Did they leave you a string of bell-buttons?" asked Cary.

Miss Bruce waxed more gracious as his irritation became more manifest. It was something new to see her theorizing, abstracted friend show such human weakness.

"Might you not feel better-natured sitting down?" she asked.

She knew the lieutenant had just returned from a walk with her cousin, and was not displeased that he did not appear to have enjoyed himself. Miss Laflin's intemperate expressions of admiration for him in the privacy of the girls' own apartment had produced their effect on Miss Bruce. They had made her resentful, indignant to the core, coming as they did at a moment when she was suffering from remorse at her own ill-treatment of him.

"You should not speak slightingly of those young men," she said gently, as Cary rather reluctantly approached and took a chair. "You were their favorite instructor."

"I did n't know a cadet ever had a favorite tactical officer. We had none in my time," replied Cary, with a short laugh.

"What an evil-disposed class yours must have been," remarked the young lady, twirling her parasol as it rested on her shoulder.

"But that was so long ago. Human nature has improved since then, no doubt."

Miss Bruce colored at this proof that her thrust was not forgotten. Cary swung an arm over the back of his chair and altered his position so that his eyes looked squarely into hers.

"Miss Fanny," he began, with determined seriousness, "I have been wanting to ask you what you think of the truth of those theories that Colonel Mackenzie propounded to us yesterday morning."

The girl had nearly asked, "What theories?" but she perceived in a flash that not enough time would be gained to compensate her for the silliness involved in the obvious evasion.

"They were quite interesting," she returned, after an imperceptible pause.

"What is your opinion as to their truth? I suppose you will have no objection to telling me?"

"Oh, none at all," she answered, hanging out a gay crimson flag in the fairness of her cheeks, but speaking airily. "I have an idea that Colonel Mackenzie is quite right."

The lieutenant looked scrutinizingly into the piquant face.

"You then, — pardon me for introducing personalities, — you, when you see the man whom you believe to be your mate, who you believe can make you happy, will choose him? How will he know that you have chosen him?"

"Oh, he can't fail to know it," declared the other, with sprightly vivacity. "I should — why, I should show it, of course. I should take *pains* to let him know it."

The eager expression in Cary's eyes faded. "Of course — naturally," he assented, in a low tone.

There was a pause, during which they both looked off to the river, where a steamer was laboriously tugging twenty-four barges in its wake.

"There is a screw loose somewhere," continued the lieutenant, his eyes on one of the barges, where a woman was hanging out clothes to dry. "I don't know whether it is with the professor's theory, or whether it is with me. The fact is,

Miss Bruce, — I don't mention it to annoy you, and I hope it will not, but it is abstractly interesting under the circumstances," — Cary looked back into her face, — " I am in love with you."

His companion flushed more brightly, and turned her head from him. "Of course it is n't the least in the world your fault. You have never been more than civil to me," he added hastily.

The twirling parasol revolved until it cut off from him the view of her rosy countenance. Cary reproached himself tardily for embarrassing her.

"Oh, please look at me, Miss Fanny," he begged. "I am not regretting it, you know. I would rather love you hopelessly than not at all. I " — He laid his hand on the obstructing parasol, when a heavy step advancing on the piazza made him turn impatiently.

Colonel Mackenzie appeared around the corner of the hotel.

"Well, young folks," he cried cheerily, "trying a sun-bath?"

Of course it was Miss Bruce who replied, restoring her parasol to its position behind her head.

"Come and sit down, colonel," she said cordially, although her voice was not quite steady. "Mr. Cary and I have been talking metaphysics, and we need you."

Cary rose, and, indicating his chair to the professor, seated himself on the piazza rail opposite, his face showing traces of excitement.

"Been having a rather heated argument, I perceive," remarked the colonel, taking the chair and mopping his brow with his handkerchief.

"Not quarreling ; oh, no," returned Miss Bruce. "We quite agree. We were speaking of the opinions you asserted yesterday morning, and we not only agree with each other, but with you."

"You did agree with him, you mean," said Cary, gazing at her steadily. "What I told you has shaken you."

The color ebbed slowly away from Miss Bruce's face, and she nodded. "Yes, it has shaken me a little, but not my opinion."

"Ah! Then you do not understand Colonel Mackenzie's position. You hold, professor, as I understand it, that if a man feels a deep attraction for a woman, so absorbing a love that he cannot keep silence concerning it, it is because she has already preferred him."

"That is my doctrine," declared the colonel stoutly.

"There !" exclaimed Cary, "you hear him ?"

"Yes," returned the girl in a low tone, "and I agree with him."

"You do not believe, then, what I just told you ?"

She nodded again slowly. "I believe you — yes," she said, with soft distinctness.

The agitation in her face and the look in the lieutenant's moved the colonel to generous indignation, which afterward it amused him to remember. "What has come over you, man? Can't you endure to be differed with?" he asked.

The young officer seemed not to have heard him. He looked bewildered and pale, but studied the girl's pure face more exigently than ever. "Then"— he began, and stopped.

Her lips trembled. The colonel looked from one to the other. "White with anger, upon my word," he thought. "I appeared on the scene just in time." Then aloud: "Cary, I want you to come over to the library with me. I have something there I want your opinion of."

The lieutenant stood upright and smiled at his superior officer with a look in his face the colonel had never before seen there. There was a clear-eyed, alert, triumphant expression about him as he leaned one hand on the back of Miss Bruce's chair.

"I'm sorry not to oblige you, professor, but the fact is — I'm — engaged."

Colonel Mackenzie stared a moment at the young man's changed countenance and began to suspect that —

Then he looked into Miss Bruce's face.

"Oh, it will keep well enough, Cary," he ejaculated, rising so hastily that he overturned his chair. "Don't inconvenience yourself at all. I'll"—

But nobody noticed that for once the genial

professor was at a loss for words to finish his sentence.   In the involuntary glance he cast back as he retreated around the angle of the piazza he saw that Cary had stooped.   Miss Bruce's parasol was shading two.

A CADET CAMP EPISODE

THE fresh sweetness of a morning in late June was perfuming West Point. Mrs. Rennard, walking leisurely up from the South Gate, under her voluminously laced parasol, paused just before she reached the Old Hospital to bestow the favor of her silent approval upon a rose-bush which stood loaded with blushing honors in an officer's dooryard.

After an instant the rustling of her invisible silk garments swished on as she continued her stately promenade. As she passed the Old Hospital, devoted to bachelor quarters, a cavalry officer emerged therefrom, and at sight of her bared his head with *empressement.*

"Good morning, Mrs. Rennard," he said, running down the iron steps. "Allow me." He took possession of her parasol.

"Ah, Mr. Woodward. The morning is perfectly charming," she returned, with a tone of majestic patronage, calculated to make grateful the very singing birds who were filling the air with melody.

"It is, indeed. Where is Miss Forsyth this morning?"

"Yonder on the Harris piazza. I left her for a few minutes while I went down to speak to Mrs. Court."

The young girl alluded to had already caught sight of her aunt and the young cavalryman, whose yellow stripes kept dutiful time to the deliberate movement of Mrs. Rennard's black laces, while one hand twisted the end of his well-kept mustache.

Phyllis Forsyth did not care much for Mr. Woodward's mustache. A good many girls lose interest in mustaches at West Point, and Phyllis was one of these. In other words, she was a cadet-girl, and this misguided penchant of hers Lieutenant Woodward regretted to observe, for he had never seen a girl more to his mind than the wealthy Mrs. Rennard's niece.

Just as they reached the Harris quarters Mrs. Rennard caught sight of something that interested her. "I think those are the plebes coming this way," she said, raising her lorgnette.

They were. "Phyllis, Phyllis!" she called, "come here quickly, please," and the young girl, obeying the elder lady, hastened her pace until they were in an excellent position to view the passing of "*Les Misérables*."

"I have been wanting a good opportunity for you to see these young men before they become disguised by uniforms," she said impressively, as the tired awkward squad passed by, periodically yelled at by the cadet corporals who were escorting them.

"Every girl who comes to West Point should have this warning object lesson.

"Look at some of those individuals! More like cowboys than gentlemen; yet next summer you might meet them as equals, provided you came to the Point. Do you wonder, Phyllis, that I have warned you to be careful what friends you make here?"

The girl's eyes looked pitiful as she regarded the strained faces and attitudes of the badgered novices, and she hated Woodward for his laughing comments on their appearance and the indifference with which he listened to the short-tempered corporals.

Mrs. Rennard proceeded with her exhortations after the plebes had vanished, and the three walked along by the Academic Building. Phyllis appeared to listen dutifully, but in reality little cared she for future camps and their vicissitudes. This one was enough for her.

She had been here for five weeks now, constantly in the company of cadets whom she had known also in their yearling camp. Needless to say her life was an engrossing one, and that she had little use for speculation.

An orderly gray procession began filing out from camp and across the cavalry plain.

"Shan't we wait here a moment and see the

cadets pass to dinner?" went on Mrs. Rennard in a different tone, as the shrilling of the drum corps met her ear.

A resigned expression stole over Woodward's face, and he tugged hard at his mustache. "Even you, Mrs. Rennard!" he said dryly.

"Certainly, even I," she rejoined. "One must admire their fine bearing even when their antecedents are impossible. But blood will tell. What a high-bred face that young Edgerley has!"

"I think you will have to move out of his way a little," remarked Woodward; and, indeed, the cadet captain, marching along the flagging abreast of his company, sword in hand, seemed, for all the attractions of his fine figure, to be about to attempt to walk directly upon his dignified admirer, who retreated as hastily as was possible.

Among all the trained forms and faces, Phyllis looked only at Edgerley, and, strangely, as he advanced, he, the partner of her walks and dances and teas, recognized her no more than if she had been invisible.

The only one of their company whom he apparently saw was Lieutenant Woodward. Without moving a muscle of his neck in his onward march, his alert dark eyes sought those of the officer, and as he passed him he raised his sword before his face in a quick salute, which was mechanically returned.

"I cannot get used to being entirely ignored by

these civil young men," said Mrs. Rennard, smiling graciously. "I instinctively bow — only to be cut, don't you, Phyllis?"

A little further on stood an old couple, evidently from the country, who had also been watching the cadets march to dinner. Excursionists are so common at West Point that Phyllis, who had fallen behind her aunt and Mr. Woodward, scarcely glanced at them, and was moving on, her thoughts full of the image of a dark face and a pair of flashing eyes, when the old round-shouldered man accosted her.

"Good day, miss. That's the road to Highland Falls, ain't it?" pointing along the way the cadets had gone, and upon the girl's assenting he beamed upon her with a toothless smile. "Them boys march pretty good, hey?"

Phyllis, amused, assented again, and the woman with the tired, pleasant eyes and the old Paisley shawl smiled too, patiently.

"Pa's been possessed to see 'em," she explained.

"Johnnie said we'd better not eat here in the park, though we've got our lunch," said the old man, showing the brown paper bundle in his wrinkled hand. "We come up in the stage, but I s'pose," looking at the girl wistfully, "it's quite a piece to walk to Highland Falls."

"It would be too far under this hot sun," she answered.

"That's what I said, wife; but," more hopefully, "we 've got our lunch, and we 'll go down the road a ways, where 't won't do no harm, and we 'll eat it. Then we 'll come back agin fer parade. Ye see, Johnnie did n't know we was comin', and he 's got somethin' to do this afternoon — when did he say parade was, miss?"

"Six o'clock."

"Well, well" — the eager old face fell — "that 's a good spell to wait, ain't it?"

"Pa, don't trouble the young lady," said his wife gently; then she thanked Phyllis and passed on. The girl saw that her aunt had strolled toward the hotel and sent Mr. Woodward back to meet her.

"What did those hayseeds want?" inquired the officer as he approached.

"Oh, only some information."

"Why could n't they have asked me?" Woodward took the girl's parasol as he turned to accompany her.

"Awed by your yellow stripes, probably. Poor old creatures! They have descended unexpectedly upon some cadet Johnnie, and I was just wondering if Johnnie was properly glad to see them and had treated them well."

"Oh, I dare say he wishes they had stayed at the Four Corners, or wherever they belong. Their appearance suggests it. A cadet's summer visitors are a great give-away sometimes. We get all sorts here, sure enough."

Arrived at the hotel, Phyllis saw, almost as

soon as she had passed the hedge, that some excitement was afoot.

Kate, Mrs. Rennard's stately brunette daughter, had met her on the piazza, and was apparently giving her some startling information. Mrs. Rennard's nostrils dilated as Miss Forsyth and the cavalry officer came up the steps. The piazza was deserted save for their little group.

"Mr. Woodward," she began, with imposing dignity, "I should like you to tell me what you know of Mr. Edgerley."

The lieutenant's smile was non-committal. He might have replied that he knew the cadet captain to be a thorn in his own side, but he did not.

"I know that he is lucky enough to be high in your favor," he returned.

"So he has been," declared Mrs. Rennard superbly. "We have been betrayed. It is a case in hand, Phyllis. You remember what I said to you a little while ago as the plebes passed by? May I ask you, Mr. Woodward, if you know anything of Mr. Edgerley's connections?"

"I do not, Mrs. Rennard," returned the young officer, who observed with satisfaction that, whatever the cause, his cadet rival's stock had suddenly taken a fall.

"Kate," commanded Mrs. Rennard, "tell them what you have just told me."

The tall girl's cheeks were glowing, and in spite of her effort toward a passive manner she was too

young to be able to quell the feeling in her bright
eyes.   Cadet Captain Edgerley had indeed cut
a broad swath socially in his First-class camp.
Even these two fastidious girls had had their secret
jealousies of each other on his account.

"Oh, well, it is no such great matter," said
Miss Rennard, striving to speak indifferently,
"only we all thought Mr. Edgerley was a gentleman."

"We know he is!" flashed forth Phyllis suddenly.

"Wait!" said Mrs. Rennard imperiously.

"Two country people have been over in camp
this morning asking for him," went on Kate, meeting her cousin's gaze.   "He came out and talked
with them.   They hailed him as their dear boy
Johnnie.   He kissed the woman."

Miss Rennard's even voice ceased.   She could
not keep it even any longer.   The shock of the
moment came back to her too vividly.

Phyllis's cheeks also began to glow.   "It was
they, then, that I met!" she said.   "The man had
on a linen duster."

Miss Rennard inclined her head.

Her cousin's gray eyes remained fixed upon her.

"You were going to walk with Mr. Edgerley
this morning?" said Phyllis.

"Yes.   I had promised to meet him in camp.
That is how I happened to be there."

"What did you do?"

Both girls had forgotten Woodward, and even Mrs. Rennard. They looked at each other with an interchange of understanding.

" He bowed to me as he came up, but his people surprised him and detained him, and — and I sent one of the men to him with word that I had forgotten a previous engagement, and should not be able to go with him this morning."

Miss Forsyth's lips compressed. " How did he take it ? "

" He looked over at me in a surprised way " —

" Im-per-ti-nent ! " exclaimed Mrs. Rennard ; and as the word fell from her lips it seemed to have three times the usual number of syllables, each one freighted with her appreciation of the luckless cadet's effrontery.

— " but after that look he sent back word that he understood."

" I only hope he did understand ! " declaimed Mrs. Rennard.

" Poor chap," said Lieutenant Woodward, twisting his mustache; " that was rough on him. It was a real Farmer Wayback who spoke to you, was n't it, Miss Forsyth ? "

The girl turned her dainty head toward him slowly. " Yes, they were evidently country people," she answered.

His people ! Mr. Edgerley's people with their lunch in a brown paper bundle ! They were going to eat it by the roadside somewhere. The patient, tired face of the woman came back to her with as much vividness as if she had known it all her life.

Late in the afternoon the audience began gathering for parade. Girls in pretty summer gowns flitted through the hedge before the hotel to join the bell-buttoned cavaliers, with whom they would chat and laugh and flirt until the very last moment would see the white-trousered legs of the cadets speeding toward camp to be ready for the preparatory inspection.

To-day there was a new subject for conversation among First-class men and their friends, — "Edgerley's surprise party," as some of them called it; for the old people were early on the scene to wait for "Johnnie," and laughter and speculation ran high in some quarters, while scorn and injured dignity obtained in other cliques.

The old man spoke to any one who happened to sit near him, asking questions or descanting on "Johnnie's" attainments, and he recognized Miss Forsyth as she passed near him in a fine, ethereal gown with elbow sleeves.

His faded blue eyes lighted as he sat there, both hands resting on his cane. "Here we air, you see, miss," he said happily, and Phyllis grew surpassingly rosy as she bowed slightly and passed on to her place.

Edgerley's movements at any time were a matter of interest, but this afternoon — how piquant the situation!

They had not long to wait. A hundred curious eyes recognized the cadet captain's advent from his company street half an hour before parade. What was he doing? Why did he not take the shortest cut toward the spectators? He turned to his right and moved across the plain to the guard tent, where he stopped an instant, then he began to walk deliberately along the line in front of the crowded seats.

It was evident that he chose to run a gauntlet. As he moved along in his spotless parade uniform, his dark eyes roved among the crowd. A few bowed to him; many more became preoccupied, and chatted faster than before. A few looked straight into his eyes unseeingly.

Occasionally his hand rose in the salute of an officer as he passed; and a climax of interest was reached as he approached the couple, who only now discovered him.

He paused before the strangers and gave a hand to each, and standing at ease, his feet planted slightly apart, he fell into a conversation with them which, if it were not interesting and happy to him, proved the young man to be as good an actor as he was student.

When Phyllis returned to the hotel after the parade, she found this note awaiting her : —

DEAR MISS FORSYTH, — My people having arrived unexpectedly, and for a short time only, I must reluctantly resign the pleasure of being your escort to the concert this evening and to the hop to-morrow night, in order that I may spend all the time possible with them.

   Sincerely yours, JOHN J. EDGERLEY.

Phyllis went with her aunt to the concert, where the fireflies were spangling the plain, and Lieutenant Woodward had never found her so gracious.

The next night Grant Hall was gay on the occasion of the cadet hop. The girls who had Mr. Edgerley's name on their cards exchanged remarks, all except Kate Rennard and her cousin.

Edgerley's air as he entered could not have been different if he had been escorting Mrs. Rennard herself. He found good seats for his people, who looked upon the scene with absorbed and open-lipped interest, while the gay music set the old father's cane to tapping the floor.

A dozen hearts in the room fluttered faster for his presence, and prepared replies in the event of his coming to claim the dances promised him. Perhaps his experience at parade had convinced him of his changed status. At any rate, he did not approach his friends.

Shortly after his arrival he moved across to where stood Colonel Burritt, one of his professors, and said a few words to him in a low tone.

Colonel Burritt responded, and Edgerley spoke again; then the colonel returned with him across the hall and shook hands with the old couple, talking with them a few minutes.

When kindly Colonel Burritt finally bowed and withdrew, the trio looked on in silence for a few minutes more; then Edgerley said something to his companions, and they rose and slowly left the hall with him.

Several pairs of eyes watched curiously the lonely departure of the three — the bowed figure of the old man in his short trousers, and the narrow-shouldered woman clinging to the cadet's arm.

A swinging waltz had just started. Phyllis Forsyth had been engaged to Edgerley for it, and she was dancing it with Lieutenant Woodward. He made some laughing comment on the strangers as they disappeared.

His partner suddenly stopped as they reached the door. She was panting with some overwhelming feeling. The lieutenant looked at her in surprise.

"Will you excuse me?" she said abruptly, her delicate nostrils dilating and her eyes pleading with him. "I am going out here a minute. Don't follow me."

Before he could reply she had vanished, and he stood looking at the door in bewilderment.

A few rods away in the radiant moonlight a carriage stood waiting. The cadet captain and his people had reached it when a light-footed white figure caught up with them.

"Mr. Edgerley," said Phyllis, breathless from

her agitation, " you have not introduced me to your people."

" Miss Forsyth ! " he exclaimed, in astonishment.

" Why, it 's our young lady, ma," said the old man. " I did n't see ye in that whirligig place, miss ! My head 's jest a-spinnin' 'round like a top, lookin' at them boys and girls ; but Johnnie, he would have it that we was to see everything 'long 's we 'd made out to git here."

" Yes, pa 's sat'sfied at last," said the wife gently. " You was very kind to come out to speak to us, but I 'm afraid you 'll ketch cold in that thin dress in the night air. Take her into the house, Johnnie. Good-by, dear," turning to Edgerley. " We won't never forget your kindness in this world." She lifted her thin hands to the tall cadet's face, and he stooped and kissed her. Then he shook hands with the old man, and tucked them both into the carriage. " I hope you 'll have a good trip back ; and don't forget . to write me," he said cheerily.

The horses started off in the direction of Highland Falls, and the smile faded from Edgerley's face as he turned toward Phyllis.

" What does this mean, Miss Forsyth ? " he asked.

" It means that I wished to meet your parents," she answered him, with soft and breathless defiance.

He continued to look at her for a time as she stood, her head thrown back ; then he offered her his arm, and they walked without speech to the hall.

When they had reached the foot of the steps, he stood still.

" Will you go in there and dance with me ? " he asked.

" Yes," she answered quickly.

He smiled down at her, a very tender and proud expression in his eyes.

" You mean to stand by me, then ? "

" Always."

The answer and the manner of it made him take her hand. The old elms waved slowly and caressingly above them, and the waltz music floated out from the open windows.

" Phyllis, until yesterday I meant to get courage somehow to tell you how I love you, but I did n't think it would come like this — when I was despairing. Have n't my people — my dear, dear old people — frightened you ? "

She looked up at him through moist eyes.

" Nothing frightens me but losing you, Jack ! "

Five minutes afterward Mrs. Rennard's face grew deeply, darkly red, for her niece floated past her in the waltz with Jack Edgerley.

The dance had been nearly over when they entered the hall, and when the music ceased Mrs. Rennard caught the look that passed between

Phyllis and "that common young man," — a look that spoke volumes to her suspicious eyes.

Her daughter soon came to her side. Kate was evidently quite as agitated as herself, but they were obliged to content themselves with meaning glances until the hop was over.

"Where is Phyllis, Kate?" asked Mrs. Rennard then, with subdued sharpness.

"She has disappeared completely. I am disgusted with her!" exclaimed the young girl.

Then Kate's escort claimed her for the stroll back to the hotel, and, Colonel Burritt happening to leave the hall as Mrs. Rennard did, the two walked along together.

Kate had been in her room several minutes when her mother entered. Mrs. Rennard's crimson and angry expression had died away, but her face betrayed some excitement still. "We have been misled, Kate," she announced impressively. "Colonel Burritt has been telling me quite a romantic story of Mr. Edgerley's family. It seems they are entirely *comme il faut*. His father was a very wealthy man, but unfortunate, and became an embezzler for a large amount."

Kate stared.

"The unhappy gentleman died shortly before Mr. Edgerley's birth, and his mother, always afterward being an invalid, frequently left her child in charge of a worthy old couple who lived in the village where she had her country house. They are the people who have just been here. Really, it is a little mortifying to have snubbed him. Ah, Phyllis," for here the young girl came in, her face pale, but the shine of the stars still in her eyes, "I must take you to task a little, my dear. Have n't you been rather exclusive with our cadet captain to-night?"

The playful tone surprised the girl.

"Then you won't make it hard for me?" she exclaimed softly, moving to her aunt and receiving from her a gracious embrace.

Kate Rennard's dark cheeks glowed and she bit her lip hard. "I hope Mr. Edgerley is not hurt by anything I have done," she said.

Phyllis glanced at her with genuine but wounding innocence.

"I don't think he cares," she answered.

A FRANCO-AMERICAN

Miss Violet Glasgow was standing near the rail of an outward-bound Cunarder alone. The startling fact that she was alone penetrated at first vaguely, then acutely, to the brain of Mr. Richard Eames, who had been dozing luxuriously in his steamer chair, a few rods distant.

During the two months since he first met her he had been more or less consciously on the lookout for opportunities like the present, and had even taken passage on the Etruria three weeks before the government demanded his return, in the undeclared hope of securing many undisturbed interviews with this vivacious maiden. Events proved, however, that he was not singular in his enjoyment of her society, and, consequently, the discovery of the present situation caused him to be alertly awake and on his feet in a second.

"Are you wearing something enchanted which makes you invisible to all men but me?" he asked, as he approached her.

The girl turned to him with an airy pose of the head. "You intend to flatter me," she said, with a slight foreign accent, "so I will take the will for the deed."

" Unfeeling young woman ! "

" I am not sure that it is a compliment to imply that I am usually surrounded by men, especially when the implication is made by a person who does not understand that I permit their attentions on principle," Miss Glasgow spoke loftily.

" I humbly beg to be enlightened. We have but one day left for me to continue my respectful study of the Franco-American character."

" Drop the Franco. I am American through and through. That is why I have contended for my rights with Aunt Margaret. I was but five years of age when she took me to France, and, as I have lived there ever since, you can imagine that I have had some difficulty to preserve purely American principles, especially since my aunt is very much affected by French ideas."

" You must have had a struggle," returned her companion, with praiseworthy gravity.

" A struggle, indeed ! Just fancy ! " Violet lowered her voice confidentially, " my aunt would like me to marry a man I have never seen, the son of a dear friend of hers. She is as extreme as that ! "

" Atrocious ! " exclaimed Eames feelingly.

" I have been busy at school most of my life, of course ; but I always knew I was going home to America some day, and as soon as we set foot on this vessel, I considered that I had already arrived."

"Precisely."

"And when Aunt Margaret demurred at the — attentions you referred to, I simply reminded her of her nationality. I intend to enjoy the rights of my countrywomen, and said I to her : —

"' *Down* with the traitor, and
Up with the Star.'"

"Noble patriot! Your aunt being the traitor, and you being the star. I see. I see!"

"I have known American girls in Paris. I know their ways. Do you suppose I am going home to behave like a foreigner? No. *Jamais de la vie!*"

At the nervous energy of the exclamation Mr. Eames could only nod a respectful agreement.

"Do you expect to remain in America?" he asked.

"I hope so. If it is what I think it is, I shall want to. I have a sister there." The brown eyes looked off musingly.

"When have you seen her?"

"Not once in all these years. A twin sister at that. Another aunt took her when we were left orphans. Does n't it seem sad that we should have been divided? But each aunt wanted us, so there was no other way. Can you imagine, Mr. Eames, what it must be to have a twin soul, — a creature so nearly one with you that separation creates a constant craving for the absent one?"

"I — I suppose I ought to be able to" —

" Why, you are just like me," interrupted the girl delightedly, her bright face, with its daintily-curved mouth, confronting him. " I suppose I ought to be able to, but, as a matter of fact, I never was. Phœbe — my sister's name is Phœbe — and I have corresponded always, of course, but she does not write long letters ; she goes to a school called Smith College, and she is very busy, and — well, there are several girls to whom I feel nearer. Now, is n't that dreadful ? "

She caught her lip between her small teeth and gazed at Eames for sympathy. He shook his head with the gravity the situation demanded.

" I think it argues something wicked in me that I am not more eager to see Phœbe. I was pondering over it when you came up ; trying to justify myself, you know."

" How were you getting on ? "

" Slowly. My sister has been brought up in a provincial village, and on that score I was excusing myself for suspecting that we should not have much in common. I was wondering how she would behave, and — and *dress*. Was n't it small and selfish ? "

Eames lifted his eyes and hands skyward in righteous amazement.

" Yes, it was cold-blooded," went on the girl. " I wonder you do not recoil from me."

" It is strange ; but then, you know, in this world it is the unexpected that always happens.

Of course you have pictures of your sister. Does she resemble you as closely as she ought to?"

The girl looked at him alertly. " Are you paying me another compliment?"

" Not wishing to be snubbed twice in the same interview — no, I am merely putting a physiological query."

" Do you suppose I would snub an officer in *our* army?" reproachfully.

" Well, I have gathered that under provocation you would."

" No, Mr. Eames; you are entirely mistaken. It hurts me to be so misunderstood. You are sacred in my eyes."

The lieutenant smiled. " Whe — ew! and such eyes!"

" Be careful!"

" Oh, well — since I am assured immunity."

" But you should n't be flippant; you should have too much self-respect. Officers in the United States army should have something better to do than to make pretty speeches to girls."

" They manage to make time for that."

" I shall shortly know more about it," observed Miss Glasgow, regarding him musingly, " for one of the first places I am going to in America is a military post."

" Indeed? I thought your destination was among the Berkshire hills."

" Yes, it was at first, but our plans are changed

since I talked to you about them. I have a cousin who is married to an army officer, and she has invited my sister and me to visit together at her house. I consider it an especially happy beginning to go first where the stars and stripes are waving."

"Auspicious, indeed! What post is it which is going to gain such an enthusiast?"

Violet's fair brow contracted slightly. "The name has slipped my mind this minute. Mrs. Jameson, that is my cousin, says it is a lovely place, on a river."

"Mrs. Jameson!" eagerly. "I suppose it is not West Point?"

"*C'est ça!*" ejaculated the girl, nodding with satisfaction. "That is the name."

Eames threw back his head, with an exclamation. "So much the better for me. That is my post at present. You know our military academy is situated there, and I am detailed as an instructor."

"What in?"

"French."

"*À la bonne heure!*" said the girl, following the exclamation with a voluble flow of words in the graceful language, against which Eames made protesting gestures, finally flying his handkerchief to the fresh breeze.

"Do you know a flag of truce when you see it?" he asked. "Are n't you aware that the best teachers of the voice can't sing a note? I don't know how it may be elsewhere, but in languages at West Point the analogy is complete."

"I have no doubt you are only obstinate," responded the girl, with a shrug.

"So that is to be the spot where you and your sister make one another's acquaintance?" mused Eames.

"Yes, and you may be sure I should not have made such confessions to you had I supposed we should ever meet again after to-morrow." She glanced at the lieutenant, and something in his gaze brought a flush to her cheeks.

"I am delighted at the prospect of observing whether your native land meets your expectations, and whether you bear up nobly in case your sister's traditions fulfill your worst apprehensions; but I shall not see you until you have had time to adjust yourself to the facts, whatever they may be. I am not obliged to report until the twenty-eighth."

"I am very glad of it, I am sure," returned the girl. "It is unfortunate that I chose you for a confidant."

"But you will still be there by the twenty-eighth?"

"I cannot say. My aunt is going to relinquish me to my sister and Mrs. Jameson for the summer — provisionally." An eloquent lift of prettily defined eyebrows pointed Miss Glasgow's words.

"I see. You let your aunt go, but you keep a string tied to her."

" What ? " much mystified.

" As they say in America," returned Eames explanatorily.

" Oh, yes." Miss Glasgow looked pleased and eager. " That is slang, I suppose, and I am so anxious to learn it all."

The lieutenant smiled. " But there is only one day left, you see."

" I know ever so much already," Violet answered triumphantly.

" Well, I prophesy that you will not need the metaphorical string. You won't want your aunt. There is something wrong with a girl who does not enjoy West Point."

" Indeed ? "

" Certainly ; and, in your case, principle will uphold you if nothing else. What more can you ask than to be surrounded by those who are already your country's defenders, and those who are learning to become so ? "

" You mean the students ? "

" Yes, the cadets. Which do you intend to be, in the society of the post, an officer-girl, or a cadet-girl ? "

" Which is more amusing ? " she asked gravely.

" That is not for me to say," returned Eames modestly.

" Is n't it proper to be both ? "

" Perfectly, but it is not always possible. It depends upon how clever you are."

"You see, I don't know how clever I am yet," returned the girl ingenuously, "I have been so recently emancipated."

Her companion laughed; but here certain others of Miss Glasgow's fellow-voyagers approached, and Eames did not see her alone again before they landed.

Mrs. Dent, Violet's aunt, had been exiled so many years from her native land that she was eager to visit certain old friends with whom her niece would have nothing in common, and, therefore, she was very willing to give her into the hands of Mrs. Jameson. "Phœbe would not come with me," announced that little woman briskly, while they were all waiting the movements of the customs officials. "She had some sentiment about greeting her twin first in this public place."

"Alas!" thought Violet, "she is sentimental."

With Mrs. Jameson — stylish, pretty, vivacious — she decided at once that she should get on admirably, and she bade farewell to her aunt in good spirits.

"Take care of her, Belle," said Mrs. Dent, in her sonorous, impressive accents. "I do trust she won't make you any trouble. Violet is a good girl."

Mrs. Jameson appeared to have no apprehensions. Indeed, hers was the cheerful, adaptable disposition invaluable to an army-woman and the army-woman's husband. She observed the effusive leavetaking of her young cousin by the latter's traveling companions, and decided that the girl must be as attractive as she looked. Among these was Mr. Eames, to whom Mrs. Jameson gave the handshake of good comradeship.

"What are you back for?" she demanded.

"More visits to make. I 'm so popular, you see. What is new?"

"Nothing but my twins. I 'll let you come and see them when you return, if you 're good."

"Wha — what! Oh, you mean the Miss Glasgows."

"Of course. I hope you have n't imbibed English slowness in two months."

"I don't know. The soil was favorable, you see, to start with."

"That is one of the best fellows in the world," said Mrs. Jameson, as she put her charge into a carriage. "He belongs to my husband's regiment, and we are so fond of him."

Violet listened attentively. She had known American women in Paris, but that was different from observing and listening to one of the envied beings in her native air and on American soil.

"I am so glad to be at home," she sighed, as the carriage rattled away to a hotel.

Mrs. Jameson laughed. "Why, bless your heart, is that the way you feel about it?"

"Of course it is," replied the girl, with dignity.

" Well, you are a loyal soul and I am proud of you."

" Is my sister well ? " asked Violet tentatively.

" Yes, she is always well."

" A regular milkmaid, I suppose," thought Miss Glasgow. " Are we alike ? " she inquired aloud.

" Very much, in feature ; but I think your style is quite different. Of course, I can't be sure yet."

" Oh, yes, you can," thought the other, with such emphasis that it is a wonder the words did not escape.

" Aunt Marion's home is so quiet it must be a great pleasure to Phœbe to see something of the world with you."

" I think she will enjoy herself. She arrived only yesterday."

The next morning Mrs. Jameson took her cousin up the river by boat. " I do not expect Phœbe will come down to meet us," she said, as the landing-bell rang for the West Point dock. " She is a girl of decided ideas, and she evidently does not choose that strangers shall witness her meeting with the sister that she has not seen for fourteen years."

Violet looked about her curiously. As the omnibus in which they sat ascended the steep, winding road, she was more engrossed in her surroundings than in anticipation of the doubtful pleasure of meeting her twin.

Meanwhile, on the vine-laden porch of Mrs. Jameson's cottage a young girl waited, looking through the clustering leaves for the first glimpse of the stage. This moment was one she had longed for ever since the decision was made that Aunt Margaret should bring Violet to America. Phœbe Glasgow had the same fine, small mouth, the same brown hair and eyes as her sister. She was dressed now in white, open at the throat, and the light of anticipation made her demure face unwontedly vivacious.

At last the plodding horses and cumbrous vehicle came in sight. Phœbe started to run down the steps, but restrained herself with an effort. The big stage stopped, two ladies dismounted, and the girl could hold back no longer.

Violet, looking up, saw a white figure flit behind the vines and then run fleetly down the steps, cool and fair in the hot August sunshine.

The stage rumbled away. "I'll hold all the parcels," said Mrs. Jameson, "while you girls put fourteen years' affection into one hug."

Violet quite forgot her doubts and fears in that moment when her sister held her in her arms. It was evident that in Phœbe's mind no forebodings had mingled with anticipation. As the latter drew back, her eyes were bright with unshed tears.

"Now, come in," said Mrs. Jameson energetically. "You have too much to say to each other for me to allow a beginning out here."

Violet kept an arm about her sister as they ascended the steps. She felt a very kindly and affectionate patronage of her.

"I hope you mean to stay in this country," said Phœbe, watching and listening to her sister as they sat at lunch, with fond wonder at and admiration of her foreign mannerisms. "Aunt Marion charged me to give you a cordial invitation to make a long visit with us."

Violet returned her look with a perturbed expression. "I mean to keep you with me wherever I go, but you ask me to make a long stay on a farm? Oh," with a winning smile, "come off!"

Phœbe held the fork which was about to convey salad to her lips poised half way, and turned her astonished gaze from her sister to Mrs. Jameson.

"Aunt Marion is very kind, of course, and I want to see her; but it is good that you could meet me here. Which are you going to be, Phœbe, a cadet-girl or an officer-girl?"

"Listen to the child," laughed Mrs. Jameson. "She talks the jargon of the place already. Oh, that is due to Mr. Eames."

Phœbe's salad reached its destination. "I shall be whichever is most entertaining, I suppose," she returned, with her usual quiet self-possession.

"Wise maiden," remarked her cousin. "To-morrow evening you will try to be cadet-girls, for I have partners for you both for the hop."

"You are very thoughtful, cousin Belle," returned Phœbe. "I hope you are not going to feel a care of entertaining us, for, indeed, we shall find it delightful enough just to be here."

"For my part, I wish to be in whatever is going on," said Violet. "I want to see everything, and I want to do everything that is proper — American-proper, I mean. I want to be in the swim."

"I shall not feel any burden of entertaining you," replied Mrs. Jameson. "There are a number of young persons who will·take that off my hands, at least while camp lasts. I have spoken to my girl friends; they will all come to call on you presently."

"There is a camp, is there?" asked Violet, looking up, with interest. "Why, it must be a jolly place."

"It is very beautiful," said Phœbe. "I am sure you must have enjoyed the ride up the river, even though you have seen the Rhine."

"Yes, indeed. The banks of the Rhine are, to my mind, disfigured by the vineyards; and I do not care particularly for those historical castles. Oh, yes, I don't think the Rhine is in it with the Hudson. Why do you stare so, Phœbe? Have I such round, shocked-looking eyes as that, cousin Belle?"

"Excuse me," said Phœbe, lowering her gaze and coloring slightly, "but it sounds so strange to hear you use such expressions."

"Oh, I dare say they are new to you, for no doubt a farm in Berkshire County is as remote as Paris from the American world's speech. Do you know how to dance, Phœbe?" The question was added rather anxiously. "For perhaps I could teach you before to-morrow evening."

Phœbe's demure little mouth smiled at her plate. "I think I can get along, but — but it is n't good form to talk slang, Violet."

Her sister laughed merrily. "Not to Uncle Isaac's cows and poultry, I daresay."

Phœbe's expressive eyes besought their hostess.

"It is not good form anywhere, my dear," said Mrs. Jameson pleasantly. "I am afraid that wretch of a Dick Eames has been stuffing you — I mean — oh, horrors, don't look at me, Phœbe!"

"Stuffing me! Is n't that amusing?" said Violet alertly.

"Not in the least!" ejaculated the hostess. "It is absurd. Those miserable expressions are as insidious as they are hideous. What I meant to say was that Mr. Eames had been gulling you — amusing himself by teaching you Americanisms."

"No, no, he did n't. Nobody taught me. The men on board talked" —

"Oh, of course the men said those things."

"And in America do not women do just what men do?"

"Not unless they wish to commit social suicide."

Miss Glasgow laid down her knife and fork and looked as though the foundations of her hostess' house were tottering.

But as days went on, and she discovered the (to her) unaccustomed latitude allowed the young girls about her, her spirits rose. She entered into the daily routine of the post life with a zest which her sister in part shared. She found that Phœbe's clothes were unobtrusive and sufficiently fashionable, and enjoyed bestowing upon her lavishly from her own wardrobe. But the patronage she had expected to feel toward Phœbe vanished. The latter was a girl, she decided, without much fun in her, but the innate dignity and natural self-possession of her sister elicited her admiration. Moreover, she learned by degrees that Phœbe was carefully educated, and had by no means spent her life in a narrow place. She even felt a little awe of her twin, whose serious, surprised gaze seemed sometimes a rebuke.

On the evening of the annual illumination of camp, the band was playing on the green when Lieutenant and Mrs. Jameson and their girls passed under the Chinese lanterns swinging from an arch in front of the tents. 'Poles were everywhere twined with colored paper. At the front of the general parade a well-grown kitten slumbered peacefully in a small wire cage, before and behind which burned rows of candles, whose warmth was apparently agreeable to the animal. The tents, all well-lighted, were decorated with chains of bell-buttons, caricatures, and illuminated texts, which affably assured the visitor that Huyler's best would not be unwelcome as a free-will offering. Gay lanterns burned wherever one could be hung, while stacked guns and draped or flying flags enlivened the scene.

Beside the kitten's cage Violet greeted the cadet whom she had promised to meet, and Phœbe walked on with her cousin. Stopping to laugh at or admire one and another evidence of cadet ingenuity, the party soon became separated.

Phœbe stopped near an officer's tent to look at a large charcoal sketch of the superintendent, executed by a clever hand, and the Jamesons strolled on. She was just glancing ahead and thinking she must hasten when a hearty voice greeted her.

"Good evening, Miss Glasgow. I felt sure I should find you if I patrolled the streets systematically. Well, how is it? Do the stars and stripes meet your expectations? And how about your sister? Did it prove that the Hayseed family have formed her on their pattern?"

Phœbe looked up, at first surprised. Before Eames had finished she recognized his identity, for Violet and Mrs. Jameson had referred several times to the officer whose acquaintance the former had made this summer, and who returned with her on the boat. Until his closing question the girl's only thought was to undeceive him as considerately as possible, but the implication surprised her. The hot blood flew to her cheeks, and mechanically she moved on slowly, Eames keeping step with her. Mrs. Jameson, looking back, saw in the dimly lighted street that an officer had joined her cousin, and went on her way.

" Did I really give you cause to speak in that manner of my sister ? " asked Phœbe.

" Ah, I see. The reality has proved so contrary to your expectations that you are surprised to remember your doubts. I suppose you and your sister are, after all, two hearts that beat as one."

" I can scarcely say that. We are fond of each other, but we are — well, different."

" Indeed ? And how is your slang vocabulary progressing ? If you add the West Point localisms to your ' sabre-cuts of Saxon speech ' you will be well equipped."

Phœbe looked at her companion closely. She liked his face as far as she could see it in the half light, and his voice was pleasant and honest.

" Do you know," she said seriously, " I think it was not at all friendly of you not to tell me that nice American girls do not use slang."

" Why — why " — hesitated Eames, surprised and crestfallen, " some of them do."

" Do you admire them more for it ? "

" Well — no."

" It seems to me," said Phœbe reflectively, " a

perfect wonder that men should not be more friendly to women."

Lieutenant Eames felt vaguely uncomfortable, and cleared his throat with very little idea what words of wisdom he was preparing the way for.

"Why does a man always think that it is perfectly legitimate for him to get all the amusement out of a girl that he can?" pursued his companion.

"Oh, come now, you know that women get even with us there," said Eames, in an injured tone.

Miss Glasgow's conscience here made a little remark, but she silenced it.

"They have learned to make the most of such opportunities as they find here and there," she responded; "but they should draw the line at their own sex. I am ashamed to think I — ridiculed my sister to you!"

"You did n't; you did n't," responded Eames hastily, made remorseful by her tone. "You must know that nothing you said gave me the right to make my poor joke. It was a poor one; mine usually are. I only meant to tease you a little. Pray forgive me."

"Well," murmured Phœbe, comforted, "I am glad." A brief silence fell between them, during which she considered the best means of revealing herself to her companion; but while she was hesitating he spoke in a changed tone.

"When we were on board ship, Miss Glasgow, I was not in a condition to give you advice of any kind. I have been affected by you in a strange manner from the day we first met. My feeling didn't seem reasonable, and I have been trying to understand it. For the last two weeks I have been broiling in the city instead of coming up here, simply in order to think it out; and there is no longer any doubt" —

"Oh!" interrupted Phœbe breathlessly.

— "that there can never be any peace for me until I tell you how I love you, how" —

"Oh, oh, how dreadful!" Phœbe stood motionless in the deserted spot they had reached, and her soft tone of horror caused her companion to retreat a step.

"How can I ever confess!" she exclaimed. "Violet never said — oh, believe me, I" — She paused, and Eames regarded the bent head and tightly clasped hands with bewilderment.

"Ah!" he said at last, with a short, sharp breath. Then he lifted his cap formally. "I am not quickwitted, as my friends occasionally remind me, but I believe I understand you. You must be" —

"Miss Hayseed, yes," said Phœbe meekly.

Meanwhile, Violet, escorted by a cadet lieutenant, had wandered up one street and down another, inspecting everything, asking questions, and prattling volubly in the manner which made her popular in the corps; for if there is one being who more than another appreciates being saved the trouble of conversing it is a cadet in the U. S. M. A.

They were passing the charcoal sketch of the superintendent when Violet discovered that she had dropped her handkerchief.

"I know where it is," said her companion. "No doubt you dropped it there in the tent where you were handling the rifles. I'll get it in a second."

He ran back, and Violet waited, regarding idly the heroic size of the features on the tall stretcher behind whose screen she suddenly heard voices.

"I don't care, she is an awfully jolly girl," said a masculine voice.

"Yes, of course," responded a scornful treble. Violet recognized the speakers as a cadet whom she knew, and his sister. "I know it is very flattering when a girl rolls up her eyes at you men, and asks you if things are 'proper.' It is very novel and pleasant for you, no doubt, to decide what the bounds shall be."

"Now look out, Jenny, Miss Glasgow is all right."

"Of course she is. How could any girl fail to be 'all right' whose conduct is prescribed by the corps of cadets! I suppose those confiding little questions of hers as to propriety could never be worn thin to you. What folly! As though anybody with common sense did not know that nice girls are nice girls the world over, and if they happen to live in a civilized part of it they are guarded with a decent amount of conventionality. It is all affectation on Miss Glasgow's part for the sake of giving and taking a little more license than the rest of us, and managing at the same time to retain your respect."

"Now let up," protested the other voice, sounding fainter as the couple moved away. "Just because she is prettier and jollier" —

"Here it is," called Violet's emissary, waving the handkerchief as he approached; then more softly, "I think you might give it to me for my trouble."

"No, please," replied the girl with pale lips, taking the bit of lawn. "Do you think we could find Mrs. Jameson? I am ill; I want to go home."

They moved to the spot where the crowd was greatest, and all at once were confronted by a tall officer of artillery, at sight of whom Violet gave a start.

"Oh, Mr. Eames!" she exclaimed, stretching out her hand involuntarily. "Could you — would you take me home?"

"Certainly."

Violet thanked her companion hastily, but courteously, and moved away with the officer. "Let us get out of the light," she said.

" What is the matter ? "

" I am ill, disgusted.   Everything is the matter. Oh, how glad I was to see you ! "

" That is good to hear.   Well, you have dis- covered America."

" Yes, and I have discovered more than that. I have learned that a nice girl is a nice girl the world over, and that men and women can't be friends anywhere.   There is a neutral ground where they may safely meet, but it is a narrow strip, as narrow here as it is in France.   When did you arrive ? "

" A few hours ago, but I have already heard of your success as a cadet-girl."

" Don't call me that.   I am through."

" It is the officers' turn, then.   I am glad of it.   What do you suppose I have been doing this evening ? "

" I cannot guess."

They were sauntering across the cavalry plain in the direction of the Jamesons' quarters, and in the darkness Violet had accepted the lieutenant's offered arm.

" I have been making love to your sister."

" To Phœbe ! " in sharp surprise.   Violet felt as though a cold hand were laid on her sore heart. " But she is already engaged; and is that consid- ered proper ? "

" I gave her to understand that I wanted to marry her.   I did not know she was engaged, but had I known it I am afraid I should have done the same thing."

Silence.

"Well, why don't you make some comment, Violet?"

"I do not understand you Americans," she answered, sighing wearily. "Won't you walk a little faster, please?"

"Cannot you guess how I came to tell your sister that I loved her?"

"Oh — why" — faintly, and with long pauses, "don't hurry quite so fast, please."

"I took her for you. Can you ever forgive me for being such a bungler?"

."It is n't your fault that I have a twin sister," said the girl softly.

"Violet!"

"No, no, don't do that. I must think. A few minutes ago I meant to go back to France and marry the man I have never seen. I wanted to be as French as possible."

"But that would condemn one man you have seen to utter misery. Think again, darling!"

"I have dreamed about you every night since I landed," admitted the girl slowly, "but — Oh, Mr. Eames," she added breathlessly, as he suddenly took her in his arms under the shadow of a huge elm, "is this prop—"

"You know very well that we shall have to invite Ellen Day here sometime, and what *is* the use of postponing it?"

Mrs. Burritt looked over toward the window where her daughter stood drumming on the glass, an impatient cloud on her face.

"I fail entirely to see why it is necessary," returned Miss Burritt obstinately.

"Your other girl relatives have all been here. Ellen's mother knows it well enough, you may be sure; and, by pure contrariness, your father never forgets about this matter, although he usually is so indifferent. He keeps at me on the subject, and I do wish, Daisy, you would make up your mind to consent and let us send the invitation, and have it over with."

Miss Burritt, *ætat* nineteen, was so supremely satisfied with her lot as the good-looking daughter of a West Point professor, that she dreaded an added responsibility which brought no glory with it. She continued to gaze down on the stately river flowing far below her.

"West Point is no place for country cousins," she replied.

"You might say that to your father," suggested Mrs. Burritt sarcastically. "No, Daisy, your obstinacy in this matter is exasperatingly selfish. We 've talked this over often, and you always put me off. I tell you, I 'm tired of being nagged at by your father and resisted by you."

Miss Burritt's lip curled.

"The idea of having to drag about with one a girl from the cross-roads, who can't dance and can't talk and has no style! The idea of having to introduce her as one of the family!"

"Pshaw! As if you never need make a sacrifice! I think you can stand it for two weeks. You know you would n't dare say one word to your father of what you are saying to me, and you think it 's nothing that I have to fix up excuses and put him off time after time. Ellen's mother being his only sister, he wants to pay her proper attention, and, in fact, he is very fond of her. It is lucky for us that family cares tie her down, or I know he would want her to be with us the whole summer."

"How pleasant it will be to have Ellen appear here in my old clothes made over! Blanche Barstow would recognize them instantly."

"Well, now, don't borrow so much trouble. Perhaps everything would go very pleasantly."

"Imagine Mr. Lorimer and Mr. Deering trying to talk to that sort of a girl!" pursued Miss Burritt disdainfully.

"Oh, she need n't have much to do with the cadets," returned her mother soothingly. "She would feel too shy and strange, anyway. She will enjoy seeing guard mount and parade, and life as it goes on here, and it would soon be over. You"—

Here both mother and daughter started, for Colonel Burritt suddenly entered the room. He was a large man, of soldierly carriage, and his direct glance now had a firmness and determination before which his wife and child were silent. He held an open letter in his hand.

"Here, Margaret," he said to his wife, "before the house gets filled up with any more guests, I want to have Ellen Day here. I 've written to her mother to let her come right along. I 'd like you to add a few words, and if Daisy feels like doing so too, so much the better. We want to make her feel a warm welcome in advance, for most likely the little girl is shy."

Well for the colonel that as he strode out of his house and closed the door behind him, he did not suspect the unfilial sentiments swelling the breast of his only child.

"There, now, we can't help it," declared Mrs. Burritt in resigned tones. "There is one possibility that you don't seem to consider. Ellen may decline."

"Any girl who gets the opportunity to visit the Point in summer, decline? I think not!" replied Daisy.

And, indeed, Ellen Day never considered declining. The cordial letter from Colonel Burritt, with its civil postscript, brought rejoicing into the little hamlet of Burrittville, where it was received. Happy, though care-laden, Mrs. Day willingly gave up her chief helper in order that Ellen might have such a holiday, and soon it was known throughout the village that the girl was going to West Point.

The local dressmaker, bosom friend to everybody, was called in to help on the slender wardrobe.

"I suppose I had better not take anything that was Daisy's, and it does n't leave me much," said Ellen doubtfully.

She had never paid much attention to clothes, for the best of reasons. Each one of her gowns had always been a matter which "Hobson's choice," not her own, decided, and that state of things having obtained through all her twenty years of life, whatever instinct for attractive plumage she might have developed had early been inhibited.

Her figure was thin and commonplace, and so was her face, but for its intelligence. Her gray eyes held a charming expression of good humor and comprehension, and her sound white teeth were easily displayed in ready smiles. She dressed her straight brown hair with the one and sole object of getting it out of the way, and as she looked at her gowns now with Miss Bascom, her thin face serious over the troublesome question of ways and means, the dressmaker picked her teeth with a needle, and wished that for the circumstances' sake, Ellen Day had been born prettier.

"They're a dreadful gay set up there," said Miss Bascom decidedly. "So I've always heard. You must have one white muslin."

"But how can I?" Something beside doubt in Ellen's tone made Miss Bascom's eyes snap.

"You must think of a way!" she said firmly. "I may get you out a black skirt with these things, and we can make shirt waists; but you must have one party dress. Now, you know very well if 't was a book you needed instead o' book *muslin*, you'd manage to get it."

The girl smiled. "Don't you think this brown and white organdie"— she began hopefully.

"No, I *don't*. 'T won't do at all. You're goin' there to your uncle's elegant house, with the aristocracy o' the land just swarmin' around. Do you think that old faded organdie would go well with gold epaulets? No, sir! You've got to have a white muslin. Your mother's told me how you read and study nights. Now, honestly, ain't you savin' up money for something?"

The shrewd though random question struck home. Ellen colored.

"You are!" exclaimed Miss Bascom in triumph.

"There is such a good, cheap encyclopædia advertised "—

" Encyclo-fiddlesticks ! " ejaculated the village oracle. " What 'll you care for such things when you are an officer's wife? You fetch that money right off, Ellen Day, and I 'll see what we can do."

So Ellen meekly watched her slowly saved dollars, earned by teaching and egg-selling, turn into white muslin and ribbon, a hat and a pair of gloves, and amid highly colored pictures of future triumphs and joys drawn by her interested friends, she at last set off for that paradise on the Hudson which has been the goal of so many more sophisticated girls.

Colonel Burritt and Daisy were at the dock to meet her on the arrival of her boat, and the heart of fastidious Miss Burritt sank within her as happy Ellen crossed the gang-plank. Her turban hat was unbecoming to her broad, bare forehead, her large waist and styleless bodice were an affliction to which her glad countenance lent the last exasperating touch.

Ellen was full of her trip. The splendid scenery of the river, the novel pleasure of the good orchestra on the boat, had ministered to her very soul.

Her uncle's hearty greeting concealed all deficiencies in Daisy's manner, and the visitor was kept busy all the way to the house answering his interested questions.

" Oh, Aunt Margaret, what a beautiful place

you live in!" she exclaimed, when Mrs. Burritt met her at the door, for her eyes had been busy on the drive up the hill and along the road that sweeps under the great trees about "Professors' Row."

"A regular aborigine; just exactly what I expected," said Daisy to her mother as soon as they were alone.

"But how happy she is!" returned Mrs. Burritt, who had been somewhat touched by the joy in the plain girlish face.

"I simply can't stand that turban!" said Daisy with set lips. "My sailor hat of last summer would look infinitely better. I shall give it to her."

"Look out you don't hurt her feelings."

"I don't think she has any, by her looks. She's hideously self-satisfied."

And when Miss Burritt carried out her threat, which she did on that first day, Ellen received the suggestion and the gift with much good humor.

"There is a little shade in sailor hats. One really needs them here," said Daisy; and her cousin thanked her, still in the first flush of her happy arrival, and full of gratitude for her good fortune.

There were poetical and artistic thoughts in plenty behind the intellectual forehead which so aroused Daisy Burritt's disapproval, and the natural beauties of the post gave Ellen deep pleasure.

She could scarcely go to bed on that first evening for the fascination of the scene from her window. Shadows lay athwart the noble, moonlit plain ; glimpses of the lights of pleasure-boats on the river occasionally slipped into view. Rounded battlements of the barracks rose castle-like behind great trees, and the band played for an hour sentimental and vivacious selections, at some point invisible, but close by the Burritt house.

On the opposite side of the plain a village of tents showed the encampment of the corps of cadets. Ellen had already seen specimens of these white-trousered and gray-coated youths moving about on pleasure or business intent, but they had not aroused her interest in any degree. What she yearned for was to accept the entrancing invitation of those mighty hills. Oh, to have the freedom of this lovely place, answerable to no one, and with no need to meet and mix with strangers who were not of her world !

Daisy had been very kind ; she had so willingly excused her from going to parade that afternoon, leaving her alone to the unpacking of her little trunk, which Ellen accomplished with frequent rushes to the window to admire the riotous roses and honeysuckle, and the close, rich ivy, which seemed to have been growing about the place for generations.

She would never forget that first night at West

Point, with the vivacious strains of tattoo, and at last the plaintive tones that sounded solemnly sweet across the wide plain as the bugles played taps. She knew the name of nothing, the meaning of nothing, but it was all part of a rich, beautiful whole, alluring to the vague fancies of a studious country girl; and the reveille gun the next morning woke her with a tingle of pleasure that a long, sweet day was before her.

Colonel Burritt warmed her heart with a sounding kiss when she came down to a good breakfast, which — novel experience — she had had no hand in preparing.

"We are early birds," he said. "It suits me, and Daisy won't miss guard mount whether she does breakfast or not. You did n't go to parade yesterday. Very well; we'll take you over to guard mount. It won't do for you to waste any more time before catching the cadet fever."

"Thank you, Uncle John. Do you mean a fever about those boys in gray coats?"

"Certainly, my girl."

She smiled pleasantly. "That sounds funny, does n't it?"

Colonel Burritt's hearty laugh waked the echoes. Here was a new sort of girl come to visit the United States Military Academy; but her ignorance would not last.

They had a happy breakfast together. Mrs. Burritt had no use for the world at 7.30 A. M., and Daisy only came down in time to take a cup of coffee standing, while the strains of "The Star Spangled Banner" came across the plain. Yesterday Cadet Francis Lorimer had performed a tour of guard duty. He would come off duty this morning. Daisy had an idea that Blanche Barstow, the commandant's daughter, intended to engross Mr. Lorimer's "old guard privileges," and she was more willing to exert herself for this young cadet captain than for any other man in the corps, not excepting the adjutant.

She cast furtive and long-suffering glances at her cousin, and wished the collar and cuffs of her shirt waist boasted more starch; but then there were so many unsatisfactory points in Ellen's costume, the only efficient method of dealing with the problem would be to ship the girl herself back to Burritt-ville, and this for the present was entirely impracticable. Daisy noticed in bitterness of spirit how well pleased her father appeared with his niece.

Troop parade was over, and the other enigmatical but interesting military ceremonies of the morning had just begun when they arrived in camp, and Ellen's bright mind began at once to take in a totally novel charm.

Pretty girls had gathered from the neighboring hotel; girls in smart, crisp morning costume like Daisy's own. Everybody knew everybody else. Cadets in fleckless uniform and with assured society manners greeted these girls gayly, only a few people paying any attention to the ceremony of guard mount going on on the plain before the tents.

Colonel Burritt took his niece to one of the tree-shaded iron seats whence she could look down the clean company streets of camp, and he explained to her a little of what she was seeing, while she listened and looked in admiring wonder.

One young man, his gray decked with crimson and gold, and his walk quite the perfection of military locomotion, moved out upon the plain before the cadet privates, who stood waiting in ranks. He lifted his white-gloved hand, and obediently the band burst forth into martial music.

Ellen wondered who this potentate might be, and asked.

"That's Deering, the adjutant. If you notice the shape of the chevrons on his sleeve, you will know him anywhere."

Here another gorgeous cadet officer in full dress, a captain, came unofficially upon the scene.

"There is the officer of the day," said the colonel.

The young man stepped up to Miss Burritt, plumed hat in hand, and greeted her.

"Here, Daisy." The colonel spoke over his shoulder. He had begun to reproach his daughter mentally for chattering with her friends, in total forgetfulness of Ellen. "Good morning, Maverick.

Come here; I want to introduce you to my niece, Miss Day."

The cadet hurried forward, and the sun glittered from his golden buttons, chevrons, and sword, and shone in the crimson silk of the sash knotted on his hip.   He bowed before Ellen.

"Delighted, I'm sure," said the young man, with an air totally foreign to Miss Day's experience.

She was not obliged to attempt what to her seemed the impossible in making conversation with him, for his duties called him out upon the field, where he took up his position with folded arms.

Near him stood now another cadet in precisely the same uniform and attitude, excepting that his white trousers lacked the unwrinkled freshness of Mr. Maverick's.

Daisy's friend, Miss Barstow, had joined her and had been introduced to Miss Day, after which the two girls talked together in what was to Ellen an unknown tongue.   She gathered, however, that this new cadet's name was Lorimer, and that he had for the past twenty-four hours been on duty and was shortly to be released.

"Yes, he's the retiring officer of the day," replied Colonel Burritt to her question.   "Now, see, they are going to pass the guard in review."

As he spoke, the two cadets removed their plumed hats, and the gray and white guard marched by, their officers saluting.   The band played gayly. Ellen felt thrilled by the martial spirit in the air.

When all was over, Mr. Lorimer, an extremely good-looking young fellow, came back under the trees to meet his friends.

Miss Day had already noted the popularity of her cousin, who ever since her advent in camp had held continual court. It seemed quite natural that now the dignified countenance of the dark-eyed young captain should brighten as he approached her.

Daisy, after receiving certain glances from her father, had been introducing to Ellen every military youth and summer girl who joined her, and now she presented Mr. Lorimer.

Miss Day looked up at him with earnest, clear eyes.

"This is the most interesting place I ever saw," she said.

It was the first remark she had volunteered to one of these strangers, and Miss Burritt laid it to the *beaux yeux* of her pet cadet, and sighed impatiently.

But Colonel Burritt had just risen and moved away, and Ellen, thirsting for knowledge, spoke to this young man for that reason. This being his fourth summer at the post, Lorimer had seen a number of feminine novices in the first flush of their pleasure, but seldom one so poorly equipped for the subjugation of the youthful military heart as this one. She was Miss Burritt's cousin, however, and he gave her a genial and responsive look, such as fell only upon a favored few from this social autocrat of his class.

"I'm glad the post pleases you, Miss Day. Miss Burritt should not introduce me to any one in my present seedy condition. Guard duty is my apology."

"I am too bewildered and fascinated to be critical," returned Ellen.

"Well," gasped Daisy, who was listening, apprehensive of some *gaucherie*.

"Would you mind telling me, Mr. Lorimer, why you didn't salute my uncle as you came up? I have been sitting here, watching every cadet salute him, even when passing distantly; but you took off your hat, like any other gentleman."

Daisy again stifled her impatience. "I should think that even she could perceive that he does n't take off his hat like any other gentleman," she thought.

"That was simply because Miss Burritt was with him," explained the cadet pleasantly. He was a Southerner, and the courtesy to women which had passed into him through many generations gave his manner a charm which impressed Ellen delightfully. Her expressive, intelligent face regarded him with interest.

"It is all so new to me; I do like to understand," she said.

Miss Burritt decided to interfere.

"Perhaps you would better defer catechizing

Mr. Lorimer until some morning when he has had a little more sleep," she said dryly. "I want to see you a minute," she added in a lowered voice to the cadet, who lifted his cap to Miss Day before he obediently followed.

Ellen's thin cheeks grew warm at her cousin's tone; now her alert ears distinguished a low laugh, and the words " rara avis " and " freshly caught," from Daisy, as she and Lorimer moved away.

The band now took up a position under a great tree and began to give a morning concert, which ordinarily would have filled Ellen with pleasure; but her happiness had been poisoned by her cousin's words and manner. She sat there quietly, looking out unseeingly on the greensward and regarding her circumstances in a transfiguring light.

Daisy's perfunctory greeting at the dock yesterday, her gift of the sailor hat, her willing departure alone for parade — all at once gained significance. All these other girls were so different from Ellen herself! Evidently her cousin was ashamed of her, impatient of her being here — had perhaps dreaded her coming.

" Don't let me be too hasty," thought poor Ellen, alarmed by the intense repugnance for her surroundings which suddenly possessed her.

Her uncle was approaching.

" Like the music ? " he asked kindly.

" It is beautiful," she answered, smiling bravely at the eagle on his shoulder-strap.

"Young folks scattered, eh? Oh, I see — Daisy and Lorimer are over yonder hatching some mischief. Well, your old uncle won't have your society long. You will be hand and glove with these boys and girls in a few days. Let us go over to the library."

Ah, if she could but have her uncle, and nobody else — what a good time Ellen thought she would have! In the dignified and beautiful library she almost forgot that sore place in her heart which a few minutes ago hurt her so.

"I suppose you know there is a cadet tea on this afternoon, Ellen," remarked Mrs. Burritt at luncheon.

"No, I did n't," replied the girl; and her hostess noticed her colorless manner in contrast to that of yesterday.

"I have n't dared tell her yet," said Daisy. "She told Mr. Lorimer this morning that he bewildered and fascinated her. I thought she was going rather fast."

Colonel Burritt perceived no sting.

"Ho, ho, ho!" his hearty laugh rang out. "Our little Ellen is getting on! Pooh-poohed at cadet fever, too! Ha, ha, ha!"

For Ellen, she felt a wild desire to rush from the table, but with a supreme effort she controlled herself. For dear Uncle John's sake she must n't. Beside, it might give her cousin too much satisfaction.

A contemptuous little smile was playing about Daisy's lips. How arrogantly pretty and successful she looked in her pale blue and white dress! A cadet's buckle, heavily monogrammed, confined the belt about her slender waist. Two or three shining bell-buttons depended from the fob of her watch. Natty, trim, correct in every particular, Daisy's costume made Ellen feel bitterly the defects in her own, and the lack of generosity in the spoiled child's treatment of herself astounded as much as it wounded her.

"If you would not think me rude," she began, "I should like to take a long walk among the hills this afternoon."

"You must n't think of it, my dear," put in her uncle hastily. "After a while you won't have to take such a walk alone. You must n't think of going to-day. Get yourself up in some pretty togs and get acquainted with the young people first."

"But I have n't pretty togs," responded Ellen bravely, and her pride made her add: "I think you have to visit a place once to know how to dress there. Perhaps you remember the demands of Burrittville?"

"Oh, you 'll do, you 'll do. Don't fret about that. Your Aunt Margaret will fix you up."

But Mrs. Burritt's vague attempts to carry out this hint were politely discouraged by Ellen herself, and she appeared in the garden among the gay young crowd in the ill-fitting brown and white organdie, — a very plain and doubtful ornament to the assembly in the opinion of all but her honest uncle, who thought the flash of her speaking eyes pleasant enough to offset any number of gew-gaws.

"That's my only sister's child, Lorimer," Colonel Burritt said to the cadet. "I'm anxious she should have a good time here, and a little afraid she won't. Her head's too full of brains for this place."

"You are hard on us, colonel," returned the young fellow brightly.

"No. I don't blame you for bidding good-by to brains in summer time, not a whit."

Ellen Day endured two hours of martyrdom on that bright afternoon. The odd person in every group, yet not daring to be found solitary by the kind and watchful eyes of her uncle, she thought she should not soon forget the agonies of a cadet tea, where all but herself were gay, and all talked a language of which she alone was ignorant.

Schooling herself to behave naturally with her hosts, it was not until the middle of the next morn-ing that she found an opportunity to satisfy her longing to run away and be by herself. She wanted to think out the situation, and decide what she should do.

This lovely spot must abound in secluded nooks. Flirtation Walk had been pointed out to her, but

Uncle John had told her it was a haven for home-sick plebes as well as lovers; and while she felt ready to mingle her stealthy tears with those of some poor discouraged boy, she meant not to shed any, but to carry her fortitude still further. Her longing to get up into the wilds of the mighty hills that guard the post and river had somehow evaporated with her other anticipations. The heaviness of one's heart communicates itself to the limbs.

Ellen walked across the plain and past the library to what looked like lonely wooded banks of the river. There she came upon a flight of steps which wound downward. Following them she found herself in a wild and lovely glade.

No one was in sight. She glanced about at the delicate flowers clinging to rugged rock walls, damp here and there from a trickling spring. She looked up into the intertwined foliage of trees. Here was a retreat full of the sweet smells of Mother Earth, and with no disturbing element.

Ellen seated herself where she could see the blue waters of the Hudson sparkle through the undergrowth, and gave herself up to thought. Alas for that heroic resolution to shed no tears! They would come as she thought of her mother's unselfishness and effort to spare her, of the happy anticipations they had all entertained. She thought of the sacrificed encyclopædia, and Miss Bascom's flattering prophecies. It seemed the height of everything desirable to take the first boat for home. It would be infinitely easier to sustain a cross-fire of questions in Burrittville than to remain here, running the gauntlet of her aunt's and cousin's criticism. Daisy evidently held her in too mean regard to believe that such slights as she bestowed could hurt; but there was another aspect to the case which Ellen was unable to ignore.

She saw how her uncle counted on her pleasure. The question was whether she were strong enough to endure pin-pricks and humiliations without appearing to be conscious of them, until the time set for her visit had expired, and so convince the dear, patient little mother and good Colonel Burritt that all their kindness had not been in vain.

It was not an easy task. Ellen felt that she should take away from the fray scars that would be carried all her life. A girl with such capacity for pleasure and appreciation must pay for it by an equal sensitiveness to pain, and what worse pain than the rôle of unwelcome guest?

Ellen grew hot all over with realization of her own plain, ill-dressed personality, of the total superfluity of her presence here; of Daisy's perfunctory introductions. What wonder that the green, sweet solitude tempted her to the indulgence of a burst of hot tears? She repented of them, however, at once, and none too soon, for scarcely had they been wiped away, when the apparition of Francis Lorimer startled her.

He had recognized her first, and seeing that she was wiping her eyes, would gladly have escaped unobserved; but her upward look made that impossible, so he bared his head with a bright " Good morning ! "

Her attitude had impressed him. In a flash there returned to him Colonel Burritt's words of yesterday. In fact, he had observed enough during Miss Burritt's tea to make him feel more than one wave of wonder at and compassion for this social stranger; and in a vague way he had mentally censured Daisy for taking no pains to make her cousin have a good time.

Now this impression deepened to an acute resentment. Lorimer had an invalid sister at home. Ellen's thin cheeks and the straight hair carried back from her wide forehead somehow made him think of her. It was a shame for the poor thing to be moping off here alone, crying. The much-occupied and popular First-class man actually felt sufficient interest in the case to make him unwilling to pass on.

" You find a good many pretty places here to explore, don't you, Miss Day ? "

" Yes," she answered in as natural a voice as her rebellious throat allowed. " I just happened upon this spot."

" Yes ? Kosciusko's Garden is one of our show places."

It was so evidently difficult for her to speak to

him, he suddenly decided that he had better move on.   Again he lifted his cap.

"Well," he said lightly, "I will leave you to your study of nature."

He had nearly reached the stone steps when he heard his name.   Turning back, he saw that Ellen had sprung to her feet and was looking after him, her face flushed.   He hastened back to her.

"Please — please don't mention that you saw me here," she said.   "You probably would n't think of it — but I should be sorry" — after another hesitation she added — "I am sure you saw that I had been crying.   That would not be pleasant news to my hosts."

The dignity and courage of her voice and manner as she finished won Lorimer's approval.

"The girl's a trump," he said to himself as he moved on his way to camp.   "This is a nice summer vacation for her!   I believe the colonel spoke that way because he wanted my help; but what can I do?"

The question was answered in the cadet's own mind by a number of flattering considerations which started his thoughts on a new tack.   Might it be possible to use his social influence for something worth while?   But again, *was* it worth while from a selfish standpoint?   How many a half hour would he have to spend away from the dainty belles who were helping to make his First-class camp gay?

Yet what a good joke it would be! How rich would be the mystification of Daisy Burritt and Blanche Barstow! Lorimer lost his cadet expression of dignified imperturbability and threw back his head in a brief, hilarious laugh. "I could n't do it alone — not make it a howling success, that is; but I 'll talk to Maverick and Deering."

Ellen Day, there in Kosciusko's Garden, had taken up her cross. She returned to her uncle's house, determined to see and hear nothing disturbing, to wear her hateful dresses, and even Daisy's cast-off sailor hat, to talk with whom she must, and to go where she was asked.

She was sitting on the piazza that afternoon in company with a bevy of girls who were ostensibly calling on her, but surrounding Daisy, when three of the brightest particular stars from camp came down the walk toward the house. They were Lorimer, Deering, and Maverick.

Ellen regarded them admiringly. They were so spick and span in the toilet just made for parade! The girls welcomed them with nonchalant sweetness as they came up on the piazza, and Ellen, who had met the adjutant at the cadet tea, bowed to them all three in silence.

How all tongues but hers flew, and what a light-hearted crowd they were! It made her almost dizzy to listen and try to follow allusions which she could not understand; so she had ceased to attempt it when Lorimer turned to her.

"Miss Day, won't you go with me to the german on Wednesday evening?" he asked.

An instant silence fell on the group. Ellen saw the glance that passed between her cousin and Miss Barstow.

"Don't frighten Miss Day to death, Mr. Lorimer," said Daisy, highly entertained. She took this amazing invitation as a subtle and indirect compliment to herself, but she must show that she recognized its absurdity.

"I am not so easily frightened," said Ellen quietly. "Thank you, Mr. Lorimer. I never even saw a german."

"Then I fancy you will find it an entertaining sight," he returned. "Perhaps you will give me the hop on Friday evening?"

His manner was so engaging and so respectful, Ellen would have been pleased by his attention but for the curious eyes bent upon her.

"I don't dance at all," she answered.

"Why, that's a shame," put in Deering, who, as he spoke, came over and seated himself near Ellen.

The effort necessary to be put forth by a cadet of the United States Military Academy to maintain converse with an embarrassed girl who is ignorant of the Point traditions and customs is something herculean, but Deering and Lorimer stuck to their task until the time came to go to parade.

Miss Burritt and her friends were obliged to share Maverick among them.

"I could only catch a word here and there of what they said to her," Daisy said that evening, in describing the scene to her mother. "They must have been very much amused. I don't doubt Ellen gave them points on poultry-raising, or some subject equally congenial."

On the following Monday evening there was a dance. Colonel Burritt would not hear to Ellen's being left at home, as she requested, so the white muslin had to be brought out.

The girl regarded it with very different eyes from the unquestioning and indifferent ones which had watched Miss Bascom fit it. She pulled out its sleeves and regarded them doubtfully. However, it was a very simple dress, and when Ellen had put it on and pulled its ribbon belt until she was conscious of its proximity to her slight person, she looked passable, she thought.

"I don't believe," she mused, seriously scanning her reflection in the mirror, "that there is anything in my looks to laugh at."

No one else seemed to think so. Daisy did not look at her after a first glance to be certain that she was not a "guy," and in the dancing-hall Mrs. Burritt gave her a seat beside herself, where she could look about at the well-carried cadets and the bevy of gay girls to whom they were so pleasantly devoted.

Little longings swelled Ellen's heart at this glimpse of a new world. The music was so inspiring that it made her foot tap under the white skirts that her encyclopædia money had bought.

She did not long to-night for book-learning. What she yearned for was to be able to sway and circle about in graceful fashion, as these young people were doing.

How pretty the dance was! Her clear eyes looked with generous admiration at the beautiful girl, a stranger to her, over whom Lorimer was bending devotedly. To think he had asked her, awkward, plain Ellen, to be his partner at a festivity like this! He must have felt very sorry for her! Well, to-night he had forgotten homely girls who cried alone in the woods; and what wonder?

It sent a warm little thrill of pleasant surprise through her, when at the close of the first dance, Lorimer, very handsome in his becoming military toilet, came straight up to her with a pleasant greeting.

"Sit down, sit down, my boy," said Colonel Burritt, rising. "I must go off and do some visiting myself."

Mrs. Burritt, busy with the chaperon on her other side, looked around in surprise when the music struck up for the second dance and the cadet captain did not stir.

"Don't let me keep you," said Ellen, wishing it were proper to tell him that she was grateful to him for this bit of a talk — just to make her feel a little more like the other girls.

"But this is our dance," he returned, smiling.

"Oh! I told you, Mr. Lorimer, that I don't know how.   I do wish I did."

"Yes, I know; so we are going to sit it out. Excuse me for not having given you your programme."

He handed her a card on which cadets' names were written thickly from top to bottom.

Ellen's thin cheeks flushed.

"What does this mean?"   ,

"Only that you are going to talk to a lot of us and get acquainted."

"Mr. Lorimer!   Oh, dear!   They will be so bored!"

Miss Day's heart fluttered excitedly.

"You are much more likely to be.   We cadets live in a narrow world, you will find."

"How very, very kind you were to take the trouble!" said Ellen, lifting her grateful, speaking eyes in a way that touched the autocratic young captain, and repaid him for the skillful generalship he had expended on the filling of this card in the busy season.

Meanwhile Daisy Burritt's sharp eyes had detected that Lorimer was cutting one of his dances for the sake of her country cousin, and noticed, too, that Ellen appeared very much at her ease and was listening and talking, her intelligent face quite good-looking in her happiness. She herself was dancing with Deering.

"Awfully clever girl, that cousin of yours," he said.

"Which are you being, — sarcastic or polite?" she rejoined.

"You need n't guy me. You must know she 's clever."

"That forehead of hers ought to mean something," remarked Daisy.

But she was surprised, and was destined to an increase of perplexity all that evening.

The music ceased, and Lorimer consulted Ellen's card.

"Gage comes next. Nice chap. Not so green as he sounds. Shall we go out of doors with the dancers?"

Ellen agreed, and, taking the cadet's arm, soon found herself on the broad stone walk, promenading with dozens of other couples beneath the trees. She could hardly believe in her own identity; but the dream was a very pleasant one. Almost every girl they passed looked at Lorimer.

At last they went back into the hall, and her companion brought to her a fair-haired young fellow, a yearling, who for the honor of doing the cadet captain a favor had gladly foregone one of his dances.

The comical side of feeling gratitude to this boy of her own age or less for bestowing upon her fifteen minutes of his society was vivid to her, yet grateful she was for the removal of all a wall-flower's consciousness by the presence of the bell-buttoned cavalier.

"I feel that it is an imposition to allow you to miss the dance," she said, as he took the seat beside her, and her fan.

"Not a bit of it," he returned stoutly. "But you should dance, really, Miss Day. It's great, don't you know."

"Too great for me," she sighed. "I'm afraid I'm too old to learn."

"No, indeed. I did n't know how till I came here. Never would learn at dancing-school, don't you know. Always went out to get a glass of water when the waltz was on. Here it's dance or get out, you know," etc., etc.

Mr. Gage's tongue was hung in the middle, as the saying is, and only a question now and then was enough to keep him going.

Ellen's next partner was no less a person than the adjutant. Then followed Maverick. These were succeeded by other First-class men, into whose ears had been dropped significant hints of Miss Day's cleverness, which she justified by her sincere desire to understand the life of the cadet, and consequent retention of the conversation in paths with which the young men were familiar.

Francis Lorimer's name was down a second time on her card.

"This was unnecessary," she said, smiling him a greeting when he came.

"Of course; but so are lots of pleasant things. You don't begrudge it to me, do you?"

Miss Burritt saw Ellen leave the hall and return with one and another cavalier, looking, with her happy face and her fresh, white gown, like a totally different being from the awkward, reserved creature who had been moving about the Burritt house the last few days.

Her father saw it, too, with deep satisfaction. He secured his daughter's ear for a moment.

"A very pretty thought of yours, Daisy, to fix up things so pleasantly for Ellen," he said, such a look of pleasure in his eyes that it required some effort on Daisy's part to disclaim his gratitude.

"Indeed, I had nothing to do with it," she answered, tossing her head in her spoiled-child fashion.

A cadet appearing to claim Miss Burritt, the colonel fell back, a cloud of surprise and disappointment shadowing his kind face. He found himself beside one of the tactical officers of the academy.

"Good evening, Dick," he said, with a short nod.

"Good evening, colonel. Is that young lady with Lorimer your niece?"

"Yes."

"I was n't certain. I 've only seen her the evening I called. Her brains don't all seem to reside in her heels."

The peculiar, gruff manner of the cavalryman was characteristic. "Queer Dick" he had been called when he was a cadet, and "Queer Dick" he was still, — a man who would have been a favorite with women but for his curt and reserved manners. His good looks attracted each new girl only for a short time. He himself said he could n't get on with girls. They certainly were quickly chilled by the reception he gave to their airs and graces. There was not an unmarried woman on the post who did not stand in more or less awe of "that bear," as Daisy and her bosom friend Blanche dubbed him.

The exasperation of it was that he was not the least shy of them. He was only bored. Unpardonable insult!

Colonel Burritt smiled at his speech now, and the lieutenant continued : —

"Must be something remarkable about a girl who can make the cadets willing to talk when they might be dancing."

"Yes; Ellen 's a bright girl. Lived in the country all her life, but seems to take to this like a duck to water. Her mother 's my only sister, and the sweetest woman God ever made — present company barred, of course. It does me good to see the child enjoy herself."

"Humph!" grunted Lieutenant Dick. "Probably spoil her for the country."

"Not a bit of it. She's too level-headed."

The pride in the colonel's tone, added to the interest that Ellen's capture of the cadets had inspired, made the cavalryman drift around after a while to her side of the room. The last dance on her card was not filled, and Mr. Dick, perceiving that the seat beside her remained empty, approached.

"Good evening, Miss Day. Probably you don't remember me. I'm Dick."

Her eyes, bright from the novel fun of the evening, welcomed him. She greeted him .with an ease that amused and surprised herself. She felt quite like a woman of the world.

"You seem to have been enjoying yourself," he said brusquely, as he took the seat she offered him.

"Why, I never had such a good time. I do so wish I knew how to dance! I never thought of such a thing before."

The lieutenant regarded her gloomily, yet curiously. Her face was so innocently eager, so natural and happy. She was a new type for him.

"What have you liked to do?"

"Read, I'm afraid." She spoke apologetically. "Read and walk — with my little hammer."

The gloom suddenly lifted from the cavalryman's face. "Do you care for geology?"

"I love it," she exclaimed, with an ardor which awoke an answering gleam in her companion's cold eyes.

"I can show you some objects of interest, I think, then," he said. "Perhaps to-morrow some-time?"

She looked doubtful. "To-morrow morning I am going to walk with Mr. Lorimer, and in the afternoon with Mr. Deering," she replied.

The lieutenant became more deeply impressed with what must certainly be the mental charms of this plain, bright girl to cause such gilded stars as these cadet officers to do so much shining upon her.

"Next day, then," he said.

"I should be so pleased," she answered, with a straightforward, hearty gratitude which made the tactical officer forget his cynicism.

Mrs. Burritt, who had been sitting beside Ellen all the evening, marveling greatly, had a private interview with her daughter before they retired that night.

"There is only one explanation for it," said Daisy, "and that is that Frank Lorimer cares more for me than I thought he did."

"Don't be too sure," returned Mrs. Burritt. "It sounded to me as I sat there as if he were greatly taken with Ellen."

Her daughter looked completely mystified.

"And look at that curmudgeon of a Dick!"

Mrs. Burritt went on. "Why, he talked to her in the most human, interested way! You know," wisely, "it is a matter of history that some of the plainest women have been the most fascinating to men."

So both mother and daughter went to bed without settling the problem.

As for the beneficiary of Lorimer's experiment, she was up betimes in the morning, with none of the heavy-heartedness of yesterday. Mingled with a real relief for her cousin's sake that Daisy need not be ashamed of her, was the natural pleasure of a girlish triumph.

Mrs. Burritt's laundress had put plenty of starch in her shirt-waist this time, and she took pains to make herself look as nice as she could to go across the lawn with her uncle and cousin to troop parade.

Colonel Burritt rallied her on her successes of the night before, and especially on the fact that the woman-hating Dick had voluntarily chatted with her. When she laughingly announced her engagement to go walking with him on the following day, her uncle's mirth was loud, while Daisy stared in genuine amazement. The story of Cinderella and that of the Ugly Duckling surely had a parallel now.

When camp was reached the puzzle deepened. When parade was over Lorimer and Maverick were pleasant in their greeting of Miss Burritt, but toward the girl in the last year's sailor hat they were eager. One established himself on each side of her. They hung on her words. Young Gage added himself to the group.

The star cadets, tickled with their success of the evening before, and pleased with the blossoming of their protegée's manner, had dropped serious and well-chosen words of praise of Miss Day among the corps whose effect showed this morning. There were plenty of men willing to see the same charms that Lorimer and Deering saw, whether they were invisible or not; and Daisy and Blanche were forced to talk to each other or to join in Ellen's court with the best face they could put upon the matter.

Fortunately or unfortunately, they little suspected that the expression of their countenances forced three of their friends later in the day to lay down their cadet dignity, and retiring to the seclusion of Fort Clinton, to give way to boisterous hilarity.

Meanwhile, during guard mount, Lieutenant Dick stood about among the spectators' seats, the usual fixed expression of misanthropy upon his countenance, and some object held in his closed right hand.

When guard mount was over, he saw his chance while Miss Day was for a minute standing alone.

He approached and greeted her hurriedly, and then displayed the stone treasure he had been guarding. The girl's eagerness and interest enchanted him. She met his comments intelligently, and made suggestions that pleased him. They would have a very good time to-morrow — that was certain!

But here Lorimer came up, with Miss Day's plain dark parasol in his hand, and the tactical officer, lifting his cap, retreated.

Nothing succeeds like success. Ellen Day's confidence and cheerfulness grew with every hour. Mrs. Burritt accepted her sudden popularity as an amazing dispensation which caused so much satisfaction to her husband that it was no matter if Daisy did have to suffer some mortification in being compelled to recognize her cousin's occult social power.

Happiness being such a beautifier, what wonder that Ellen's cheeks began to fill out? And her puzzled relatives looked askance at her and wondered if she really were such a plain girl, after all.

The most astonishing of her conquests was that of Queer Dick. Far from dropping off, or scaring Ellen, or being bored, he was always coming over to Colonel Burritt's with a new treatise on geology, or starting off with her, hammers in hand, on a drive or a tramp. Indeed, the tactical officer's attentions gave Lorimer and his fellow-conspirators a means of graceful and gradual withdrawal from that ultra-devotion which was so much fun while it lasted, but would have palled in time.

The cadet captain did not lose his interest in Ellen, however. He regarded her changed appearance and Daisy's changed manner with much self-complacence.

"When a cadet-girl starts out to be an officer-girl, there is no use in trying to stem the tide," he said one day to Miss Day before her cousin, with much assumption of sentimental injury.

So it came about that all the rosy prophecies of Ellen's Burrittville friends came true, and when finally she appeared among them again, many were the compliments that brightened her laughing face.

She was a sort of Scheherezade in the village for weeks to come, and her mother's worn face brightened in the sunshine of her child's happy memories.

"The question is," said pleased Miss Bascom, "did that white muslin do the business? Are you engaged, Ellen Day?"

"No, indeed," answered the girl decisively, but the postmistress told Miss Bascom in strict privacy that a letter came to Ellen every week postmarked West Point.

"It may be her relations, though," the dressmaker warned her. "Her cousin Daisy, you know."

"Pooh! Nobody's cousin Daisy ever wrote like that," was the scornful reply.

Winter's snowy blanket had wrapped the little

village when a stalwart stranger one day descended from the afternoon train at Burrittville and asked his way to the Day cottage.

Seven different women could swear to seeing him go in there, but nobody saw him come out. He was a genteel man, and walked as if he was marching, they said. They all held afterward that they suspected from the first that he was military.

Ellen's little sister let him in, and he was ushered into a parlor where a bright coal fire was burning.

Ellen herself appeared almost immediately, and her cheeks were very red. " Why did n't you tell me you were coming ? " she asked.

" I thought I would n't," he said, holding her hand so that she could n't release it, and studying her face earnestly. " I imagined if I surprised you that I should find out something of the way you feel toward me ; but I don't. The way I feel toward you I have learned perfectly. I 've been a starving man ever since you left the post."

" But our letters have been such a comfort," she said, feeling very warm and surprised and happy.

" Have they ? " he exclaimed delightedly. " I 'm a Queer Dick ; I know it. Everybody knows it ; but will you have me, Ellen ? "

She did n't know what she said, but it was satisfactory ; and fifteen minutes after they had sat down together he took from his pocket a little velvet box containing a flashing diamond ring.

"Dear me!" gasped Ellen, half in delight, half in resentment. "You were very sure of me."

"No," returned the lieutenant, regarding the jewel admiringly; "but I thought if you refused me, we should enjoy looking at the stone together."

His fiancée laughed gently, tears in her eyes.

As soon as the tactical officer returned to the Point his engagement was announced. Everybody was astonished, but pleased, as well there as at home in Ellen's village.

Miss Bascom plumed herself triumphantly. "I knew I made that white muslin real pretty," she said.

In the barracks up on the Hudson Francis Lorimer clapped the cadet adjutant on the shoulder. "It's a first-rate match," he declared. "I like it; and I'll bet a hundred dollars to a nickel Queer Dick would never have spied the little thing if we hadn't boomed her."

And Deering refused to risk his nickel.

THE NEW ORGAN

Miss Lida Hasbrook had played the little organ and held general direction of the music in the Congregational church at Stapleton for twenty years, when her complaints of the asthmatic old instrument began to be heard. Not even then could she move the men out of their indifference. The wheezing of the bellows was a part of their Sunday worship, and they accepted it with the composure of long habit, turning a deaf ear to the little woman's hints and suggestions.

Only her nephew Jasper sympathized with her woes. She kept his house, cooked his meals, and mothered him generally, so doubtless she earned the right to his attentive ear. At all events he was forced to listen three times a day to his aunt's excited statements, and as he threw in a soothing or a hopeful word here and there, Miss Hasbrook derived comfort from his passive sympathy.

"It is a shame and a disgrace to the village to have such music in church," she exclaimed one day while they were at dinner. Jasper had heard the same remark a great many times, and assented in his quiet way.

"And it 's my belief that we women of the sew-ing-circle will take hold of it, if the men won't," she added defiantly. "We 've got the minister on our side, anyway."

The young man surveyed his aunt with some curiosity in his grave brown eyes. Although it had been a matter of course all his life that Aunt Lidy should lead the music on Sunday, he had only lately come to a realizing sense of the depth of her interest in that weekly occupation. Her thin cheeks were flushed now. After regarding her a few seconds thoughtfully, he remarked : —

"Well, Aunt Lidy, if your heart is so set on this thing, and you believe that the ladies want to take hold of the matter, you may tell them that I will give you fifteen dollars as a sort of nest-egg to begin with."

"Jasper Hasbrook, you dear, generous boy ! " ejaculated Miss Lida, looking across at him with eager, sparkling eyes. She knew that uses for the young farmer's spare dollars were many ; and if he had a surplus to spend on luxuries, it would always go to buy books, if he pleased himself.

"That is probably exactly what 's needed, to give a little spur to the whole thing," she added with joyous gratitude. "You 'll see we shall have that organ now, Jasper Hasbrook, and it will be all owing to you ! "

Miss Hasbrook proved a true prophet. The new organ became an accomplished fact, but not for many a long month. The minister prayed for it, the congregation talked about it, the sewing-circle worked for it, a fair was held in its behalf, and at last, after much straining, the amount of its cost was nearly achieved. A deficit of twenty-six dollars remained to be made up, and a hard-drawn subscription began to be taken. The last difficult five dollars was wrested from Mr. Nicholas Peabody himself, an old gentleman who enjoyed the reputation of being the " nearest " as well as the most prosperous member of the Stapleton congregation.

To Miss Hasbrook belonged the honor of securing that portentous five-dollar bill, but by the time the longed-for cash rested in her hand, a blow had fallen which robbed it of its value, and blanched the rosy prospect to ashen gray.

It happened in this wise. A lady of the sewing-circle had written Mr. Peabody a suave and persuasive letter, as being the surest way of reaching an individual so practiced in eluding committees of ways and means. The letter informed him of the nearly reached success of the church's project, and besought Mr. Peabody to provide for himself the pleasant memory of having finished a work so well begun; inasmuch as the society was determined that not one penny of debt should hang over their purchase and blight its beauty.

The sewing-circle had been waiting nearly a week for the reply to this appeal, when Miss Hasbrook, returning one afternoon from its session, caught a glimpse of Mr. Nicholas Peabody approaching along the village street.

She had been mentally deploring the lateness of the hour, fearing that Jasper would be kept waiting for his supper, and wishing that she had thought to slice the cold ham before she left home; but at sight of "old Nick," as Mr. Peabody was dubbed by the graceless boys of the village, Jasper was forgotten, and the ruling passion rose uppermost. From the moment when she had, a year ago, informed the sewing-circle of her nephew's gift, she had been a leading spirit in the work for the beloved object. To be sure, she had an incentive which others lacked. The new organ stood in her view as a prospective honor and joy to herself. More joy than honor. Her hard little hands longed toward its shining keys!

The energetic woman picked her way more recklessly through the slush of the country sidewalk. A bird in the hand is worth two in the bush, she thought, hurrying because she feared her neighbor might elude her if she allowed him to reach the post-office corner before she did.

"Oh, Mr. Peabody, I'm so glad I met you," she called, speaking before she had quite reached him, with an amazing forgetfulness of her usual regard for the proprieties. Suspicion soured the man's face at once, but Miss Lida proceeded undaunted.

"The ladies were wishing this afternoon they could get your answer to their letter about the organ. The amount is almost complete, as we told you."

Miss Hasbrook tilted her head to one side in a birdlike fashion, and smiled confidingly up toward the scowling face so far above her.

"It's a fool business, the whole of it," vouchsafed the old man curtly.

"Cross-patch!" mutely soliloquized Miss Hasbrook, but her eyes widened innocently. "I didn't know anybody thought *that*," she answered.

"Why, of course 't is. A big, new orgin 'll be nothin' but a white elephant if you do git it. Work 'n scrape 'n pinch 'n git it paid for, 'n what then? It 'll be an everlastin' expense to git somebody to play it."

"Oh, no," responded Miss Lida, a conscious, happy glow pervading her. "I don't know why it should cost the congregation any more to have a good instrument played than a poor one." She tittered a little in the excess of her satisfaction.

"What ye talkin' about?" exclaimed the other irritably. "I hear ye calc'late to have peddles and two or three times as many keys as the old orgin 's got." He glowered at the little woman with entirely impersonal exasperation. It did not occur to him that this individual was a part of the present *régime*. The important and momentous

periods of what Miss Hasbrook was wont to call
the professional side of her life had never made
any impression upon this member of her audience.
Had Mr. Peabody been asked who played the
organ in his church, he would have meditated, and
might have responded that he guessed Lidy Hasbrook did usually.   He had no idea of the dagger
each subsequent word planted in the innocent breast
of his listener.

   "I s'pose you'll admit that somebody's got to be
hired that knows how to work all them fandangoes,"
he sneered, "and a nice time you'll have of it.
You all talk about it as chipper as though Stapleton was full o' these orgin chaps.   I've seen 'em
play in the city churches, yankin' them stoppers,
they call 'em, in an' out, an' stompin' on the peddles faster 'n faster till their feet look like a shoe-
shop in a hurricane.   Them that want that kind
o' business in church can have it an' pay for it,
too.   I don't.   Here's your five dollars, though,"
slowly producing the money from a shiny old wallet.
"Take it, an' your foolishness be on your own heads.
Don't expect any more from me."

   Miss Hasbrook received the money in a nerve-
less hand.   Her tongue was unmanageable, and an
unintelligible sound was all she could utter by way
of thanks.   Old Nick grunted in return and went
his way.

   His stunned victim, like one in a bad dream,
splashed home through the dismal, dismal streets.

It had never once occurred to her before this afternoon that the coming of the new organ meant the elimination from her life of all its poetry.

Jasper noticed her pallor and silence that night, but she evaded his questions until, accepting her reluctance to confide in him, he turned to the ever-welcome subject of the organ. To his perplexity, at the sound of the word his aunt's hands began to tremble among the teacups.

"Don't talk about it to-night," she said shortly.

"The plan is n't given up?" he ejaculated, certain that nothing less awful could so have discomposed Miss Hasbrook.

"No."

Miss Lida caught her lower lip between her teeth and studied the tablecloth. It was scarcely whiter than her face when she spoke again, her light eyes meeting the thoughtful brown ones of her nephew.

"Jasper, who do you suppose is going to play our new organ?" she asked.

"I had n't thought as far as that," he answered. "First catch your organ, you know."

His aunt's eyes fell away from his kindly, curious gaze.

Then it was not an impossible, cruel idea to him that she might not continue in the office, which to her was the chief reason for her existence. A moment she brooded gloomily on the facts; how, little by little, the plan formed by the leading spirits had enlarged and become ambitious, and how she had enthusiastically led them on, not realizing that the " first-class instrument," toward which they proudly looked, might baffle her modest powers.

Her companion's voice broke in upon her meditation.

" Why do you ask? Has the question of an organist come up yet? "

" Not — not really."

" I should think it was somewhat premature. By the way, Aunt Lidy," continued the young man, trying to introduce a cheerful topic, " Mrs. Lindsay told me to-day that Grace would not go back to the academy another year. When she comes home in June, it will be the end of her schooling."

" Yes," responded Miss Hasbrook abstractedly. What was Grace Lindsay, or indeed any earthly interest to her now!

" Mrs. Lindsay said Grace spoke of you in her last letter," Jasper went on, and he did not find his subject uninteresting. On the contrary, it made him unobservant of the fact that Miss Hasbrook's expression did not brighten. " Grace said she should love you and be grateful to you all her life, Mrs. Lindsay told me, for having given her organ lessons so many years."

Miss Lida gave a little cackling laugh. " Then I was of some use in the world once," she said.

Now her nephew did stare at her. If she had .

broken out with a remark in Latin it would not have been more uncharacteristic than this speech, and Jasper would have understood her better; for he knew a little Latin and he did not know Miss Hasbrook at all in her present mood.

It was not until the next day that the cause of her trouble dawned upon the unimaginative mind of her nephew. The idea came to him all on a sudden, as he was returning from the village store, and he stopped stock still to give a low whistle. The young man loved his aunt sincerely, and he glowed with compassion in a moment; but when he reached home he did not refer to the subject, although Miss Hasbrook was still white and listless, and he saw that she moved about her work as though the mainspring of her old, energetic activity were broken. Jasper had always been a kind and thoughtful fellow, so although he was especially gentle to-day, even patting Miss Lida on the shoulder as he passed her on his way to the table, she believed her secret was still her own. A new ambition had replaced the one so long cherished in her breast, and was entertained with even greater fire: it was to prevent any one from suspecting that she had ever expected to preside at the new organ.

Affairs moved on without a hitch after the reception by the committee of Mr. Peabody's five dollars. Time flew by, at least so it seemed to Miss Hasbrook, with cruel swiftness. Her wound

had not healed, when one fair June day she was
invited to join a triumphant and select few to take
a first view of the new organ at last in its place
in the church.

What would Miss Lida have given to stay
at home!   But such a course was not to be considered. "Folks would talk," indeed they had
talked already; for her altered looks could not
pass unnoticed, and more than one sympathizing
fellow-worker expressed a fear that the new organ
had about killed Lidy Hasbrook. So it had, agreed
the ex-organist in her own proud, hurt heart, but
not in the way they thought.

She attended the " private view," a red spot
burning in either cheek. Jasper was present as
the starter of the enterprise, and Mr. Peabody
as its finisher. The latter was complacently conscious of his honors, and he indulged in a broad
smile of satisfaction as he passed the ends of his
stubby fingers over the polished wood above the
stops of the new instrument.

"It 's a fine orgin," he said, drumming on the
dumb white keys.

Near him, in an irregular semicircle, stood the
chief workers in the cause, mostly women, their
faces expressing in their several ways the relief
and satisfaction of success crowning endeavor. On
Miss Hasbrook's lips was a smile, which she had
rehearsed before her looking-glass for days.

A shaft of sunlight striking through a neighboring window illumined Mr. Peabody's bald head, and intensified his air of being the organ's patron saint.

"Brother Morse, I guess we've got about the right thing," he remarked, turning to the minister with a look that suggested his having accomplished the undertaking single-handed. Evidently the beauty of the new possession had charmed into quiet the fears lately entertained of the new expenses it implied.

"I long to hear the capabilities of the instrument," replied the minister, whose patient, kindly face quite glowed with satisfaction. "Miss Hasbrook, won't you allow us to hear the voice of our beautiful new friend?"

Jasper regarded his aunt with covert anxiety. "Do, Aunt Lidy," he urged with the habitual respect of manner which made people call him a model nephew. "I'll be very happy to blow for you," and without waiting for Miss Hasbrook's reply, the young man disappeared into seclusion behind the organ.

He worked at the bellows with a right good will; but the stored wind was allowed to escape without the wings of melody. Still Jasper began pumping again. He believed if he remained out of sight and hearing, Aunt Lidy would allow herself to be persuaded. He knew she must long to touch that tempting keyboard.

At last, in the midst of his exertions, he heard

the pulling of stops. "There!" he said to himself with satisfaction, as the music began.

But what music was this? It was solemn, full, unfamiliar. Jasper pumped away mechanically, his whole amazed, bewildered soul given up to listening. He had expected to hear some of the tunes he knew and loved. This was inexplicable. Suddenly, delicate and smooth runs began to lace themselves in and out among the chords of the first theme. What had happened? Had the new organ proved a veritable inspiration? Had fire from heaven descended upon Aunt Lidy and gifted her with new and marvelous powers?

Jasper could scarcely wait for the time to emerge from his hermit cell; and when the last chord had died away, he hastened forth. His big eyes and eager questioning countenance elicited some laughter from the group who were standing about commenting.

"I guess that raised your hair some, Jasper," remarked Mr. Peabody airily, waving his hand toward the organ-seat, which a young woman had just vacated.

"Who — what?" ejaculated the young man, gazing at the fresh face of the girl, who bowed to him.

"Miss Grace, that was n't you!"

"Why, yes, 't was, Mr. Hasbrook," said Mrs. Lindsay, with a delighted laugh. "We came up here just as you were going out of sight, and being

as I was telling brother Nicholas last night about
Grace's advantages, he insisted she should show
what she could do; and she 's astonished me, that 's
a fact." The woman evidently tried to repress her
effervescent love and pride, but in vain.

Her daughter's earnest, modest face looked very
sweet as she turned toward Miss Hasbrook, pale
and rigid.

" Miss Lida was about to play herself, I thought,"
she said, " and I should not have consented to take
her place had she not added her command. I
learned long ago to obey Miss Hasbrook implicitly
in musical matters, for what I owe to her I can
never express."

This tactful confession of allegiance struck warm
to Jasper's heart for his aunt's sake. Miss Lida
felt an unacknowledged balm in the words of her
old pupil, and relaxed unconsciously. The girl's
performance, although nothing remarkable to cul-
tivated ears, had smitten her with wonder and a
species of despair. She had never heard anything
so fine, so hopeless to emulate.

" It is very good of you to remember that you
owe me anything," she murmured. " You have
left your poor old teacher far behind."

The girl's kind heart grasped intuitively much
of that which was passing in Miss Hasbrook's
mind. All her life she had known the latter as
the musical authority of Stapleton.

" If I can do anything in return for you," she

said softly, " you know how happy it would make me." It was all she had time for before her old friends closed around her.

Mr. Peabody seized the lapel of Jasper's coat as they were leaving the church.

" It does seem 's if 't was almost a providence Grace comin' home jest now with so much lightnin' in her fingers, as ye might say," he remarked. " Sister Lindsay was tellin' me last night how it come about. I was all sot ag'in Grace spendin' so much time at that academy, but it seems ther' was a girl there without any head to speak of fer 'rithmetic; an' Grace she tootered her, as they call it, an' the girl's brother, bein' the best orginist o' the place, paid her back in lessons, an' give her a chance to practice. Now it 's in my mind, Jasper, that the committee — you 're one of 'em, I take it — could n't do better than to hire Grace Lindsay to play the new orgin. Ye can get her cheap. Now you think on 't. Ye can get her cheap."

Jasper nodded his head and disengaged himself from the detaining hand. The old man's eagerness disgusted him. He could read in his unusual complacency the relief of the miserly soul in seeing himself delivered from the necessity of coming to the further aid of his widowed sister.

Jasper observed his aunt attentively when she returned home that afternoon, and was relieved to see a look in her face more natural than any it had worn for many a day.

When they were seated at the tea table she spoke : —

"You have n't said a word about Grace's playing."

"No; I was waiting for you. I have n't the courage to comment on music until I hear what you have to say about it."

"Fiddlesticks!" Miss Hasbrook passed him a cup of tea. "What do you suppose I found under the cushion of the organ-seat in the parlor yesterday? I thought I 'd been hearing you play some unfamiliar tunes lately. I guess you 've got some independent ideas about music."

Her nephew smiled at his plate with quiet amusement.

"I was n't hiding that Episcopal Hymnal from you. I thought it might be an unorthodox sight for some of the neighbors."

"Well, Jasper Hasbrook, let me tell you that was a fine performance of Grace Lindsay's to-day."

"It seemed so to me."

Miss Lida cleared her throat. "She 's offered to give me some lessons," she said; then, as her nephew observed a non-committal silence, added, "I don't know as I should look very well taking lessons at my time of life;" but the trembling of Miss Lida's hand belied her indifferent words as she seized the pot and spilled the tea into her saucer while she poured.

"Nonsense to talk about your time of life,"

returned Jasper heartily. "Turn about 's fair play. It might interest you to learn the use of the pedals."

Miss Hasbrook looked up furtively. A crimson tide rose in her face, and longing she could not repress shone in her eyes.

There was a moment's silence, then Jasper spoke again : —

"Did any plan for Grace come into your mind while she was playing, Aunt Lidy?"

She looked at him sharply, suspiciously now, and her face grew pale again. "Speak out, if you have anything to say," she said coldly.

"No," he answered calmly. "I have n't."

Miss Hasbrook began crimping the edge of her napkin by pinching it in fine folds. "I should think you or Mr. Morse or any other of the music committee who was there might have had thoughts if you 'd been bright," she said at last, with evident effort. "It 's plain enough that Grace Lindsay can play that organ; and she 's right here in town."

"It is a good idea," returned Jasper quietly, "and coming from you will have weight. There is to be a meeting of the committee to-morrow evening. I thought it would be well, perhaps, for me to be able to tell them that it was your suggestion that Miss Lindsay be engaged as organist."

Miss Hasbrook gave him one quick look, questioning and comprehending all at once. She pushed her chair back from the table and came around to his place. Then she embraced his neck and nervously drew his head close to her fast-beating heart for one instant.

"Thank you, Jasper," she said unsteadily.

There was no dissenting voice in the matter, and Grace Lindsay at once assumed her new duties. Twice every week she and Miss Hasbrook had what she termed a little practice together, and making acquaintance with the beautiful, resourceful instrument caused the sun to shine again for Miss Lida.

The sun shone more brightly for her nephew, too, now that Grace had returned; and yet he felt as though she had grown away from him in those years of city experience, which had clothed her with a subtle something that divided them. They had been boy and girl sweethearts. His sled had always been at her service, his biggest red apple was always saved for her; but though her development in all directions now appealed more and more to the natural refinement of his nature, he dared not expect to please her with his plodding home-staying ways.

She came out from the church where she had been practicing, late one warm July afternoon, and, locking the door after her, turned quickly, and saw Jasper stretched in the shade, book in hand.

"Do you mind this eavesdropping?" he asked, as he met her surprised gaze.

"Oh, no." Grace spoke quietly. She always had, from her demure little girlhood.

"What was that last thing you played?" he asked again, rising.

"A Communion by Batiste."

"It was beautiful. I want to thank you, Grace, for your kindness to Aunt Lidy. I don't believe you know how much it is to her and to me that you have brought so much pleasure into her life. I have n't had a good chance to speak of it before."

The girl's eyes looked away from the warmth of the young man's gaze. "You make me very happy by telling me so."

"The idea that I should be able to make you happy, even for a moment, Grace!" he burst forth, with such ardor that the delicate flush in his companion's cheeks deepened. "I fear you find Stapleton duller than it used to seem before you went away," he added.

"It is the same old place," she answered, "and there 's no place like home, you know, Jasper, especially," she added with a smile, "when there is a good organ in it."

"Then bless the organ!" he ejaculated.

"Good-by," she said with some haste. Her old playfellow's eyes were rather too expressive.

He looked after her as she went, not daring to

follow her this time, although on many a subsequent occasion when she found him, book in hand, waiting for her on the steps, he walked home with her to the gate, to the alert interest of all the neighbors.

These interested friends exchanged notes and came to the decision that Jasper ought to speak long before the young man himself mustered sufficient courage. It was after Christmas before he decided that for his peace of mind he must force the demure guard with which Grace Lindsay always defended herself, and find out what was her real feeling for him. She was so friendly so long as he was friendly, and so startled and shrinking the moment he displayed the least ardor, that it is little wonder he dreaded to cross the Rubicon.

His love had in it such an element of tenderness, he so respected the timidity from which he suffered, that when the moment arrived beyond which suspense became unbearable, he would not put his question to that grave, blushing face, but one Saturday wrote Grace a letter. He urged his suit warmly, and at the last said: "You will want a day to decide. If there is hope for me, play, at evening service to-morrow, my favorite Batiste Communion. I shall understand."

He sent the letter by a messenger to Mrs. Lindsay's cottage, and waited with what patience he could command for the morrow. On Sunday morning it was not altogether a pleasant surprise to see enter the church with Miss Lindsay a strange young man, who ascended with her to the organ loft, and remained seated near her throughout the service.

Jasper, following his own plan, made no effort to speak or even to bow to Grace. He walked home from church alone, — Miss Hasbrook was ill with a cold, — a prey to forebodings. The strange man was evidently an intimate friend. What might his coming mean? What did Jasper know of the ties the quiet girl he loved might have formed during her long stay afar from Stapleton? As the slow-moving afternoon wore away, possibilities which it crushed him to credit became more and more probabilities to the young man's mind. By the time for evening service he scarcely felt courage sufficient to take him to church; but he finally went, heavy hearted and heavy footed. He was a little late when he reached the door, and as it swung back to admit him with a rush of icy winter air, an electric shock ran through him. He seized the door-post an instant and turned faint in the warm, bright light. The familiar chords of the Batiste Communion filled the church. Firm, joyous, solemn, the theme rang out. Jasper bowed his head, and what his thoughts were in that ecstatic moment of reaction, only his Maker knows.

He stood until the last loved tone melted into silence, then turned and went out again into the night. He walked, he knew not and cared not whither, and the keen, frosty air was powerless to cool his glowing cheeks.

This very night he would see her, if only for a minute; and at the time he judged the folk would all be returning from church he turned his fleet steps toward the Lindsay cottage. A light was burning in the parlor. His intimacy at the house warranted his entering unannounced, and by so doing he might succeed in seeing Grace alone for a golden moment.

He quietly went in and opened the parlor door. His dearest hope was realized. There sat Grace by the table, alone. One moment he stood gazing at her, with adoring, proud eyes.

She glanced up. " Jasper ! " she exclaimed, startled and springing to her feet.

In an instant he was beside her, and she was clasped in his arms. He kissed her lips, her brow, her hair.

" My darling ! My darling ! " escaped from his overflowing heart.

" Jasper ! " she exclaimed breathlessly, pushing him from her with both hands.

" What ! Not yet ? " he said fondly, possessing himself of the two trembling hands. " You are not vexed that I did not wait to walk home from church with you ? I could not. Your guest " —

" I — I have n't been to church to-night."

" *What !* "

"Oh, what is the matter, Jasper? Don't! You frighten me."

His eyes looked fierce in his pale face, and when he spoke his voice was husky. "Grace, the Communion was being played when I went into church to-night. Is this some trick?"

"Indeed, I knew nothing of it," returned the girl, trembling, and not attempting to release the hands he still held. "I was ill, and my teacher, Mr. Harvey, was here on a visit and offered to play in my stead. I never thought of his choosing" — her head drooped.

"Then I have only to ask your pardon," said Hasbrook dryly, dropping her hands.

She buried her face in them.

"Oh, I know you're sorry for me, Grace. It was a little mistake that couldn't be guarded against, I suppose."

"I didn't know," stammered the girl, her face still hidden. "I wasn't sure until " — she looked slowly up — "Then it was because of that mistake that you — you kissed me so?"

Hasbrook stood, tall and unyielding, regarding her stonily. "I have apologized," he said shortly. "What more can I do? I can't take back those kisses."

She looked at him with a rapt expression. "Yes — you can," she breathed, and with a sigh that was half a sob she glided into his arms.

When another June came around they were

married.   It was a day full of sunshine, and no wedding march ever rang more joyously than that to which the young couple left the church; for Miss Hasbrook played it with a will, and she was not the least happy of the wedding party, for her little feet trod laboriously but surely among the pedals of the new organ.

A THANKSGIVING REVIVAL

"It 's only a dinner," said Charles Maynard, Jr., in tones of impatience. Charles Maynard, Sr., stood over against him on the hearth-rug trying to forget for the time being his admiration for the stalwart proportions of his only child.

"I tell you it 's a good deal more than that, young man!" he returned emphatically. "It 's a sacred rite, is Thanksgiving dinner, commemorating all the fortitude and trust of our forefathers; and it is n't going to be kicked into oblivion by a lot of sporty rascals with more muscle than reverence; not in my house, anyway."

Charles junior's lips twitched.

"We only want to kick it along from one o'clock to six; not into oblivion," he replied. "This football game is a matter of local pride," he added.

"And Thanksgiving dinner is a matter of national pride and loyalty," retorted Mr. Maynard.

"Would n't do away with it for the world," said Charles. "Altogether too many fond memories cluster around it."

Maynard senior raised himself on his toes and shook his head. "The trouble with the rising generation is that they have too many turkeys and

too much plum pudding. You 're all *blasé*. You
little know what it is to look forward for weeks to
the annual feast that was such a treat in my young
days."

This was too true. Charles junior took a new
tack. "The Lansings are going to dine at six," he
hazarded.

Mr. Maynard snorted contemptuously.

" Yes, and you inquire into it and you will find
that they 'll have ice-cream for dessert. Ice-cream,"
he repeated with fine scorn, "on Thanksgiving
Day! I tell you it has come to this : It 's Man-
hattan Field *vs.* Plymouth Rock, and I 'm for
Plymouth Rock if I have to sit down to my one-
o'clock dinner sole alone."

" You must n't do that, sir ; I 'll dine with you
myself first."

The young man's face was serious enough now,
and indeed his father knew that a little matter of
martyrdom at the stake was not to be compared
with this offer of sacrifice.

He laughed. " It is n't so bad as that, my boy.
You must go to the game with your sweetheart, of
course."

" But neither May nor I could enjoy it under
those circumstances."

Mr. Maynard lost himself in momentary thought.
He was recalling the days of his youth.

" We did n't know much about football in Berryville," he said. He smiled as memories clustered

upon him thick and fast, but Charles junior continued to look serious.

For a long minute the two stood silent in the richly furnished room. The youth was chafing under his elder's conservatism and obstinacy, but at last a flash lit up the countenance of Maynard senior. " I have it ! " he said, and he brought his hands together with a resounding slap. " Go on to your ball game with May Lansing, and eat ice-cream with her afterward."

" But you " —

" Don't waste a thought on me, my boy."

" You 'll come to the game ? "

" Not much I won't !   I 'll take care of myself. Ask me no questions.   I 'll tell you all about it afterward."

Mr. Maynard laughed again.   His new idea had evidently cleared away all his pessimism regarding the rising generation.

Miss Lucinda Parsloe was a respected citizen of that Berryville to which Mr. Maynard's thoughts had so wistfully returned, and no one respected her more highly than Miss Parsloe herself.

The neighbors all fell in meekly with this self-esteem, — all except, perhaps, Mrs. Mortimer; and that coquettish widow, having lived her married life away from the little New England village, had lost some of its habits, an unquestioning submission to Lucinda Parsloe being among them.

She and her sister Abbie and Lucinda had in their youth been inseparable companions until Ella Deering's attitude toward the opposite sex aroused Lucinda's righteous wrath. Men and boys had always been few enough in Berryville, and whenever one of the rare birds approached this trio, collectively or individually, it was always Ella who succeeded at last in monopolizing him.

Abbie never thought of resenting this.

"You know Ella has such a pretty dimple and such a way with her," she used to say.

But Lucinda glowered, fully believing that her wrath was all on account of gentle, forgiving Abbie, as in one case, and that the most flagrant of all, it certainly had been.

Only Ella's sudden marriage to a Mr. Mortimer, whom the volatile girl met while on a visit to Boston, saved the friends from coming to open rupture.

Now twenty years had passed. Ella was a plump and pleasing widow, this autumn at home on a visit to her sister. She still had the dimple, and still the alluring "way," and she thought Abbie an absurdly quiet little mouse, and told her so.

"Berryville is a hole, nothing but a hole; it ought to be spelled Buryville, and Abbie runs back into it just as fast as I get her to Boston," she complained to Lucinda, when the latter came to call.

Miss Parsloe did not relish this contempt for the place of her birth and residence.

"Tastes differ," she remarked dryly. "Why don't you revenge yourself by running back to Boston when Abbie's back is turned?"

"Oh, you snubby old Lucy!" rejoined Mrs. Mortimer gayly.

Lucinda was not sorry when one day soon afterward she saw Abbie Deering come into her gate alone.

"Ella had a headache," explained Miss Deering, when greetings had been exchanged.

"That's all right," was Lucinda's rather startling response, and they sat down for a cozy chat. "Ella's the same old sixpence, ain't she?"

"I don't think she changes much," replied the guest gently. There are few people so preëminently gentle as Abbie Deering. If it were only a matter of picking up the scraps from a littered carpet, she seemed to caress each raveling.

Miss Parsloe was her opposite in every respect. Thick-set, strong, almost brawny in build and muscle, she sat, regarding her slender, fair-haired maiden guest with the bridling suspicion which the neighborhood of Mrs. Mortimer always awoke in her.

"Ella having as good a time as ever?" she asked.

"She seems as happy as the average. She has her down days."

" Yes, when there ain't any men around to flirt with." Miss Parsloe thought it. She did n't quite dare to say it. She felt in Abbie's atmosphere a defense of Ella.

" I 've always thought, and I always shall think, that I have her to thank that you ain't my cousin this minute. You need n't purse your lips. I ain't backbiting her. I 'd just as soon say it to her face."

The lace in Miss Deering's sleeve trembled visibly, and she lost color so suddenly that Lucinda was startled at the effect of her own words.

" I am surprised at you," said Abbie, sitting up stiffly. " You would n't — you could n't hurt me more than by speaking of that to Ella."

" I won't, then." Miss Parsloe replied hastily with the feeling that she had been guilty of out-rageous intrusion. She talked on with unwonted embarrassment. " There 's no gainsaying that it is a power to have Mrs. before your name."

" We have done very well without it, Lucinda," returned the guest. She had regained her poise with quick self-control.

" Oh, I 've no complaint to make," replied her friend, with a toss of the head, " but it 's queer, all the same. Take a widow; she 's ten times as likely to get married as a single woman the same age."

Abbie Deering colored a little, and her eyes had a gentle twinkle. She was getting up her courage to say something funny. " ' He that hath a goose shall get a goose,' you know," she remarked at last.

Miss Parsloe's laugh was deafening applause. "Pretty good, Abbie," she responded. "Only in this case it ought to be changed to 'She that hath had one goose shall get another,' *ha, ha, ha!*"

Miss Deering joined, blushing, in her friend's noisy mirth, and her ears were the quicker to hear a determined thumping at the back door of the cottage.

"Somebody at the door, Lucinda." Miss Parsloe rose, and her laughter trailed through the kitchen as she went, then it died suddenly. In a minute she returned, her face long, and in her hand a yellow envelope, unfamiliar to her experience.

"It 's a telegram, Abbie," she said in a changed voice. "I thought I 'd rather be with somebody when I opened it."

Her guest sat up, wide-eyed and sympathetic, as the message was unfolded, but Lucinda's stern face was at first inscrutable. Gradually it relaxed. The telegram was a long one, and with a suppressed exclamation she re-read it, then looked with a strange smile at Abbie.

"No bad news?" said the latter tentatively.

Miss Parsloe started. "That boy 's waiting. I must send an answer."

She scribbled something on a sheet of paper. "Mine is n't so long as the other," she remarked; then she held it off and read aloud the six words she had written : " You guessed right the first time." With another triumphant look at her guest she left the room.

It was an extraordinary telegram certainly, but Miss Deering was determined not to show any curiosity. She knew Lucinda's love of having and keeping a secret, and she " would not give her the satisfaction."

" You 're not going ? " protested her hostess, returning.

" Yes. I promised Ella not to stay long."

" Well, I 'm sorry. Look here, Abbie, you have n't forgotten you 're to dine with me on Thanksgiving Day ? "

" But now that Ella is here " —

" All the more reason. We three will renew our youth and have a good time."

" Thank you then, Lucinda, if you really want us."

Left alone, Miss Parsloe again opened her telegram and read it with lively appreciation : —

"I am coming to eat Thanksgiving dinner with you. Turkey, white and sweet potatoes, squash, boiled onions, cranberry sauce — plum pudding, mince, pumpkin, apple, and cranberry pies. Cider, nuts, and raisins.
CHARLES MAYNARD."

" It 's ten years since I laid eyes on him," she mused. " He 's a lone, lorn man if he *is* rolling in money. I guess he 's homesick at last."

Then the consideration of her own concise wit
in the framing of her reply overcame her, and she
yielded again to breathless laughter.

Was it right to surprise Abbie so? The amount
of feeling her friend had shown at the mention of
that old-time rivalry made her hesitate an instant.

"Oh, I 'll risk it," she decided. "Abbie did n't
want any unpleasantness. That was all."

It was after eleven o'clock, Thanksgiving morning, when Miss Parsloe's strong hands were locked
in those of her cousin, and she pumped his arms
up and down, while they scanned each other's faces
in a high state of contentment.

" I thought most likely you would n't think about
church, so I stayed home. It 's. all on your conscience, Charles."

" I have n't any conscience to-day. I 'm all
stomach, Lucinda."

" Have you seen anybody you knew? "

" Not a soul. New man at the station. Everybody else .at church, perhaps; but the village is
here. I don't see how I 've stayed away so long! "

Mr. Maynard crossed over to the base-burner
stove and stood before it with his hands crossed
behind him. Chill airs crept around the windows,
and the colors of the ingrain carpet were crude.
The furniture was covered with haircloth.

In his New York house the atmosphere was
evenly and moderately warm by favor of the latest

heating appliances. The carpets were thick and the furniture luxurious; but Mr. Maynard was not homesick. He looked about him in wonder that decades could pass and no appreciable change be found in the condition of his native village. Lucinda must have some new chairs. That was certain.

He turned to meet again the eyes that had been gazing at him with such admiring delight, but during his short reverie Miss Parsloe had disappeared.

"Glad to see you, girls!" he heard her strong voice say. "Lay off your things in the bedroom."

He heard a buzz of reply and a quick frown gathered on his brow. His anticipations were demolished. How colossally stupid of Lucinda! She had invited guests. Girls, too! Oh, bore of bores! Why had he set this trap for himself and walked into it?

His genial face and attitude had disappeared; it was the starched and repellent man of affairs to whom Lucinda now ushered in her guests.

She was too triumphant in her successful *coup* to observe the change in him.

"Well," she said, beaming upon the women, "I don't suppose I need to make any introductions here."

Mrs. Mortimer's face lighted at sight of the surprising apparition of a correctly dressed man; but it was plain that neither recognized the other.

Lucinda's glance traveled back to Abbie, who came last, and whose changed, pinched face gave her a shock.

"I'm a fool!" she thought, with a pang. "Here; go back, go back," she said, pushing Miss Deering out into the friendly shade of the little hall. "One at a time!"

Then, returning into the parlor: "Do you two folks mean to say you don't know each other?"

The stony mask of the man's face had begun to soften. There were mischievous lights in the widow's eyes, and her dimple began to play.

"Why, Charlie — Mr. Maynard!" she exclaimed.

"Ella Deering, as I live! But you married somebody."

"So did you!" The smiling retort was accompanied by a decided squeeze of the banker's fingers. "But I am Mrs. Mortimer, if plain 'Ella' won't do any longer."

"As if anybody ever dared call you 'plain Ella'! Then the other lady was your sister."

Here Abbie glided silently and with a sort of desperate swiftness into the room, and met his outstretched hand with her own cold, thin one.

"This is a great surprise, Mr. Maynard," she said, scarcely lifting her eyes, and wondering, oh, *wondering*, at Lucinda's brutality. "She could n't have known. She could n't have understood," thought Abbie.

Her sister chatted on volubly, and as they all moved on to the dining-room, Ella monopolized the guest of honor.

For once Lucinda was grateful to her. That independent and stirring individual was sustaining an unwonted attack of humility. She regained her forces, however, as Abbie regained hers.

The dinner, Mr. Maynard averred, was ideal and orthodox in every particular.

Mrs. Mortimer and Miss Deering, being as intimately associated with his youth as Lucinda herself, were an assistance, instead of a drawback, in that season of reminiscence which he had promised himself; and three of the quartette continued to talk with undiminished relish until late into the afternoon, Abbie Deering listening with gentle and responsive attention, and answering when spoken to. She wondered at her sister's ease and volubility. " It might be different, though, if one had not cared for him," she thought wistfully.

Mr. Maynard walked home with the sisters. When they reached the gate Mrs. Mortimer returned his cordial hand-clasp with interest.

" Let us see a great deal of you while you are here, won't you ? "

It was the first time that the thought had suggested itself to Mr. Maynard's mind that he should not go immediately back to New York.

" Thank you," he answered vaguely; then turned toward Abbie.

She had stepped inside the gate, and to an inconvenient distance for shaking hands, so he stood with his hat off and smiled at her.

"This day has been a great pleasure. Would you have believed we could look so clearly across a chasm of twenty years?"

"Yes. I have not forgotten."

The sight of him standing thus stirred such memories that the answer was wrung from her; and a ring in her quiet voice sounded in his ears all the way back to Miss Parsloe's cottage. "It's a wonder Abbie never married," he thought.

As he strolled on in the frosty twilight his memory continued to unfold scenes of that time when these women were girls, and when ambition had stirred him to go to the great city where his employer's daughter fell in love with him and laid the foundations of his fortune. A sweet woman, his wife, for ten years now only a memory.

His thoughts had veered back again to a farther past by the time he rejoined Lucinda, whose brain had been in commotion during his absence.

Her dinner had been more of a success than she had anticipated. The only shadow across its brightness was the thought of Abbie and the evidence of shock which she had overcome so bravely. In striking contrast had been Mrs. Mortimer's happily excited face and sparkling eyes. All the little resentments of the past seemed seething together in Lucinda's breast as she dwelt upon it.

All her jealousy for Abbie, all her defense of her, were in arms when her cousin came in.

"I don't know when I 've had such a good time," he said heartily. "It is n't often a man can reminisce so amicably with two old flames at once. New friends can never take the place of old ones."

He took the armchair Miss Parsloe had drawn forward for him.

"Oh, you remember they were your flames, do you?"

"Of course. I 'm a little mixed," humorously, "as to which one favored me the more."

"You are, are you?" Lucinda's tone made him look up surprised. "Oh, I suppose it ain't your fault. Men are built that way. There 's poetry that talks about love being part of man's life and woman's whole existence. I 've laughed at it, but there are women it 's true of."

Miss Parsloe warmed to her subject. While sitting here alone she had been recalling half-forgotten events big and little, which, added to the overwhelming feeling exhibited by Abbie to-day, satisfied her conscience as to assuming more than she was absolutely sure of. Charles was in a softened mood, tender with memories of the past. If he would ever be susceptible to such flattery as she had at her command now was the time to bring it to bear.

He looked at her with dawning interest.

" Ella did like me pretty well," he said.

Lucinda flashed scorn upon him for a silent moment. " Yes, that 's just what she did; liked you pretty well while you were in sight. Out of sight, out of mind, instanter! 'T ain't her fault. Her mind 's only just big enough to hold what it 's looking at. Charles Maynard," solemnly, " we ain't young folks. There ain't a reason with any common sense in it why I should n't tell you that there has n't been a day for twenty years that you 've been out of Abbie Deering's mind. I, like a fool, let her come here to-day unprepared. Ella did n't know you at first. Abbie did, and like to fainted away where she stood. She 's had one good offer that I know of, but she sent the man off, so 's she could go on worshiping where her heart was, in secret and silence. I don't know as you were worth it; I don't know as any man is, but I 've told you this because I 've been stupid and cruel to-day, and you must n't go on and do worse. I lotted on having a visit of several days from you, but now I want you to get back to New York to-morrow by the first train that 'll take you. You know it comes hard on me to say it."

It was a risky card to play. Lucinda knew it. She would be ready to bite her tongue out if he took her at her word. At the same time it would be worse still to see him remain to be entertained by Ella Mortimer. If he stayed now it would be to see Abbie.

He was staring at her, dumb with surprise, while she made her rapid consideration.

"I think you exaggerate," he said at last.

"Think so, then!" she retorted, fierce with hope and apprehension.

The banker's sleep was disturbed that night. He was haunted by the tone in which Abbie had said that she had not forgotten; haunted, too, by the delicate face and the dove-eyes that had avoided his except at the moment of parting.

Bits of poetry found unwonted paths through his brain, and this was one of the scraps: —

> "For beauty is easy enough to win,
> But one is not loved every day!"

The next afternoon the Deering sisters were sewing in their room when Mrs. Mortimer gave a joyful exclamation and jumped up: —

"Here's Charlie Maynard in a buggy! I did n't know there was as decent a rig in Berryville. Do tell me, Abbie, do I look best in my violet hat or the black one? Get out my fur cape for me, will you, dear? Men hate to be kept waiting."

Abbie hastened to wait on her sister, her heart beating fast, and by the time the little servant came to their door Ella was pinning her veil.

"Mr. Maynard wants to know if Miss Deering will go driving with him."

"Yes, I 'll be right down," replied Mrs. Mortimer abstractedly. "Where *are* those tan gloves?"

"No, it's Miss Deering he wants," repeated the little maid grinning.

The widow turned about sharply.

"Very well. She will come," she said, and slammed the door in the small face.

"Oh, I can't, Ella!" said Abbie breathlessly.

"You can, and you will." Mrs. Mortimer's eyes were shining strangely. She dressed Abbie in her own cape, put in her bonnet pins for her, then turned her around and gazed into her eyes.

"Would n't it be strange, Abbie!" she said.

"It does n't mean anything, my dear." Miss Deering was striving for her equanimity.

"I used to play you selfish tricks," said Ella with sudden feeling. "You 've cared about him all along. I 'm glad it 's you."

"But it is n't I!" protested Abbie, so prettily flushed as she went fluttering down the staircase that Mr. Maynard, waiting at the door, looked long at her, his head uncovered.

Hours had passed before they returned; and the spot they visited ought to be discovered, for there they must have found the fountain of youth and drunk long and deep; for the light that shone henceforth in Abbie's eyes was of that eternal youth which reigns only where love itself is life!

"Good-morning, Mr. Dobson," said pleasant-faced Mrs. Billings, standing at the back door of her seashore cottage as the carpenter went by.

"Good-mornin'," he answered, the smile on his shrewd, humorous countenance so genial as to make one forget that in some localities it is customary for a man to remove his hat in addressing a woman.

"When are you going to fix my screens, Mr. Dobson?"

"Dunno. Got a jawb on hand now fer an old maid down Lowell way. Don't dast let up on it fer fear she'll make me balder 'n I be. Got a red-hot must after me these days, you bet."

In spite of this profession of haste, Mr. Dobson pushed his hat back, leaned against a piazza post, and crossed his feet leisurely while he changed a quid of tobacco from one cheek to the other.

"A new cottage? Who is she?" asked Mrs. Billings; for on this little island in Casco Bay a new cottager usually meant either a disagreeable interloper or a new member of the family. "I do hope she's nice. Old maids — it's the thing to call them bachelor maids, Mr. Dobson — they usually are nice."

" Well, this one means to stay a bachelor now, and don't you forget it.   Hain't you noticed that cawtage we 've started up thar near Stony Beach ? Must be ye did n't have yer magnifyin' glasses with ye."

" Why ?   Is it small ?   Who is she ?"

" A woman by the name o' Blaine.   House don't remind me o' nawthin' so much 's a snail shell. Miss Blaine can carry it off home on her back if she wants to, come autumn.   I reckon she don't cal'late to have no visitors."

Mr. Dobson was right.   Miss Lucilla Blaine did not calculate to have visitors.   On the contrary, while perhaps she would not go so far as to rig a spring gun on her piazza to greet possible guests, she intended to repel with decision any attempts to be neighborly on the part of the cottagers already settled on the island.

What Miss Blaine did want was to get away from people ; to be beholden to nobody ; to exchange ideas with nobody ; to think her own thoughts, to read her own books, and to cook her own meals undisturbed.   That is, she believed she wanted this.   She was very weary of her life, and longed for something wholly novel.   This existence would be wholly novel.   As the last scion of a highly respectable and well-to-do New England family, she was, at home, always more or less under inspection.   She often said to herself that she never had any real privacy.   Even when, a few years before, her niece Marion, her adopted daughter, ignored her commands, and, marrying an impecunious teacher, went off with him to Boston, she could not openly yield to the blackness of her impotent grief and anger, but was obliged with heroic struggles to conceal from her servants and neighbors the extent of the catastrophe.

Here then, on Gull Island, she had at last found the place she wanted. Not a servant should spy upon her. With a sort of fierce triumph she furnished the new house, steamed the clams for her first dinner, and then sat out on the piazza facing the sea, casting suspicious glances to the right and to the left, and armed to the teeth with mighty snubs to be delivered to the first comer who should attempt to invade her tiny castle. Down here she had no reputation to lose, and she was determined to reward herself for bygone repression by a lawless riot in honesty.

She had seen to it that she would have no near neighbors. "Moreover, the fools will all believe me poor," she said to herself, with a grim smile. "I dare say I shan't have much trouble."

She did not have much trouble. The cottagers at the unfashionable little resort were there for rest, and Miss Blaine found that a mere hint was sufficient to secure for herself uninterrupted solitude. She relaxed her guard, and for a while enjoyed carrying out to the letter the plan of. her dreams; but when monotonous weeks had passed, she sometimes caught herself looking up from her book as she sat on the piazza to watch the groups of happy friends crossing the fields. She had often noticed in her distant observations that the habitués of the island were either related to one another or else were congenial spirits.

"God setteth the solitary in families." The text slipped into her mind one sunshiny afternoon as she sat there alone; but she shook her head. "I am no more solitary than I was at home," she thought, with sudden defense; " not so much so ; not so much so!" Then she dropped her book and clasped her hands over her eyes with a climax of feeling that life was sorrow.

Thus she sat for a minute, lost in what was not thought, rather the feeding of the mind on the bitter herbs of discontent, longing, and regret.

When next she looked up she found herself observed. Astonishment at the figure which met her view held her for a moment in silence. It was a small boy who paused beside her piazza. He wore coarse blue overalls which covered him from shoulder to feet, and made him look tall for his four years. On his head was a cap with a visor. It was rather small for him, and set slightly askew on his close-cropped hair. His feet were incased in the species of rubber shoes known as "sneakers," and their tread on the soft grass had been so noiseless as to be undetected even by Miss Blaine's suspicious ears.

Clasped in both dimpled hands the child carried a faded and streaked parasol, the old covering of which had come loose from two of its ribs and slipped up, revealing their black bareness.

Variety shows were not in Miss Blaine's line. Had they been she would have seen that this handsome boy looked like a miniature character artist just come upon the stage to sing in broken English a song concerning the "Vaterland." The russet and rose tints of his complexion, the bewitching curves of his grave mouth, and above all, the direct gaze of his deep-blue eyes with their strongly marked brows, arrested her attention, while his garb raised only the disapproval under deep layers of which her sense of humor lay buried.

Surprise holding her silent for an instant, the child spoke: "I thought you were crying," he said.

"What have you come here for?" she asked, and her brusque tone would have frightened most children. This one was naturally fearless and entirely inexperienced in harsh words, and he continued to regard her.

"Because I hurt the baby," he answered.

Miss Blaine was bewildered, as much by the direct, unabashed manner, as by the reply.

"How did you hurt it?" she asked involuntarily.

"By accident."

"What did you do?"

“ I slapped her.”

The unexpected response came near to stirring that buried sense of humor; but after all it was only surprise which Miss Blaine felt. She drew back in her chair and made a strange grimace, — a sudden drawing together of her features, which caused her eyeglasses not to drop, but to leap from her high-bridged nose in a manner which her visitor found diverting. His gravity vanished, and he laughed aloud with every evidence of lively interest.

“ Please do that again,” he said.

Miss Blaine started. She had no idea to what the child referred. In her bewilderment at his amusement, she replaced her glasses, the better to see what it was all about.

Her guest suspended his laughter, and waited with open-mouthed anticipation to see his request granted.

“ You ought not to have come here,” said Miss Blaine, feeling at a disadvantage, and speaking curtly.

“ My mamma knows I came. She told me to take a walk and I would feel better.”

There was an unusual exactness about this child’s speech ; precision which gave every syllable its due. Miss Blaine observed it with wonder.

“ Aunt Jane Billings has given me this parasol to use as long as I am at the island,” he pursued, looking first at his streaked possession with fond admiration, and then at his new acquaintance; "but I shall not carry it back with me to America."

Miss Blaine started again, and again her glasses performed their acrobatic feat.

The boy broke into appreciative laughter, looking at his entertainer delightedly. Miss Blaine, still not connecting his amusement with her unconscious habit, felt herself grow warm, and wondered if this might be a half-witted child whom ill-luck had sent her way.

"I don't know who your mother is," she said sternly, "but you must never walk in front of my house. I am Miss Blaine. Everybody knows that I don't want people walking on my grass."

The boy looked at her doubtfully. He could hardly believe that such a diverting person could be serious. His prolonged gaze found no reassurance, however; so the blue legs started off meekly toward the back of the house.

"Good-by, Miss Blame," he said over his shoulder. The innocent shaft struck home.

The lady looked after the quaint little figure until she saw it reach Stony Beach and sit down among the pebbles.

"Good-by, Miss Blame." The phrase looked up at her like an accusation from the book she tried to read. She had never thought of herself as a bad-tempered person. Had she been unnecessarily severe to that queer-acting child?

She did not stop wondering about him, and when Mr. Dobson came the next day to put some additional shelving in her kitchen, she introduced the subject of her visitor in a manner which she considered artful.

"Oh yes, I know who ye mean," replied the carpenter, smiling. "Little chap's a German; leastways his father is, and the boy's heard tell so much 'bout his relations t' other side the ocean he thinks 'cause he come 'cross the water in a boat to git t' the island that he's in Europe now. Funny little bugger. I like to hear him talk. He ain't any common sort of a baby. His mother's visitin' up to Billin's. Mis' Billin's ain't any relation, they tell me, but the boy — Hermann his name is — he calls her aunt."

All things considered, Miss Blaine decided that it was well she had been stern. Any kindness to the child might lead to becoming involved with the neighbors.

But the charm of her hermit life was waning. The old restlessness was asserting itself, and when next day on her solitary walk she happened to meet the intrusive child in his outlandish rig, and he gave her a smiling gaze of recognition, she returned his look curiously.

"I have been feeding the pigs," he announced, in a tone which showed that the operation had been a very satisfactory one.

"You enjoyed that, did you?"

" Yes ; " the child's face beamed. " I left some apples in their den to remuse them. Mamma says apples are apt to remuse pigs."

" Humph ! Very apt to," returned Miss Blaine. The friendly blue eyes held her with a novel charm. " I guess you 're having a pretty good time here," she said, lingering.

" Yes." Hermann became suddenly thoughtful. " The balloon man does n't come here," he continued. " At home in America he comes very often ; but," with a little sigh and a cheerful look at Miss Lucilla, " there are so many happinesses here we don't need balloons."

" Ahem ! No. A— good-by, Hermann," said Miss Blaine, and stalked on, pausing soon, however, to turn and look back at the child.

After this she began to watch from her window for the blue overalls, the small cap, and the parasol, for the purpose, of course, of making sure that the boy with the luminous dark-lashed eyes did not dare disregard her commands and pass in front of her house. Children were so lawless. No one except their own infatuated parents could be expected to like and put up with them.

The first time she caught sight of him after their last interview she darted to the side of the window and reconnoitred through the blind.

On came the sturdy little figure toward the house, and when he drew near, without glancing up — somehow it gave the watcher a queer sensation that he did not look up and try to see her — he marched around, making the circuit of Castle Dangerous and taking his way on down toward the beach. When she had seen the last of him, Miss Blaine, feeling singularly dissatisfied, hurried to her bookshelves to find the most interesting volume in her possession.

The pebbles were a strong magnet to her little neighbor, and he sought them almost daily, but he never trespassed upon Miss Lucilla's lawn. One morning, as she recognized the dilapidated parasol coming across the grass, she was suddenly seized with the recollection that she ought to brush the spider webs down from her piazza roof. Forthwith she caught up the broom and hastened outdoors in time to intercept Hermann as he was sheering off from dangerous ground.

"Good-morning," she said shortly.

He looked up. The lady was being funny again. The child's jolly little laugh bubbled over irrepressibly as her grimace relieved her of her glasses.

"How do you do that?" he asked, standing still and regarding her.

Miss Blaine grew warm under his admiring gaze.

"How do I do what?" she asked.

"Make your glasses jump off so."

"Oh," said Miss Blaine, feeling rather sheepish as she suddenly understood his repeated diversion. "Are you still having a good time on the island,

Hermann?" she asked with some embarrassment, dabbing vigorously at the spider webs.

"Yes."

"'Yes, ma'am,'" corrected Miss Blaine quickly. "Does n't your mother tell you to say 'ma'am'?"

"No.   Keo does not either."

"Who is Keo?"

Hermann looked reflective.   The faithful nurse had been in the house when he was born.   He knew she was as much a part of the family as papa; but she was no relation to him.

"Little boys should answer when they are spoken to," said Miss Blaine.   "Who is Keo?"

The child looked at her with his usual honest simplicity.   "I don't know how to teach people that," he returned.

"Well, if I ever!" was his hostess's mental comment.   The unconscious, quaint little being attracted the lonely woman wonderfully.   Her secret question now was not whether it would be wise to detain him; it was by what means she could do so.   Hermann made a sudden exclamation.

"Oh, see this, Miss Blaine!" and down went the cherished parasol as he stooped to the grass and touched something gently with the tip of his chubby finger.   "What is it?"

The lady drew near and looked with interest. The treasure-trove was a brown and yellow furry caterpillar, making the best time it could make to get away from the investigating finger.

" That is a caterpillar, Hermann."

" Will it bite ? "

" No, indeed.   You can take it up if you wish to."

The child promptly took gentle hold of the creature and let it crawl from one of his dimpled hands to the other.

" When you are a big boy," went on Miss Blaine, at last on familiar ground, " you will study about all these little animals.   I have studied a great deal about such things, and it is very interesting."

" I will take it and show it to mamma," said Hermann, his face beaming with pleasure.

Miss Blaine would have scouted the idea that she could be envious of an unknown woman ; but she wondered about the mother of the sturdy figure while she stood still to watch him as he withdrew, the parasol hanging precariously over his shoulder as he kept careful eyes on his prize.

She had gone into the house when her ears were assailed by a series of shrieks, coming faintly from a distance.

" Some young one fallen on the rocks, proba-bly," she muttered.   " I hope it is n't Hermann ! " The eager thought followed quick at the heels of the indifferent one, and she even hastened unde-cidedly to the window; but with an impatient " Pshaw!" moved away and went into the kitchen.

In a few minutes she heard a soft knock at her back door.   She opened it, and to her astonishment there stood the small familiar figure, his cap rather more awry than usual, and signs of tearful woe in his solemn face.

"I have lost my caterpillar," he announced, making a manful struggle not to break down.

Miss Blaine felt odd sensations about her heart. "It's too bad!   How did you lose him?"

"A boy took him away from me, and he hurt him."   The corners of the little mouth twitched down.   "There was — was" — the child hesitated with horror and compassion, "there was blood on the boy's hand.   Then he ran and threw my caterpillar away."   The corners of the lips twitched so they could scarcely speak.

"He was a very naughty boy!" exclaimed Miss Blaine severely, more warm than she had been in any cause for many a year.

Hermann, still quivering under the shock, began to cast about in his infant mind for the consolation that did not come from without.   "Perhaps," he said hesitatingly, looking appealingly up into his hostess's face, "perhaps it was not blood.   Perhaps the caterpillar was a little *sick*, and" — he lowered his voice in acknowledgment of the indelicacy of the suggestion — "and he — spit up something!"

Miss Blaine cleared her throat in heroic preparation to throw veracity to the winds for the first time.   "I guess that's what it was," she replied; "the caterpillar was sick."

The clear, dark eyes were upon her. "I came to see if you would help me find another. You have studied about such things," said the boy in his quaint fashion.

"Yes, I will, Hermann. You just wait till I get my hat on;" and Miss Blaine's hands fairly trembled with eagerness as she pinned on her green veil.

After that it was a dark day to the maiden lady when she had no interview with her little lad. She began to develop ingenuity in interesting him, — she who had never been in intimate contact with a young child in her life.

No alarming intrusion from neighbors followed upon her indulgence, and it came to be that she stepped outdoors to meet the boy occasionally, or invited him in to look at her pictures.

"You have not a picture of my emperor. He is very handsome — my emperor," he said one day; and although Miss Blaine's glasses leaped off at this shock to her republican principles, she did not attempt to lecture the child, who she had found could speak but a word or two of German, and was destined to grow up a good American.

Even when he talked to her, as he often did, of what he used to do in America, and what he intended to do when he returned thither, she did not correct him. Probably his people thought the mistake was amusing and innocent. Perhaps it was. At all events, Miss Blaine knew that a subtle sweetness crept into life when those serious rosy lips addressed her, and all her severe principles were merged in the one desire not to repel him.

"You little missionary!" laughed Mrs. Billings, one evening when Hermann came home bringing a ginger cake which his new friend had given him. "Have you been out again, converting the heathen?"

"What is heathen? I have been on Stony Beach with Miss Blaine," returned the child. "She has studied about pebbles."

Miss Blaine actually began to hum about her work in the tiny kitchen. Nothing occurred during the day but that she considered whether it could be turned to account to interest Hermann.

One morning she met him with a mysterious nod.

"What do you think happened here last night?" she asked.

"What did?" returned the little boy, sitting down cosily beside her in a place she made for him on the piazza.

"It began yesterday. I was sitting by the window, and I heard a rustling noise across the room in my waste-basket. 'Dear me,' thinks I to myself, 'is that a mouse?'"

Her listener's eyes were upon her, full of interest, and she awkwardly took hold of his hand, which nestled contentedly in hers.

"And was it a mouse?"

" Yes ; and pretty soon what do you think that mouse did?   He came up and sat on the edge of the basket and looked at me with his bright eyes, just as cunning as could be, and his little ears stood up like two fans. I said to him : ' You silly mouse, what makes you do that ? Don't you know if I see you I shall have to set a trap and catch you?'"

Hermann's eyes grew so large that the narrator was elated. " So last night I set a trap near my desk, and this morning the mouse was in it."

The expression which grew on the listener's face gave a disconcerting blow to Miss Blaine's self-esteem.

" Was he dead?" asked the child solemnly.

" I — I think — yes, he was."

She felt her face grow warm. Oh, why had she made the hero of her tale so engaging ! She waited guiltily.

At last Hermann looked up hopefully.   He had, as usual, found consolation for his tender heart. " Perhaps it was not the same mouse," he said. " Perhaps it was the same *color*, and cut out the same *shape*, but perhaps it was a different one."

And his companion, her integrity completely undermined, eagerly grasped at this solution of the difficulty, and assented.

For a day or two afterward it happened that the child did not appear in the neighborhood of Miss Blaine's cottage. How long those days were, only that lady knew. On the third one the solitude became unbearable. She put on her shade hat and went to walk, not, as usual, seeking the wild and uninhabited portions of the island, but turning her steps toward the other cottages.

As she crossed the unfamiliar ground she cast sharp glances to right and left, but not once was she rewarded by a glimpse of blue overalls, now very baggy at the knee, and with a general appearance of such disrepute as to match the parasol.

She kept on her way down to the jagged rocks in whose pools at low tide were revealed the little creatures of the sea in crystal clearness. A fascinating, if dangerous, playground for a child; and on climbing down the boulders in a spirit of investigation Miss Blaine caught sight of her little German. He was standing on the slippery seaweed, stooping over a pool. One sleeve was stripped up above his dimpled elbow, and his arm was plunged into the water.

No one else was in sight.

"What an idea! To think of letting a baby like that come here alone! Why, he might be killed a thousand times, and break his leg and sprain his ankle into the bargain," thought the indignant woman, too excited and fearful to be careful of her own steps as she leaped and slid toward the boy.

"Hermann! Be careful!" she exclaimed, with such sudden vehemence that the little fellow started, slipped, and fell, giving his head a hard bump on a projecting rock.

He was stunned during a long enough instant for Miss Blaine to catch him in her arms, and, seated, to hug him to her breast, before his lungs asserted their good healthy condition.

His cry of pain brought a woman speeding over the rocks. " Why, Hermann dear, did you fall ? " she called.

" Now, you just keep away, whoever you are," exclaimed the excited Miss Lucilla. " If you don't know any better than to leave a child alone in this place you have n't got sense enough to be trusted with him.   Where is it, my lamb ? " she asked lovingly, although Hermann was making it very evident where it was by rubbing his short dark hair with a very wet hand.

As for the snubbed young woman, she paused behind Miss Blaine's shoulder, caught her lip between her teeth, and clasped her hands, her eyes shining moistly, as starved Miss Lucilla pressed kiss after kiss upon the firm rosy cheek on her breast.

It was Hermann's habit when he received a sudden hurt to cry; but he never cried long. There were too many interesting things to be attended to.   Now he ceased his wails, and, still rubbing his head, addressed his comforter.

" Miss Blame, did you ever (sob) ever study about (sob) starfish ? "

" Yes, my lamb, and the next time you come here I 'll come with you myself. You must never — do you understand, Hermann ? — never come alone like this."

" I did not come alone. My mamma came with me." The boy struggled into a sitting posture and looked up over Miss Lucilla's shoulder. " There is my mamma."

The young woman came silently around into sight, and when Miss Lucilla met her gentle appealing eyes she gave such a start that Hermann looked at her questioningly.

Quick, bitter suspicion filled the elder woman's heart. This child had been a bait, a tool. While she was still held dumb by a painful conflict of feeling, the mother spoke to her boy. " I thought those little sneakers were getting too old and slippery," she said, gently taking hold of his foot as she seated herself near him.

" Can't you afford to get him new ones ? " demanded Miss Blaine suddenly. " Look here, Marion, I wish you would give me this child. I 'll do well by him. You have another."

Marion shook her head gently. " We are very well off, thank you, Aunt Lucilla. My husband has a good position in the Institute in Boston and a number of private pupils. You can see that he could not spare his boy."

" This is not Aunt Lucilla ; this is Miss Blaine," said Hermann explanatorily.

" Who is Aunt Lucilla, then ? " demanded the spinster of the child. " Now I 'll catch her," she thought fiercely. " This baby is my own flesh and blood. I 'll find out what she 's told him about me."

" She is my Aunt Lucilla," he responded.

" What kind of a one, — a cross old aunt, is n't she ? "

" No, she is not cross. My mamma loves her. Sometime papa and mamma and the baby, and me too, are all going to have dinner on Thanksgiving Day at her house."

Miss Blaine's lip quivered, and her niece's cheeks flushed. Somehow their hands met, although they did not look at one another.

" Hermann ! " she squeezed him; " I don't want to be ' Miss Blame ' any more. I am your Aunt Lucilla."

" Pretend ? "

" No, really your aunt, and you are going to eat Thanksgiving dinner with me this very autumn. Will you kiss me and say ' Aunt Lucilla ' ? "

The boy kissed her willingly, and obediently repeated " Aunt Lucilla ; " then jumping up and pulling her toward the pool, he added : " Have you studied about sea urchins, too ? "

A MISTAKE IN CONSONANTS

"I suspect it is the witching hour of night when ghosts troop forth," said Frances Kennard, as she and her sister entered the house after parting from the friend who, in their aunt's absence, had been their chaperon for the evening.

"I could believe it to be morning," responded the other wearily. "Why cannot people who give musicals begin their programmes at a reasonable hour?"

"Why, May, it was a beautifully managed affair," said the younger, as she turned up the gas in their room, disclosing the sparkling depths of her own happy eyes.

"Two points of view," remarked May, with a little laugh.

"How different our temperaments are!" said the other, still smiling at her pleasant reminiscences.

"Very," replied the elder dryly. "What sort of an effect would it have on my temperament, I wonder, to be the rose that all were praising for — say one evening?"

"Why, May, you *were* the rose that all were praising. You never sang better than to-night.

I saw half a dozen people wiping their eyes when you finished. Even Jack Huntington said it was a marvel that such a cold girl as you always seemed could sing with such fire and passion.”

“ Indeed! That sounds like the sort of compliment my friends reserve for me.” Miss Kennard’s colorless cheeks flushed.

“ He went on to say that he had always understood that it required a deep experience either of grief or love to give a singer such thrilling power as you possessed.”

May approached her dressing-table. “ Jack has a marvelous fund of general information,” she returned.

“ Don’t make fun of him,” said Frances, regaining her gayety of demeanor. “ Old friends are best.”

“ So I observed that you thought this evening, for scarcely any one but Mr. Huntington had an opportunity to come near you.”

“ He amuses me more than the rest,” admitted Frances, “ and then it is such fun to see the others glower!” She stifled a merry little laugh, in deference to the lateness of the hour.

“ What did you answer, Fay, to Jack’s original proposition ? ”

“ What about ? ” asked the pretty young girl abstractedly.

“ My deep grief and my love.”

The deliberation and unsteadiness of the low

tone were impressed on the inattentive ear sufficiently to cause Frances to bestow a light kiss upon
her sister's cheek in passing.

"You *are* tired, dear. Hurry into bed. I forget just what I said, but it was something to the
effect that you were the exception that proved the
rule. The bare idea of hidden grief or a grand
passion in connection with May Kennard!" The
girl laughed and squeezed her sister affectionately.
"Jack knows, as well as I do, just what a steady-
going, level-headed, even-tempered, reliable girl
you are. Why, it would turn the whole world
topsy-turvy if you were to become erratic, so I
am very glad that you do not require any such inspiration for your singing."

The older sister gazed at the other wistfully.
"You remember the staid farm horse of the fable,
don't you, Fay, who became jealous of the graceful
pet dog belonging to his master? In the same
way I come occasionally to a climax of jealousy of
you, my dear. Being plain and serviceable fails at
times to satisfy me, and I pine to be a belle."

The younger girl's eyes widened in surprise, and
she hesitated in doubt how to reply to this unprecedented confession.

May laughed rather bitterly. "I fancy the
master of the dissatisfied farm horse gazed upon
him with somewhat of your present expression.
At all events you remember that when the animal
attempted to gambol about in imitation of the little

dog, he received blows for his pains. I have n't forgotten that feature of the experiment, and my worst enemy cannot accuse me of ever attempting to be kittenish, however tempting the circumstances."

"I — I did n't know you cared for frivolity," stammered Frances, rather abashed by the light burning in the gray eyes, usually so gently quiet.

No more words passed between them until the gas was out and they were in bed; then Frances turned and spoke with some eagerness to console : —

"I was nothing beside you to-night, May. I wonder you were not elated at having made such a success. You were such an assistance to the hostess in other ways beside your singing. She said you had been invaluable to her. People are always being grateful to you, you are so capable."

"Yes," returned the other, in the weary tone which her sister found so novel. " ' Be virtuous and you will be happy,' ' Pretty is that pretty does,' and so forth, and so forth. I know the whole list by heart, Fay. All the same, I should like to go to a party sometime and not be of any use to anybody, but sit off among the palms with Jack Huntington."

"With — Jack!" gasped Frances. "Why, you have n't seemed to approve of him at all since he returned from his travels. You 've said " —

"Oh, well, somebody with a fair mustache and

adoring eyes," interrupted the other recklessly. " What do I care who it is so long as he admires me enough. I want to be utterly useless and pretty like " —

" Like me, perhaps," returned Fay, with swift-offended pride.

" Oh, no, dear, no. Never mind my nonsense," and May patted her sister apologetically.

" Poor Jack is n't a bit well," declared the latter, after a minute. " The doctor has given him his choice of two or three prescriptions, and he has chosen a walking-tour."

" Indeed? When does he start?"

" Very soon. He bade me good-by to-night, and told me to tell you that you would not have a chance to reform him for a month."

The next morning no reference was made by either of the sisters to the elder's brief and astonishing mutiny. Frances, seeing May go about the house with her usual reticent serenity, attending to the cares which devolved upon her in their aunt's absence, half wondered if she had not dreamed the little scene of the night before, and shortly forgot all about it; for Frances Kennard's life was too full of pleasant realities to admit much time for speculation. She was a beautiful young creature, in the zenith of her popularity, and her matter-of-fact, sensible sister was an indispensable aid in the various undertakings of the society girl.

Life ran on for them in the usual grooves for

about ten days, and then a little letter written on pink paper and addressed to Miss May Kennard in a painstaking hand, fell like a bombshell among the clouds of tulle and lace which Miss Kennard's skillful fingers were altering to suit the fastidious maiden for whom it had just arrived from the dressmaker. Frances, waiting rather impatiently while May hurriedly ran her eyes over the letter, was astonished to see her sister flush violently, and then turn very pale as she re-read the contents of the pink note. Her astonishment increased when May, after a thoughtful moment, during which she seemed to put a constraint upon herself, dropped the letter and turned her eyes, dark with some emotion, upon her.

"Fay, do you love Jack Huntington?" was her startling query.

The younger sister was silent, and her fingers toyed nervously with the ribbons of her ball-gown. Of a certain sort of confidence little subsisted between the sisters. Their intimacy confined itself largely to the externals of life. This being the case, Frances was the more amazed by May's direct question.

"If I did, would you expect me to tell you here and now?" she asked.

"Yes, dear, as you value your happiness," said the other, with no abatement of her solemn intensity.

"Do explain yourself," said Frances, half impatiently. " I should n't expect you to be theatrical. What is in that letter ? "

" If you care for Jack you will not care to see it."

" Ah, it is some slander of him then."

" No. Oh, tell me, Fay. Be honest." May turned paler, if possible, as she spoke beseechingly. " Does your happiness depend on Jack Huntington ? "

The belle of the season lifted her chin proudly. " Do I seem like a person whose happiness could depend on the favor of a man who has never said he loved me ? "

A radiant smile began to tremble on the other's lips.

" Those words would be a lash to my pride if I still felt pride concerning Jack," the elder sister said, " but, Fay," a glory of happiness transfigured the speaker's face until it looked unfamiliar to her astonished companion, " I am the most blessed woman in all the world, for I love him with all my strength, and he loves me." She extended the letter with a gesture and gaze Frances never forgot, and the young girl mutely received it.

In language as prim and precise as the handwriting, she read that Mr. Huntington lay ill at the writer's house. He had proceeded on his walking-tour as far as the village of Swanley, where he had rescued two little children from drowning in the river. The writer supposed that, the spring weather having been unusually wet and bleak, Mr. Huntington had endured much exposure, to which the struggle in the swift current of the river had put the finishing touch.   At all events he was attacked with fever, and the writer, Miss Azubiah Reed, had received him into her house and was at present nursing him to the best of her ability.   The patient alarmed her by his delirious state.   She had had no idea where to send to his friends; but the young man called frequently upon " May — May Kennard," with protestations of affection which, Miss Reed stated, could not be misunderstood.   She had that morning found Miss Kennard's card among his effects, and decided at once to send this account to her address, hoping that it would be the means of acquainting Mr. Huntington's friends with his whereabouts and condition.

" That blessed card ! " said May, as her sister looked up from the letter with a dazed countenance. " Do you remember my giving it to him one of the last evenings he was here, with that reference to a page of Ruskin written across it ?   But for that who knows how long I might have remained in ignorance ; for I was always cold to him, Fay, as he said.   I feared his discovering that in all the world there existed for me but one man.   I feared your discovering it, too, dear, for until now I thought you cared for each other."

" How very ill he is ! " said Frances mechanically.

" Yes, but I will nurse him back to health," and
a radiant confidence glowed in the speaker's face
as she rose.

" You are not going down there yourself ! "

" What else can I do ?   He has neither mother
nor sister to go to him, and he has called me."

" But what would Aunt Susan say ? "

May seemed not to hear the feeble remon-
strance.   She went hurriedly to her room, followed
by Frances, whose thoughts were in a hubbub.
Jack Huntington, she had been sure, was devoted
to herself.   She had a hundred proofs of it which
her sister did not suspect.   In the first rush of
bewilderment and surprise it seemed to her that
his loss was a heavy blow.   Why, then, had she
not been frank when May catechized her ?   That
look in the latter's face as she put her questions,
now that it was explained, gave the pleasure-seek-
ing beauty a glimpse of noble heights of unselfishness which she herself had never dreamed of.   Her
own pangs of mortification were for the moment
swallowed in amaze at the discovery of her sister's
transfiguring affection and proposed abnegation.

" Of course I shall go with you," she said
briefly.

" Thank you," rejoined May, taking her sister's
face between her hands and giving her such a kiss
as Fay had never received from her before.

" No wonder she can sing ! " 'thought the
younger, still marveling.

A few hours later Miss Azubiah Reed was pleasantly excited by the arrival of a telegram, promising the prompt appearance of the young lady whom her interesting patient had been calling with such impassioned fervor. Miss Zuby, as she was known throughout Swanley, though neither young nor comely, had a secret streak of romance in her nature which would have been gratified by current events were it not for the trepidation which her patient's ravings caused her. When the Kennard girls appeared at her hospitable door, the kind soul welcomed them anxiously.

"I did hope his ma 'd come," she declared.

"He has no mother," replied May; "we are as near to him as any friends he has."

Miss Zuby fixed her eyes on the younger girl admiringly. She was a fit mate for handsome Mr. Huntington.

"I 'm thinkin' the sight o' your face 'll do him good," she said bluntly.

Frances glanced involuntarily at her sister and blushed, but did not reply.

"He 's better, anyway, to-day. He 's slept quite a spell, and he hain't hollered since mornin'. What shall I call your friend?" pursued the hostess, still gazing approvingly at Frances' long-lashed eyes and finely-tinted complexion.

"We are sisters," responded the girl; "this is Miss May Kennard to whom you wrote."

"Oh, jus' so, jus' so," said Miss Zuby, much

embarrassed by her mistake. " Won't you lay off your things ? "

For a long time afterward she scolded herself for her stupidity, and before many hours had elapsed came heartily to sanction Mr. Huntington's choice, so pleased was she with the sensible, helpful, capable way in which the elder Miss Kennard assumed the duties of nurse. The latter put into effect a dozen devices for the patient's comfort of which Miss Zuby had never thought, and the change in the young man's condition continued in the right direction.

One day he opened his eyes from the stupor which had followed his fever. May Kennard was sitting near the bed with some needlework. He recognized her, and in his feeble condition the surprise was so great that his eyes closed again. The girl, who had not perceived his look, approached him quietly, and making some change in the covering, knelt beside the bed, clasped her hands together, and adored. The look of pure love and yearning in her face should have waked the sleeping; and Mr. Huntington, not being asleep, but, on the contrary, making up his mind for another essay at comprehending his surroundings, lifted his heavy lids and met the beautiful tenderness of her gaze.

She saw the light of recognition in his eyes, and a low, inarticulate sound broke from her lips.

" Jack, you know me," she said very gently, and

she took the hand that lay on the coverlid in her own soft one, while such a radiance beamed in her face that it was the greatest of the sick man's many marvels.

"I don't understand," he said feebly.

"But you will soon.   Don't try now.   Just rest," she replied, with the intonation a mother might use to her baby, and a soothing serenity of manner which made the young man give up all his multiplying conundrums, and fall asleep clinging to her hand.

Happy tears gathered in the watching gray eyes and fell unheeded on the coverlid, and the spontaneous burst of thankfulness which ascended to God from that fast-beating heart must have been a song in heaven!

That afternoon when the old doctor came he found his patient awake, and this was his peroration as he was leaving the room.

" Well, sir," cheerily, " you will have enough to do the next month or two, to express your thanks to this young lady; not an unpleasant duty, I suppose.   Ha, ha, ha!   I wish we could keep her here in Swanley.   She is the sort of woman there ought to be at least one of in every town; but there ain't, young man !   There ain't enough of 'em to go round, and I suppose you 'll agree with me there.   Now, you 've nothing to do but grow strong. Let 's see you be quick about it.   Good-night."

The doctor's knowing manner was also a conundrum, and May's color and half-smiling lips gave a girlish prettiness to the quiet strength of the face Jack had known so long. He thought he had never seen her so attractive, and he lazily enjoyed watching her as she made the preparations for his comfort during the coming night. Once as she stood near his bed he reached out his hand and taking hers carried it to his lips.

"You know I am grateful to you, May," he said fervently; "I never heard of such kindness as yours in coming down here, and caring for me. I simply have no words in which to talk to you about it."

She beamed down upon him with the sweetest expression, and joy in the touch of his lips sent a glorious color over her face and throat.

"I never appreciated May Kennard," thought the young man, as his lifted eyes beheld the beautified woman.

The next morning as May was removing his breakfast tray, she said, "Fay wants to see you to-day."

"Is Fay here?" That was her patient's brief reply, but her eyes were on his face. Had they not been, his tone, unawares as she had taken him, would have been enough.

A slow, terrible pain crept mercilessly around her heart, seeming to threaten her very life. The dishes on the tray rattled together as she bore them from the room.

Frances was in the kitchen playing with a couple of kittens that Miss Zuby had just brought in from the wood-house.

"Come to our room a minute, Fay," said May.

Her sister looked anxious at sight of her and followed without a word.

"Is he worse?" she asked at last, when her sister had closed the door behind them. "For pity's sake, May! Oh, my dear girl, you are worn out!"

"No, no; sit down here," pushing away the camphor bottle; "I 've something to tell you. It is you Jack loves."

"May!" gasped Frances, frightened by the pinched white face, and suffering the most unselfish pang of sorrow she had ever experienced; even while — so subtly constituted is the human heart — somewhere underneath the compassion a gratification sprang to life.

A nervous smile twitched her sister's pale lips. "Miss Zuby did not hear quite right. She made a little mistake in consonants. That is all. My card helped on the delusion. The delusion! O Fay!" the dry manner changed, and the girl bowed her head in her hands in tearless anguish. "My heart is breaking!"

To do the popular, pretty Frances Kennard justice, she at last lost sight of herself entirely. This episode in her life made a woman of her. She represented to Miss Zuby that her sister's strength had given out, and that they must return home at once. She wrote a cheery little note to the sick man, signed by both sisters' names, in which she said they thought best not to excite him by personal good-bys, but hoped soon to see him in town ; and all the way home in the cars she edified herself with a mental review of the years of her sister's unostentatious, helpful life and her own careless exactions.

As for Mr. Jack Huntington, he was greatly disappointed by this slip 'twixt cup and lip. The catechism he put to Miss Zuby failed to elicit more than he already knew — namely, that Miss Kennard's card had been the means of her being sent for to come to him. Frances had had the forethought and cleverness to persuade Miss Zuby to say nothing to the patient concerning his ravings.

She had not, however, sealed the lips of the village doctor. When, later, Mr. Huntington and his few traps were *en route* to the depot, the old gentleman met him and bade him good speed.

"Going to follow your sweetheart, eh? You show your sense, young man. She's a girl worth following to the ends of the earth."

This well-meant speech served to rouse again all the mysterious doubts and suspicions which had become allayed with returning strength. The memory of May Kennard's strange looks and behavior, often dwelt upon during Jack's monotonous days of convalescence, came back to him vividly. He remembered how the doctor had spoken before her on the last evening she spent with him, and that she had shown neither surprise nor resentment. On the contrary, that last eloquent, down-pouring gaze of tenderness, as he kissed her hand, thrilled him in retrospection. He remembered his own excitement at the sudden information of Fay's presence in the house, and that that was the end of what now seemed a fantastic, improbable dream.

"There is no telling what I said or did while I was off my base, there," he mused as the train sped on. "I am going to the bottom of this thing."

Mr. Huntington's card was handed to the Kennard girls the following day. They looked at one another. They had not mentioned his name since their return to the city.

"Now we begin a new chapter," said May to her sister. "I want to say to you, before we see Jack, that if you should ever come to care for him as he does for you, I do not want you to hinder your happiness by a false idea of loyalty to me."

Frances met the steady gray eyes that looked large above the thin cheeks. "I 've been too busy all my life wondering if people were in love with me to care deeply for any one," she answered. "I might, under other circumstances, have come to be loyal to Jack; but as it is I can be loyal to you, May, and I always will be, dear, as long as I live."

Then they kissed each other, and went downstairs to congratulate Mr. Huntington.

The three had not been together long before Frances was called out of the room. She bestowed a hasty glance on her sister before reluctantly answering the summons.

Scarcely was she gone when Jack changed his seat for one nearer May.

"I am glad to see you alone a minute," he said. "As you may imagine, I must always have a new feeling toward you since your great kindness to me. No sister could have done more for me than you did."

His handsome, pensive eyes were gazing straight into hers, but she did not shrink.

"You look worn out still, poor, dear girl." He tried to take her hand, but she gently withdrew it. He regarded her reproachfully, and continued: "I came to-day to ask you to marry me, May. Will you?"

Jack had a pleasant voice, and his most commonplace words had power to thrill her. It was a wonder that the girl had strength enough to preserve an appearance of serenity now.

"Certainly not, Jack," she said kindly. "You do not owe such a return to me any more than you would to the sister whose place I took."

Were these calm eyes the ones that had last looked on him? Was that hand whose touch was forbidden him now the one which had yielded itself

lovingly to his feeble grasp, and smoothed his brow
with a tender, lingering touch? The implication
in her words made him blush ; and the hasty return of Frances was as much a relief to him as to
May. The latter was not a girl to be lightly won.
He told himself that he might have known that.
An intense, mysterious creature was reticent May
Kennard, affording glimpses of her glowing soul
only when she sang. For some unfathomable reason
the curtain had been lifted for him in that sick-
room ; but now it was dropped and impenetrable.
Well, it was over. He had acted upon his determination, and now found himself free to pursue
the lovely girl who was absorbing his fancy at
the time his illness laid him low. He turned
to her now, and until he left the house addressed
himself principally to her. Yet, when he took
his leave, it was with a sense that the prettiest
débutante of the season was showing her winter's
dissipation in a certain loss of freshness in body
and mind.

"She has n't May's brains. She never had,"
he mused, and then he thought of May with a
sensation of pique and vague discomfort.

Later in the season he took an extended cruise
with some friends in a yacht, and daily he lived
over those strange experiences in the country village. Again he thrilled at the pressure of a
magnetic hand, and more and more there grew
in him a longing for a repetition of those dream-

like occurrences which had become sacred in memory.

One day, as the yacht was cutting through the sparkling blue waters of Casco Bay, he suggested to his companions that they stop at the island where Miss Kennard's aunt had her cottage. As there were on board several of Frances' admirers, this suggestion was cordially adopted.

The yachtsmen received a hearty welcome from the Kennards, and Mr. Huntington watched for his opportunity to be alone with May. It came at last. The whole party had been inspecting the yacht as it rode lightly at anchor in a picturesque cove of the island.

"I've done a lot of thinking on that boat, May," said Jack, as they climbed the hill together.

"It seems to have agreed with you. I think you may venture to keep on," she answered banteringly.

"You must decide that, for you have been the subject of my cogitations."

"Don't return to that, Jack," said the girl, with a serious, hurt look. "Once was all very well. I appreciate your intentions — but under the circumstances — I should think — I should think "—

Huntington was watching her eagerly. He liked better this embarrassment and changing color than the baffling serenity of last time. "What *are* the circumstances? I 'll be hanged if I know," he burst forth, as she paused. "Won't you explain?"

"No. Why puzzle yourself? You were feverish. It is all past now."

"But I can't forget. I dreamed you loved me. Oh May!"—they were in a copse of little trees which must have grown for their especial benefit, so thick a screen did they form—"why was it worth your while to bewitch me if you meant to throw me over after all?"

There was no mistaking his earnestness. May lifted her eyes and looked guardedly into his face. She saw there nothing but honest perplexity and love. Jack was a sufficiently commonplace man, but the simple fact was that if he did really and spontaneously love her, it made a paradise of the world, a joy of life.

"I believed you cared for Fay," she said, her hard-won caution not yet broken down.

"I admire Fay," was the prompt answer, "but I love you."

This simplicity won. Down went the tottering wall of caution, swept away in a flood of happiness. The soft eyes filled again with the rapturous light he remembered and recognized with an eager thrill.

"It was not a dream!" he exclaimed.

A few months later, when Miss Zuby put on her spectacles to read the engraved invitation to the wedding, there was some complacency in her down-curving smile of satisfaction.

"That there pretty little Fay critter tried to throw me off the track when they was goin' away," she soliloquized, "but, law, I guess I can trust my own ears, can't I?"

A NEUTRAL THANKSGIVING

"Miss Esther ought to be home by this time," said Deborah anxiously, going to the window again to peer up the street as the sound of a trolley car diminished in the distance. "What has become of the child? It'll be dark before the next car comes along."

The child she was watching for was forty years of age, but that mattered nothing to the faithful woman who for twenty-five years had kept house for the Wainwrights, and taken care of Esther's physical comforts. To Deborah she was still the same girl who had been the youngest, brightest creature in the house when she came into it a quarter of a century ago, and who now was the only one left.

Esther's sister Lucy had married, and lived in the city adjacent to the suburb where the Wainwright homestead was located. Recently Lucy had died after years of invalidism, leaving a daughter nineteen years of age, and it was at a summons from the dead woman's lawyer that Miss Wainwright had gone into the city to-day.

"Poor dear! I'll be glad when it's all over," soliloquized Deborah. "Miss Esther hain't had,

so to say, a scrap o' comfort since Mrs. Dyett went
— stayin' there at the house with Kitty, and seein'
after things, puttin' away and givin' away. It's
the saddest work a body can do. I s'pose she'll
bring the child right home here, and after a while
things will be real pleasant. It'll be grand for
Miss Esther to have a young companion in the
house instead of nobody but an old woman like me
to talk to from mornin' till night."

The good creature was conscious of a twinge of
jealousy, — one that had been oft repeated in the
last few days as she meditated over the changes
that were sure to come.

While she still cogitated she caught sight of a
straight, slender figure walking with firm, quick
tread up the street.

"There she is now, and Kitty ain't with her —
yet!" she muttered with relief.

"But you do look tired, child!" she added, as
Miss Wainwright came in; and with motherly fingers the housekeeper began unbuttoning the jacket
of her mistress's snug tailor suit, her old heart has-
tening apprehensively as she saw signs of unusual
agitation in the beloved face, now pale and with set
lips.

"Indeed I am tired, Deborah," replied the newcomer dejectedly. "I have but one ambition —
tea!"

"Dear heart, if tea is all!"

The old woman waited on Miss Wainwright with

devoted attention as she sat at the well-spread table, speaking from time to time to coax her mistress to try some dish, or to have more of some dainty, but Esther shook her head.

"More tea only, Deb, more tea. I've been driven to drink." She shook her head, and poured again from the dainty teapot with a hand that was unsteady.

"It's those lawyers, drat 'em!" returned Deborah indignantly.

"Not altogether. I suppose Lucy is to blame more than the lawyer."

The housekeeper stared and grasped her clean apron with both hands, astonished at a reference in this tone to the departed. "Why, what has Mrs. Dyett done?" she asked.

"She has put a request in her will that — well, it has surprised me."

"I see it has, poor dear. Do try some o' the salad."

"I have looked forward to taking Kitty as my own daughter" — Miss Wainwright examined her delicate cup as she spoke — "to planning her life and making her happy."

"Just so; I s'posed you had."

"Well, it seems I shall be obliged to share her with another guardian."

"Why, who is it?" The housekeeper fell with righteous indignation into her mistress's mood. "Kitty hasn't got anybody else but you — you,

her own aunt, and she the very livin' picture o' you.
Mrs. Dyett always admitted it."

"The picture of what I was, perhaps. I can see
it myself ; but I 'm forty, Deb," — the declaration
was made wearily, — " and to-night I feel ninety."

"You 're just as pretty as you ever were," returned Deborah stoutly. " There 's nobody should
know better than I do how you look. You 're quiet
in your ways. You spat back your hair flatter 'n
you used to, and wear your hats too plain ; but if
you 'd give yourself a chance like the other girls,
and let your curls out, you 'd hold your own with
anybody."

Miss Wainwright's smile had a trace of bitterness.

"Yes, Miss Esther, I tell you if you 'd fix up
and wear kind o' ruffly things and feathers, Kitty 'd
only be the bud and you 'd be the rose. Don't
talk to me about feelin' ninety ; I ain't but sixty
myself. Now do tell me, Miss Esther," her tone
changing from aggression to sympathy, " what you
mean. Come, sit in the big chair by the fire and
heat your feet. You 're just beat out."

Miss Wainwright, her head leaning obediently
against the cushioned chair, and her eyes on the
blaze, gave a long sigh.

" Yes, I 'm disappointed to the core, Deb."

" But Mrs. Dyett did n't have any friends close
enough to give Kitty to 'em. You 're all the aunt
she 's got in the world."

" You forget she has an uncle."

" You don't mean to say " — incredulously — " she 's left that little girl to a gay, worldly bachelor?   Lucy wa'n't crazy, was she ? "

" Kitty is n't a little girl except to us."   Miss Wainwright spoke in an even, monotonous voice. " She is nineteen years old."

" But in the name o' common sense ain't you her natural protector and guide — and she the image of you ? "

" I am to have her half the time and he half."

" Land o' liberty !   What did Mrs. Dyett do that for ? "

" Probably out of loyalty to her dead husband and his family."

" It 's a fool arrangement," announced the housekeeper.   " Why, he won't know what to do with the girl.   Perhaps," hopefully, " perhaps he 'll refuse to act."

" If only she were n't so pretty," said Miss Wainwright regretfully.   She would willingly have dispensed with her niece's dimples, have seen the curling tendrils of her hair straighten, — aye, even have been willing those merry eyes should squint, if such plainness and obliquity would have alienated Judson Dyett's critical admiration, and made him willing to give her full possession of their joint ward.

What had beauty ever done for herself ?   It had not prevented her from losing the lover of her youth, even before the world knew that they had plighted their troth. The bliss, the misery of that time swept over her in a strong wave now, and she caught her breath in sudden agitation.

Deborah was smoothing the ringless hand that lay on the arm of the chair.

"I used to like Mr. Dyett," she said thoughtfully, "in those old days when he came with the other fellers sparkin' you, Miss Esther. I 've thought sometimes if you 'd ever given him any encouragement he might have been a different man."

"Different in what way?" Esther's usual energy seemed to have vanished altogether.

"Oh, more of a man, and not so — oh, you know what I mean; he 's only a grown-up boy now, playin' with boats and horses and such doin's. I don't want to hurt your feeliu's, Miss Esther, but do you s'pose," she hesitated, looking at Miss Wainwright lovingly, "do you s'pose perhaps Mrs. Dyett was thinkin' about money? They do say Mr. Judson 's made a lot speculatin'."

"No, I 'm sure there was nothing mercenary in her mind."

Miss Wainwright said no more, and the housekeeper, seeing her thoughtful mood, gazed at her wistfully; then, sighing, left her and went to clear off the table.

Esther sat still, staring at the fire and trying to reduce her thoughts to order. The grief and resentment toward her sister which the discovery of the latter's wish had caused were subsiding. Her cooler judgment told her that Lucy, merely knowing that she disliked Judson Dyett, had concluded that they two would be more likely to reach an amicable agreement if such a request came to their knowledge after she was gone.

Nearly a year had elapsed since Esther had seen this man. When they did meet it was only in formal fashion. Although he lived but a few miles away, their interests, their friends, their paths, were widely diverse. He had been expected to be at the lawyer's office to-day, but some business having detained him it had been left to Miss Wainwright to consult with him as to their new duties at her own convenience.

Where and when should she talk with him? Evidently at the Dyett house. In a few days that would pass into the hands of new owners; then the interview must take place soon, while that rendezvous remained to them. Not for any consideration or reason would she ask him to come to her own home. Why, had it not been in this very room that —

Esther Wainwright looked about her furtively, with frightened eyes. Memory had her in its power to-night.

The next day her weakness had passed. Deborah's brow cleared as she saw by her mistress's self-possessed manner and the expression of her face that her usual ability and common sense had reasserted themselves.

"I expect to bring Kitty home with me to-night," said Miss Wainwright to the housekeeper, and the latter lingered in the doorway to look after her mistress, while Esther took her quick way down the street.

" Would n't bend a grass-blade if she stepped on it," was Deborah's comment, " but I never knew before how she despised Mr. Dyett. Thought one spell she favored him more 'n any of 'em. But none of 'em got her, not one." Deborah finished triumphantly; the mere fact of Esther's monotonous life failed utterly to convince her that all the eligibles in the city would not flock to the Wainwright door provided Esther's bright eyes ever gleamed encouragingly.

Those eyes gleamed now, and the curved lips were firmly set when Miss Wainwright reached the Dyett house and ran up the steps.

" Is Mr. Dyett here, Maggie ? " she asked of the maid who answered her ring.

" Yes, ma'am. He 's waiting for you in the parlor."

Esther moved unhesitatingly to the little drawing-room, whence the ornaments had been removed. As she passed between the portières she saw at once the object of her search.

He was standing, his feet apart and his back to her, examining a painting on the wall. One of the hands crossed behind him held the gloves he had just taken off, and his silk hat lay on a bare table near by. He was well dressed, and, as he turned, his clear-skinned face had a care-free look rather unusual in a man of forty-five.

"Ah, how do you do, Esther?" he said cheerfully. He stepped forward, and their hands met perfunctorily. "You're not selling that Corot with the house, I hope," and he turned back for another appreciative look. "That was always a pet of mine."

The color flew to her cheeks; yet what other greeting did she expect from Judson Dyett? She wished to propitiate him while there was a shadow of hope that he might yield to the request she had determined to make.

"No doubt Kitty will be glad to have you store it for her until she has a home of her own," she replied.

"A home of her own!" He gave a short laugh. "Won't you sit?"

She accepted the chair he placed, and he took one near; and his eyes ran quickly over her neat figure.

"How old is the little rascal?"

"Kitty is nineteen," said Miss Wainwright laconically.

"Ha! We thought ourselves grown up at nineteen, did n't we?" His look interrogated her pleasantly.

How did he dare! Esther felt tremulous as she leaned back and loosened her feather boa.

"I know now, at any rate, that a girl of nineteen is a child," she replied. "What is your response to the word I sent you this morning?"

"I was always glad to do anything I could for Lucy. I am glad to still. Kitty and I are great chums."

"But the care of a girl at that age would be really inconvenient for a man situated as you are."

Mr. Dyett raised his eyebrows at her tone.

"You disapprove of the arrangement?"

"It seems to me wholly unnecessary."

"Then you did not coöperate with Lucy in the plan."

Esther's eyes flashed at him. "I did not!"

He smiled at her thoughtfully, striking one palm softly with his gloves. "I believe you," he said at last.

She felt with anger that she was coloring to the roots of her hair. "It is excessively disagreeable to me to act with — with any one in this matter," she said hurriedly. "I was prepared to do everything for Kitty myself, and — and Lucy of course only appointed you out of a sense of duty to her husband" — she paused.

"Very kind, and very proper," returned her companion, with the same irritating composure. "I 'm fond of Kitty. I have no child of my own. It was very thoughtful of Lucy to rescue her for half the year from a home where I should never have been asked to peep at her."

"Judson, you know — you know I would never have been so unjust."

"Why should I?" was the quiet response. "We can only judge of the future by the past."

Miss Wainwright rose to her feet. "There is no need to prolong this interview," she said quickly. "I had a slight hope when I came in that you would be willing to decline to act as Kitty's guardian." She paused and looked at him. "If you will do so, I promise to send her to visit you four times a year."

Dyett rose also, his eyes still resting on the slender black-clothed form before him.

"I believe you have n't a gray hair, Esther," he remarked musingly, meeting her fleeting glance.

She bit her lip at the irrelevance. "This is a serious matter to me," she said. "Was there ever anything in life serious to you?"

"Did n't I say you were unjust?" he asked quietly.

She looked full in his eyes. "Then you insist on your rights in this matter."

"I see my chance to share something with you at last. You would have me refuse merely to please you."

"Yes, I would." She smiled at him bitterly. "A small reason, surely. Not worth mentioning for a moment."

He nodded. " The same tongue, the very same. Oh, what a fool I was to have minded it in the long ago. If I had been a little older and wiser at the time, I could have gotten over that trouble of ours, Esther." He returned her smile as it faded. " By this time you would have been done with sharpness," he added.

For a moment she stood dumb at his audacity. " Perhaps you will agree to leave this question to Kitty?" she went on when she could speak, standing very straight and ignoring his speech.

" Why, yes," he answered slowly. " I think that would be safe." She took a quick step toward the door. He placed a detaining hand on her arm, and she shrank back from it. " One moment, please. It 's as well not to prejudice the child, eh? Let her think that we are — er — that we are " —

" Friendly, of course, yes. You agree that if she chooses to live wholly with me you will not object ? "

" Ye–es, provided, of course, I have the run of the house. I must keep an eye on my brother's child. On the other hand, if she elects to live with me you will at all times be welcome under our roof."

Miss Wainwright regarded him, mute, and he raised himself gently on his toes, his hands crossed behind him, as he returned her gaze with a faint smile.

"I see that nothing will induce you to treat the situation otherwise than facetiously," she said coldly.

"Certainly, I will be as serious as you like. Name your own terms if you object to mine. I will see if I can agree to them."

"If you have a spark of kindness — if you are not positively malicious, you will agree to them."

"In that case I surely shall."

"Then this is the way it shall be. Provided Kitty elects to live with me, I send her to visit you at stated times and seasons; if she elects to live with you, you shall send her to visit me at intervals; but if she prefers to abide by her mother's request and share our care equally, you shall see nothing of her during my half of the year, and I will see nothing of her during your half of the year. Do you agree?"

He shrugged his shoulders. "I suppose so, knowing nothing of unkindness and malice."

Miss Wainwright again caught her lip in her teeth and regarded her companion with less tension. "Thank you," she said, "and one thing more, Judson. I wish you would agree to one thing more." She dropped her eyes, and so did not perceive the kindness of her companion's gaze. "Let me take the child home with me for a fortnight before we talk about it to her. Let her rest and recover a little from her loss. I, of course, will during the time say nothing of this."

"Very well, then ; as I understand it, in two · weeks' time you would like me to come to your house."

"No, no," responded Miss Wainwright quickly. "We will appoint a place. We will come in town and meet you. I would not trouble you to come so far."

The man's smile deepened, and a humorous light came into his eyes. "But it would be no trouble, I assure you. It would be at once a duty and a delight."

The expression of Esther's face was as hard and repellent as its color was soft and winning.

"There is no occasion," she said coldly. "We will come to you."

"At my house, then. I 've a decent enough apartment, Esther, and Kitty is at home in it."

"At your office, if you will allow it," rejoined Miss Wainwright stiffly.

At his office it was that they met a few weeks later. Miss Wainwright and her niece were ushered into a private room, and there Judson Dyett soon joined them, — fresh, smiling, debonair, looking on such good terms with himself and the world that Esther felt again, as she had at their previous interview, suddenly older, plainer, more humdrum than usual. Her rigid pose made the contrast of Kitty's manner the more sharp. As her uncle entered the room the young girl jumped up and threw her arms around his neck.

"Dear Uncle Jud! Why have n't you come to see me?" she cried.

He retained her hand, or she his, as she drew him toward the divan where Esther was, and made him sit down, placing herself between the two.

"It is n't so far on the cars, is it, Aunt Esther?"

The latter stirred uneasily, and pretty Kitty, with a loving glance, took her aunt's hand with her free one, and looked content at holding both her relatives captive.

"To tell the truth, I 've almost forgotten the way to your Aunt Esther's house. Her latch-string is not for the likes of me," said Dyett.

The girl looked up doubtfully at the quiet tone.

"Your uncle is a very busy man," said Miss Wainwright briefly.

The situation was not at all comfortable for Esther. Kitty was but a slender barrier between her and the person who kept sending calm glances at her over their niece's head; and moreover the girl was doing the most foolish and risky things with the hands she held, beating them softly up and down in her lap, and almost striking them together. Esther was in poignant momentary dread lest hers should be forced against that large strong one, still brown from the summer's cruising. Yet she would not forcibly withdraw her hand. She was too jealous of the love that had welcomed her rival, and she was glad to keep a hold on Kitty.

"I have n't told you yet what we are here for, my dear," she added seriously.

"Anything but to see Uncle Jud?" inquired the girl naïvely.

Miss Wainwright's lips contracted. "You may tell her if you prefer," she said to Dyett.

"I fancy you would state the case better," he returned. "At least, you would be better satisfied. I am willing to give you every advantage." The smile that accompanied this was so boyish, and there was such a teasing twinkle in the man's eyes, Esther felt that she hated him. Moreover, at this moment Kitty, looking up in her curiosity, absent-mindedly dropped her uncle's hand upon her aunt's, and it rested there.

Miss Wainwright started. "I wish to lean back, Kitty," she said quickly, and relinquishing her niece to the enemy, she withdrew herself and sat back in the corner of the divan.

From this retreat she stated the situation to her niece, and gave the girl her choice of the alternatives already agreed upon, while Judson Dyett, pulling his fair mustache, looked from one to the other in silence.

"But how unkind!" said Kitty piteously, when she had finished.

"What is unkind?"

"To ask me to choose between you."

Miss Wainwright bit her lip, surprised.   Dyett
regarded her in mild triumph.

"You see, I'm in this, Esther," he remarked.
"I did n't think you had all the facts."

"But even if I do take turns living with you
half-years about, I suppose we should all three be
together a good deal anyway, naturally, should n't
we?" asked Kitty.

Dyett pulled his mustache more industriously,
and fixed Miss Wainwright with a curious regard.

"No, my dear," she replied, "for this reason:
Your uncle and I have very different tastes, very
different friends.   No matter how much we might
determine to be sociable" — Mr. Dyett coughed,
and Esther's New England conscience winced ;
nevertheless she procceded firmly — "we should
not really see much of each other.   But I don't
urge you, Kitty.   He can" — her voice broke a
little — "he can give you a gayer life than I can.
Your — your mother trusted him."

"And that is more than you do, Esther, eh?"
For the first time his face lost its nonchalance.

"Well, but at certain times," persisted Kitty.
"There are certain times when families *must* be
together, like Thanksgiving and Christmas and
birthdays, you know."

Evidently there was no recognition in her mind
of the fact that these two who stood in such close
relation to her were unrelated to one another, and
that she was their only tie of interest.   "Here

comes Thanksgiving now in three weeks. If I
spend my first half-year with you, Aunt Esther,
of course Uncle Judson will be with us on Thanksgiving day."

" Ahem — no.   Ahem — yes," replied Miss
Wainwright, taken very much by surprise and in
sore straits.   Kitty's large, surprised eyes were
upon her.   " Deborah, you know — Deborah is n't
well this fall.   She " —

" I 'll have the dinner," said Dyett, his lips
twitching.   " Come to my house.   If you will
honor my humble roof — I mean ceiling — I don't
suppose a flat can be said to have a roof — I 'll
get the biggest turkey in town."

" Yes, yes," said Kitty, " that 's what we 'll
do ! "

Her aunt kept silent, but her breast heaved and
her color rose, and Judson Dyett knew her.

" Is it agreed, Esther ? " he asked.

" I will come," she answered rather breathlessly
and at bay, " unless I am ill."

Her adversary looked at her and her eyes fell.

" Don't you think," he asked dryly, " that you
would be less liable to be ill on Thanksgiving if I
took a room at N—'s " (naming a famous caterer)
" and we met on neutral ground to celebrate the
day?   Come, we want to make this little girl have
a good time, don't we ? "

. Miss Wainwright blushed painfully.   " That
might be a good arrangement," she answered.

Kitty stared first at one and then at the other. "How strangely you both act," she said.

Her uncle replied, and for once her aunt was grateful to him. "We're a little bit jealous. Can't you see it, Kitty? You're a bone of contention, little girl. You don't look it." He scanned her approvingly. "I admit that there's nothing bony in your appearance."

"But you simply must n't contend over me. You must n't," she replied. "I love you both."

"Then we eat turkey at N—'s?" said Dyett, looking at Esther.

She nodded. "I agree," she answered.

Kitty raised her eyebrows. "That's certainly funny," she said doubtfully, "but it might be fun."

The girl meditated often on this interview before Thanksgiving arrived. There were some incidents in that talk that started her fancy to dreaming dreams.

But it was such a strange idea to think of two quite old people — people who had looked just as they did now ever since she was born — being shy of each other, or feeling — oh, *that* way, you know!

If Uncle Jud did admire Aunt Esther, he should see how pretty she could look, that was all. Kitty overrode all Miss Wainwright's objections, and fluffed out her hair and insisted on decorating the front of her aunt's black waist with her finest lace, and anticipated the novel celebration of the day openly.

Poor child! It was so many years since her mother had been able to share a Thanksgiving dinner with her, she had not the usual associations to overcome; and her curiosity was aflame to see her uncle and aunt once more together.

To Esther Wainwright that dinner was a dreaded ordeal. Calm, unruffled life could only begin again when it was over. For Kitty's sake she determined to suspend all memories and all defensive tactics; to try not to chill the genial mood of their host to-day.

"Of course there are things I don't understand about this," said Kitty, when the two were on their way into town. "Deborah seems very well to me, and — I don't see why you should want to snub Uncle Judson."

This bluntness brought a color to Miss Wainwright's pale cheeks which remained there for her host to see and approve. "You can't expect to understand everything," she answered; "and your uncle and I have been strangers for too many years for me to dream of snubbing him."

A couple of hours later, as the three were eating the varied dessert of a regulation Thanksgiving dinner in the cosy private room at N—'s, with the waiter dismissed, Kitty Dyett leaned back in her chair and looked from her uncle to her aunt approvingly.

" Aunt Esther promised she would be as sweet as peaches to-day," she remarked disconcertingly, " and I think she has been, don't you ? "

Mr. Dyett bowed seriously. " She has kept her word nobly."

" You see, I just dread to have this day over," went on Kitty plaintively ; " you 've both been so dear, and the bone of contention has had such a happy time. I don't want to feel that there are n't any more such coming. Are we always going to be obliged to meet in a restaurant or a trolley car or some other neutral place before you two can be nice to each other ? "

In the long moment that followed Miss Wainwright blamed herself despairingly for not having taken this chatterbox into her confidence, and thereby restrained her tongue.

" That was nonsense," went on the girl, " was n't it, Uncle Jud, about you and Aunt Esther being jealous of me ? " she added wistfully.

" I don't know," returned her uncle musingly. " I 've been thinking while we dined to-day how wonderfully you, Kitty, resemble the girl I loved when I was a youngster."

" Did n't she love you, the goose ? "

" Quite as well as I deserved. Not enough to come halfway and meet my advances after I had been ass enough to take offense at something she did. She never forgave me — never." He finished slowly, and the fingers of one hand drummed softly

on the tablecloth as he gazed thoughtfully into his
niece's bright eyes.

" Then I hope you forgot her as she deserved ? "

" No, never for a day."

" Then, of course, she married somebody ? "

" No, I think she forswore mankind in my person."

" Uncle Jud ! " The depth of contempt and
reproach that looked at him from the wise eyes of
feminine nineteen !

" What 's the matter ? "

" The matter is that you 've simply wasted —
well, fifteen years anyway — that is, if she 's
alive."

" What makes you so sure ? "

" You said she looked like me. She would have
married somebody — *sure* — if she had n't liked
you just — exactly " — Kitty emphasized her words
on the tablecloth with a small fist — " as much as
you wanted her to. Oh, poor silly Uncle Jud ! "

He kept his gaze on the speaker, nor stirred an
eyelash toward the flushing, paling woman on his
other hand. But Kitty suddenly turned toward
her. " Aunt Esther, I can't spend my first half-
year with you," she exclaimed. " It 's my duty
to stay with this poor, half-witted man and help
him find that dear woman who is thinking about
him all this time — I just know she is."

" But she is a faded old maid by now," said
Miss Wainwright faintly.

“ Like you, perhaps,” jeered Kitty. “ Does n’t she look like a rose, Uncle Jud ?”

“ Better stay with your aunt, Kitty. You ’ll find her easier by living with her,” said Mr. Dyett.

“ What ? *Oh !* ” ejaculated the girl, with a start, apparently overwhelmed by this enlightenment.

“ You have us both at your mercy, Esther.” The man looked at his old sweetheart now. “ I confess that I urged Lucy into this arrangement for Kitty. I have n’t been able to forget, but you were always repellent. This was my last chance. I ’ve nothing to plead for myself but that you hold the place in my heart to-day that you always had.”

“ Oh, if there were anywhere I could go ! ” mourned Kitty, jumping up distractedly. “ It ’s all the fault of your wicked obstinacy again, Aunt Esther. If you had entertained us nicely at home I could slip upstairs now, and you ’d never know I ’d gone — but here, in a restaurant — why, I just *can’t* do anything but turn my back.” She suited the action to the word.

“ It is too late, Judson,” said Miss Wainwright, trembling. “ I am too set in my ways. So are you. We ought not to think of it.”

Silence fell, and Kitty turned stealthily to spur the dejected lover with a glance; but Mr. Dyett had Esther’s hand in his, and his lips were pressed upon it, and the girl jerked hastily back again in silence.

" I 'm quite sure I 'm doing wrong ! " exclaimed Miss Wainwright tremulously, at last. " It can't possibly be right to —   I must think."

" Dear me, Aunt Esther," came from Kitty's averted curly head, " you 've thought twenty years, and, added to that, it 's almost as much more that I 've been kept standing here. One thing sure," after a pause, " if you don't have him I shall live with him *all the time* — the poor darling ! I could n't do less."

Silence again. Kitty waited a little, and then turned slowly. What she saw was a glimpse of heaven through the open gate of love. Her eyes filled, and a sort of awe stole over her.

" It *is* Thanksgiving day, is n't it ? " she said softly and timidly.

" Yes, dear," said Judson Dyett, holding out his hand to her, " it is Thanksgiving day ! "

"I'm all fer peace. Mary Annie ain't." Solon Bryce let the reins hang loosely from one hand whose arm was supported on his knee as he slouched down in the habitual position which had bowed his back and which threw into striking contrast the strong, erect figure of the young man beside him.

"I guess you're abaout the last boarder she'll hook this year — g'lang, Bess — and so I told her. Fishin''s ben pretty good — better'n I expected, I must say — but it's nigh onto September naow, and it's abaout over. I ain't sorry, nuther. It's some wearin' haulin' folks backerds and forrards to the cars — no offense, young man, but they've all ben women up to naow, and I like to speak my mind naow I've got a man to speak it to. Trunks, too! The trunks alone is enough to make a body-sweat to think on 'em."

At the gloomy, introspective frown on the old man's face his companion's half smile became more pronounced. "I see," he remarked; "you are taking boarders against your will."

"Not much I ain't a-takin' 'em — g'lang, Bess; it's my niece. Women's allers at the bottom o' trouble, and you'll find it aout sometime if you

hain't a'ready. I'm all fer peace, myself; Mary
Annie ain't. She kep' school last winter over Lawrence way, and though I missed her I got along,
and took comfort, too; but come toward spring
Mary Annie wrote me she was goin' to come home
and keep boarders this summer. I diskerridged
her. I wrote back that boarders was vanity and
heaviness o' sperit, and what more did she want
than enough to eat; but there ain't any way o'
headin' off Mary Annie. She answered in her
way — kinder light and playful — that she had
her future to think of. She wanted to lay up
money to buy *trousers*. I jest groaned. I allers
knew Mary Annie was too full o' sperits and head-
strong, and naow here she was turnin' aout to be
one o' these new women, plannin' a'ready to wear
trousers! She came right home after that, and I
faced her down with it. She laughed and said
I had n't read it right; said petticoats was good
enough for her if she only had enough of 'em. But
she got as red as a beet, even though she would n't
give up her plan, not an inch of it."

"Your niece was writing about her trousseau,
perhaps," said the new boarder, much entertained.

His companion nodded. "You 've got it. That 's
what she claimed. I guess that 's yer aunt on the
piazza," added the old man suddenly, as the wagon
turned in toward the farmhouse. "She 's ben in a
great takin' to git ye here. Ye don't look so sick
to me."

"No, I 'm about right again; but Mrs. Pomeroy has insisted for weeks that a fortnight of Miss Bryce's entertainment would do me more good than months at the seashore."

"Owen, my dear boy!" exclaimed the plump little woman on the piazza, coming down the steps at that moment.

Owen Chalmers had seen his room, and was now being personally conducted by his aunt to where the afternoon sunshine sifted through the branches of a huge old elm tree.

"Is n't this ideal?" she asked. "Miss Bryce has had these seats fixed so ingeniously to get the best shade; but then, she always sees the best way to do everything."

Chalmers stretched himself upon the rustic seat his aunt had indicated. "That is where you and Uncle Solon differ," he remarked, repressing a yawn, and thinking wistfully of a certain gay circle he had abandoned the previous evening at the seaside.

"Uncle Solon!" repeated Mrs. Pomeroy impatiently. "I suppose the poor old fellow has droned you nearly to death. He is no more Miss Bryce's uncle than you are. He is some distant relative that her father left on her hands when he died. But she is as good to him as an own daughter could be."

The warm interest in the speaker's voice surprised Chalmers mildly.

After a moment's silence he followed the bent of his thoughts and began speaking of mutual friends. While he was talking there came across the grass toward him a girl on a bicycle. Her dark skirt, high, trim leather boots, and dark hat were relieved by a light shirt waist whose sleeves fluttered breezily as she swiftly advanced.

Owen's speech grew slower. There was a style about this girl. As she passed them he caught his breath. He felt the conscious power of her pose and expression. He flushed at the brief, smiling glance she flung at Mrs. Pomeroy.

" I thought you said all the boarders had gone ! " he ejaculated.

His aunt watched him closely. " They have."

" Don't tell me *that* is Mary Annie ! "

" There now ! I thought I was n't in my dotage," said Mrs. Pomeroy triumphantly.

Chalmers did not hear her. He had turned in time to see the lithe figure jump from the wheel and pause to give directions to a workman who was mending a fence.

" Well, Lawrence is a good deal of a town," he said at last.

" What ? "

" Lawrence is where she teaches, is n't it ? I suppose she is engaged to somebody there."

" Indeed she is n't. She told me herself she did not meet a man the whole winter whom she preferred to a book."

“ Then where is he ? ”

“ There is n't any he.”

“ Certainly there is. Uncle Solon confided in me. It seems it is already a question of the trousseau.”

“ For pity’s sake, Owen Chalmers, tell me at once all you know about it. I have spent hours cogitating over that girl’s future ! ”

“ Nothing, absolutely. If I had seen her then, I should have been tempted to draw him out.”

Mrs. Pomeroy was sitting up very straight, and her eyes had a far-away look. “ That would n’t be right,” she said decidedly. “ Miss Bryce must have some powerful motive for reserve, for we have had many talks together when it would have naturally come out. I am very much astonished and — yes, disappointed.” The lady gave a short laugh. “ I might as well make an open confession now.”

Her nephew returned her look curiously.

“ Go ahead, Aunt Jane.”

. “ I sent for you with the cold-blooded intention that you should fall in love with this country flower, — this nonesuch, as the people about here would call her.”

“ Oh, my subtle aunt ! ”

“ Yes, I was prepared to combat your mother and sisters if necessary. Let me tell you, young man, that it is the greatest compliment I ever paid you that I thought you worthy of her.” ·

Owen smiled. “ A glimpse was enough to see

that she is a queen. I perceive that I have had a
narrow escape from at least aspiring to Mary Annie
the First, and incidentally to Uncle Solon."

"I hope you will always be able to treat the situation humorously," returned Mrs. Pomeroy with
such impressive gravity that her nephew, seasoned
society man that he was, had difficulty in refrain-
ing from laughter.

The supper that night appealed to a hungry
man, and lent added charm to the hostess who dispensed it. There were but the three of them at
table.

"Uncle Solon likes supper of a different sort
and at a different time," explained Miss Bryce
when Owen in expansive mood mentioned his drive
home from the depot in a manner which implied
that making the acquaintance of Mr. Bryce had
been one of the social events of his life.

His aunt's countenance betrayed resignation as
she observed that Mary Annie was making the
impression that she had hoped for.

The folds of the girl's thin green gown inclosed
her beautiful figure as the calyx does the rosebud.
Before the meal was finished Chalmers, in spite of
his knowledge that the rose had been gathered,
grew restive under the entirely cool attitude she
maintained toward him.

"She *is* a queen," he repeated to his aunt when
they were again alone. "Do you suppose she con-
descended to make that shortcake?"

"I know she did," replied Mrs. Pomeroy tragically.

"Heavens! That settles it.

> "'To know her is to love her,
> And love but her forever.
> For Nature made her what she is,
> And ne'er made sic anither!'"

"Oh, Owen, don't joke! Who can it be?"

"How can I guess? It is enough that it is somebody. A pretty trick you have played me."

Chalmers had no mustache to twist, so he tortured his watch chain as he stood, his feet planted apart, a half humorous, half earnest smile playing over his face as he recalled the sweep of Mary Annie's lashes and the curves of her velvet lips.

The next morning Owen, in knickerbockers, was on hand when Miss Bryce brought out her wheel.

"Perhaps you will let me ride with you," he said, rolling his bicycle to where she stood.

She shook her head decidedly, and her smile might have been intended for the cat that rubbed against her well-fitting boot. "It is not pleasant where I am going, but there are pretty rides about here. You will enjoy exploring. I have a business errand to do myself. Wheels are a wonderful saving of time and strength, are n't they? Good morning," and she was off.

Chalmers looked after her with a distinct grievance. "Run away, little boy," her manner seemed to say. "You have time to play. I have n't."

He mounted his bicycle and rode a few minutes aimlessly. Soon he wheeled about and returned to the house. A vision of Solon Bryce sitting on a log and whittling had passed through his mind. The vision proved a reality, and the young man took a seat beside this rough bit of lichen which dwelt near the rose.

"Miss Bryce seems full of business this morning," he hazarded.

"Yes, we 're all some busy," responded Uncle Solon, changing the straw he was chewing to the other side of his mouth. "I 've got some kindlin' to chop presently. Mary Annie 's workin' the farm on shares this season. It 's ag'in my judgment. Takes a lot o' lookin' after. I 'm all fer peace myself, but Mary Annie ain't. She 's gone over in the plowed ground naow. She 's got to understand every last plan Woodward 's got." Uncle Solon chuckled with deliberate enjoyment. "One thing I 've got to be thankful for, anyway: I ain't Woodward !"

Chalmers was astonished at the number and intensity of emotions which suddenly ran riot beneath his calm exterior. The only idea which cleared itself in his mind was a suspicion followed by a yearning to relinquish the identity of Owen Chalmers, the favorite of Fortune, and be one Woodward, standing in the plowed ground with Mary Annie, and responding to the lights and shadows in her eyes.

His aunt approached restlessly, hesitated, then spoke to Chalmers in a low tone. "It must be somebody near by. I always carry the mail myself, and always call for it."

Uncle Solon glanced up as, after this oracular utterance, the lady disappeared.

"Seems if Mis' Pomeroy had somethin' on her mind; but women don't take no peace anyway. If 't aint one thing, 't is another."

"It *is* somebody near by," said Owen to his aunt when, later, he had followed and found her. "It is one Woodward, who works the farm for her."

"I don't remember the name," said Mrs. Pomeroy, her lips nearly quivering. "Did Uncle Solon tell you so?"

"No, but she has gone to see the man now. She refused to let me go with her. Everything points to it. I am going fishing," added Owen abruptly.

"To see if there is truth in the adage?" Mrs. Pomeroy's smile had a tear in it. "There is not. There are n't as good fish either in sea or brook as she is; but — I 'll try not to be angry with her."

Owen had to try, too, as days passed. Mary Annie was such a will-o'-the-wisp! She was the busiest person he had ever known. He believed she made errands to avoid him.

One afternoon — he could hardly believe his good fortune — he beheld her sewing out under the elm tree. She wore the green gown. It was the color of the tiniest, youngest leaves above her, and he thought of dryads as he hurriedly approached.

"So you do sometimes behave like ordinary mortals?" he said, as he took the vacant chair near her.

"Always," she returned, with that sweet, rare smile whose curves he was always watching for since he had begun to live. He had an unnamed contempt for the aimless wandering which he had called life before the day when he met Uncle Solon at the little country station.

His eyes fell on the fine hemstitched band she was sewing. "Is that for the trousseau?" he asked bluntly.

Her eyes lifted to his with wonder. "Yes," she replied. "What in the world made you think of that?"

"I guessed it." His eyes had a gloomy fire, his voice a ring which sounded over-serious even to his own ears.

She shook her head. "Do you always make such uncanny guesses? I shall be afraid of you."

"I wish you wouldn't," he said simply. He took an end of the long band as it hung near him and examined it. "Do you call this tape?" he asked.

He had never heard Mary Annie laugh before, and a 'wondering smile banished the Byronic gloom from his countenance as the girl's infectious amusement burst forth.

"Was I so very funny?" he asked.

"Yes, you were very funny," she assured him.

"It must be a wonderful thing to be going to be married," he ventured, after watching her deft fingers awhile in silence.

"Yes," she agreed, without lifting those lashes. "It is a very serious thing, certainly; almost an awful thing."

She looked so adorable as she said it that Chalmers's heart tightened. The muscles of his brow contracted, too, but that was because he saw Uncle Solon approaching. There was a fatuous smile on the old man's face, a smile of content at having discovered Owen. The latter had not considered that the friendliness which he had displayed in often seeking Mr. Bryce's society might prove a boomerang which would recoil upon him and ruin a rare *tête-à-tête*.

"Do you know what struck me jest naow as I was comin' along?" asked Uncle Solon.

"No," returned Chalmers, wishing that, whatever it was, it had hit harder.

"I 've ben wonderin' ever sence you come who you put me in mind of. I 've got it naow. Mary Annie," addressing the girl, "it 's that feller was on your burer. Mr. Chalmers is the very livin' image of him."

The startled girl glanced up at the weather-beaten face. "You are mistaken. There was no photograph."

"No, 't wa'n't a photygraph. 'T was done aout in pen and ink. Don't you remember it? 'T was the day 'fore Mr. Chalmers come. I went to your room 'cause I 'd cut my finger, and I see it then. Wall," exasperated, "if you hain't ever noticed that that picter favors Mr. Chalmers you hain't got eyes. It 's ben pesterin' me ever sence he come. I 'll g' right upstairs naow and git it." The old man was turning away with unprecedented energy when the girl detained him.

"No, no," she said hastily. A scarlet flood poured over her face. "It is n't there, Uncle Solon. It has gone."

"I tell ye I kin find it, and I 'll prove I 'm right."

"No, Mr. Bryce. Why take the trouble?" put in Chalmers. His heart was beating madly at sight of the agitation in the face and attitude of the always cool, always poised girl, but he spoke calmly. "Don't go. I 'll take your word for it."

"Like ye as two peas in a pod," grumbled the old man crossly. "'T would make ye laugh to see it."

There was a constraint over the cosy party at supper that day, and in the evening Owen announced to his aunt that he should return to town the next morning.

"But you have only been here a week," faltered the lady.

"I know." Chalmers was walking up and down the room, his tall form making the ceiling seem lower than ever. "The thing I have always scoffed at has come to me. There is nothing for me to do but to get away."

Some sight suddenly drew him to the window. The sun had sunk from the cloudy sky, but the moon was rising. Stooping, he passed out through the low window upon the piazza.

"Do you ride without a lantern after dark on these country roads, Miss Bryce?"

"It will be moonlight, and I know every inch of the way."

"Sha'n't I go with you? I"— He hesitated; it would seem such an irrelevant fact to her. "I go away to-morrow."

There was an instant's silence before the answer came. "No, I thank you. I must see Mr. Woodward about something I forgot; but I shall be back in half an hour."

She had not returned in half an hour nor in an hour. Chalmers was watching. Whatever her motive for going to Woodward even at evening rather than to allow him to come to her, he thought she was running a risk. The moon she had relied upon was long ago obscured.

"There ain't no call to fret," remarked Uncle Solon when Owen went to him. He looked up from his newspaper and grinned. "Mary Annie may have took a notion to visit the selectmen and labor with 'em abaout good roads. She's got that bee in her bunnet naow."

"Can you tell me where this Woodward lives?" asked Chalmers gravely.

"Straight east till ye strike the fust crossroad. Turn to yer left and it's the fust house."

Two minutes later Owen's bicycle lantern was sending its little stream of light along the country road as he sped on an errand whose foolishness he suspected until he was hailed by a woman's voice. There in the dark, by the side of the road, sat Miss Bryce, her wheel lying beside her.

"Your knife, please. Cut my boot," she said breathlessly.

He brought the lantern and knelt beside her, freeing the swelled foot with all the skill he could bring to bear.

"I'll never go wheeling again without a knife," she said faintly.

"Or a lantern. Are you in great pain?"

"It feels better already. I ran into a stick of wood that must have fallen from some wagon. I was thinking of — something else, and — oh, I was so glad to see your light!"

The warmth of her voice, her nearness and help-lessness all stirred him.

"Shall I go and get Mr. Woodward?" he asked constrainedly.

The lantern revealed her beautiful, surprised eyes.

"I thought perhaps you would rather he helped you than I."

She caught her lip in her teeth. "Oh, I don't think I could let him — he is a real good man, but I'd rather he did n't — touch me."

Chalmers was still on his knees. He leaned toward her. "Then who is it?" he asked desperately. "A great misfortune has befallen me. It is cowardly, perhaps, for me to speak of it; but I go to-morrow. Who is the man?"

"What man?" faintly.

"Why should you mind telling me? The man the trousseau is for."

"Oh!" Silence. "That ruffling was n't for me; I'm making it for a girl in Lawrence."

"But I know — Mr. Bryce told me — you wrote him of your own trousseau."

Mary Annie colored finely there in the dark. "Did he tell you *that?*" She smiled. "That was only nonsense."

Owen began to breathe as if he had been running. "Then is n't there anybody?"

"N—o," hesitatingly, then decidedly, "No."

"Mary — you have the loveliest name in the world — Mary, you have known me only a week."

"Oh, I have known you much longer. Mrs. Pomeroy talked — and then she had your picture. I — I made the sketch of it that Uncle Solon saw."

"Mary!" ecstatically.

"But I tore it up the day after you came."

"Mary," dejectedly. Then, rising with sudden remembrance, "I am stupidly selfish. You are suffering. I will carry you home."

"Oh, no, indeed. Help me on my wheel. I can pedal with one foot. This is not a bad sprain, I am sure."

He lifted her carefully into the saddle. "You will have to let me support you," he said, as the wheel moved slowly. "Don't pedal. No need of it."

"And your machine?"

"Can lie there. Mary, may I change my plan about going away?"

"If you like."

"What does that mean? I love you."

"But how can you?" She objected in such a sweet and unsteady voice that Owen held her closer. "You don't know me."

"We will get acquainted now," he returned. "Are you willing to try me, dear? Do you care — just a little for me?"

"It is n't at all according to my theory," she answered slowly, happiness struggling with the doubt in her voice, "but I 'm afraid — I do."

Mrs. Pomeroy did not have so much trouble with the relatives as she feared. She had Mary Annie at her house that winter in Boston, and showed her off to her heart's content.

An arrangement was made for Uncle Solon's continued comfort at the old farm. Indeed, he rather anticipated the unruffled future which he foresaw would succeed the wedding.

This took place in June; and the last thing the bride did before the ceremony was to come, looking like a fresh white rose, to the old man's room to inspect his unwonted toilet.

"That tie won't do, Uncle Solon. Here is a better one." She tied it in place herself, took his wrinkled cheeks between her hands and kissed him affectionately, then flitted down the narrow stairs to where Chalmers, radiant, was waiting.

Mr. Bryce followed, wriggling his neck uncomfortably in his stiff collar, and as he descended a murmured soliloquy was on his lips: —

"I 'm all fer peace. Mary Annie ain't."

" For, sir, my daughter Helen's a match for any man," said Farmer Burchard, his hard face harder as he spoke. " She won't go to her husband empty-handed either. I cal'late to give Helen Forest Farm if she marries to suit me; and Forest Farm, Ezra Fairfax, is the prettiest property in Middlesex County."

The farmer and his hired man were driving along the road to the station, for Mr. Burchard was going off on a week's trip to buy some cattle.

Ezra made no reply to this boast. He had heard it a number of times, and as he loved Helen Burchard with his whole heart it was not pleasant to listen to, especially as he understood at this time it was a warning note intended to prevent any philandering in his employer's absence.

" I shall never have Forest Farm if that is the price I must pay," declared Helen herself a few hours later, looking into her lover's honest eyes. The two had grown up together, the children of neighbors. " I shall marry you or nobody, Ezra. I love father, but his ambitions can't make wrong right. Had he been the one to die instead of your father when we were children I might have been your mother's 'help' to-day." The girl smiled in a way that warmed Ezra's despairing heart.

"If there were only something I could do to change matters!" he exclaimed. "I hate the name of Forest Farm! I wish Hosea Hinkley had never sold it."

"He would n't if he could possibly have done without the money, that is certain," remarked the girl. "What a triumph father felt it to be when he secured it before good Mr. Hosea died."

"Yes; if that scamp of a brother of his had got hold of it, I guess Mr. Burchard might have whistled for Forest Farm. Jim Hinkley 's the biggest rascal unhung, and he hates your father. He 'd have liked to spite him by selling to somebody else. Well," Ezra heaved a mighty sigh, "for my part, I 'd be willing Jim had got it. I ought not to let you cling to the thought of me, Helen; it will spoil your life."

The girl gazed at him with frank tenderness. His sturdy form and bronzed face filled all her horizon. "Can you stop thinking of me?" she asked simply.

"God knows I can't," he answered, and then he lifted his old hat with a reverent gesture and kissed her.

The next day he was plodding along the street to the village filled with the problem that always absorbed him, when a stranger accosted him. He looked up and beheld an elderly gentleman with the stamp of city life upon his face, clothing, and manner.

"Young man," the latter began, "can you tell me the whereabouts of a place known as Forest Farm?"

"Yes," replied Ezra. "Walk right ahead and take the first turning to the left, and as soon as you cross the creek you 're there;" then, with a bluntness which amused his interlocutor, he continued: "Were you thinking of renting it?"

The stranger smiled leniently and tapped his hand with a legal paper he held. "No, I was n't thinking of renting it," he answered deliberately; "I am thinking of buying it. In fact, I — have just bought it. My daughter saw the place and thought she would like it for a summer home, and I have come down to take a look at it myself. My deed here will assist me in locating boundaries. I 'm much obliged to you."

The kindly stranger bowed and moved on, leaving Ezra to stare after him, his lips parted, his thoughts in a turmoil.

His face reddened under its bronze. In some uncomprehended way had his chance come? Might he do for Allan Burchard some service which should win him Helen?

He made a swift movement to follow the stranger, as suddenly changed his mind, and charged up the village street at a pace which scattered the children before him like leaves in the wind.

Squire Winslow, sitting at the desk in his second-story office, looked startled as steps dashed up the wooden stairs and the young man burst into the room. "Well! What's the matter, Ezra Fairfax?" exclaimed the old man, pushing his chair back, images of dire catastrophes crowding through his brain.

"I don't know," gasped the other, dragging a seat to the desk and falling into it. Then with catches of the breath he told his story.

The squire pushed up his spectacles and listened, frowning. "Certainly, I remember the transfer of Forest Farm," he said. "I drew the deed. You say Mr. Burchard is away. Could n't he have" —

"No, he has only been gone since yesterday, and he told me the day he left he was going to give the place to his daughter. Jim Hinkley's at the bottom of this, somehow or other."

Squire Winslow found time even amid his problem to admire Ezra's keen, set face.

"There's only one thing that could have made it possible for Jim to meddle, and I suppose that is just the thing that has happened," said the squire, after grasping his stubbly chin in deep thought. Ezra scrutinized him eagerly.

"I remember now. Mr. Burchard met Hosea here in this office and paid the money and took the deed. When I offered to mail it to the registry, Mr. Burchard said he wanted to show it to his wife first. He said he had business in Lowell the

next week and would take the deed to the registry
then himself. Now, perhaps, he forgot it; then,
knowing Hosea's honesty, put it off from time to
time, and it has never been recorded. Jim Hinkley has wanted money pretty bad lately, and they
do say Satan takes care of his own. Anyway, he
must have put that very idea into Jim's head.
Jim probably looked the matter up, found things
just as he suspected, got a customer for Forest
Farm, and sold it." Squire Winslow misunderstood the abstracted thoughtfulness that changed
his visitor's face.

"Brace up, my boy," he said kindly. "Get
back the grit I saw in your eyes a minute ago, and
perhaps we 'll beat Jim yet." He caught his
watch from his pocket. "No," he ejaculated,
"you can't get the deed and catch the last train
to Lowell."

"What — what 's the idea?" asked Ezra, sitting up, alert again.

"Why, the stranger said he 'd just bought Forest Farm. It 's likely he 's taking a look at the
property before recording his deed. If he records
his first you 've lost the farm; but if you could
any way get yours in " —

"I see!" Ezra sprang from his chair, a light
flashing all over his face.

Squire Winslow still had his watch in his hand
and his mouth open when, three steps at a time,
the young man was fleeing downstairs.

"Bless me!" muttered the lawyer, and his own hand trembled with excitement as he reached for his hat and followed after, as swiftly as his older limbs would carry him.

Ezra reached home in an incredibly short period. Mrs. Burchard saw him coming, and was startled by his look. She had a kindness for her daughter's lover, but did not dare to side with him.

"Where's the key to Mr. Burchard's desk?" he cried.

"In its place," she answered apprehensively.

"So it is," he gasped with relief, feeling behind the secretary and producing it. "I saw Helen out by the barn. Tell her to saddle Mark quick, please."

"Has Mr. Burchard" — she began.

"Quick!" implored Ezra, rummaging among the papers with desperate eagerness.

She obeyed and returned. "Where are you going, Ezra Fairfax?"

"To Lowell."

"On Mark? What will Mr. Burchard say? You know how he feels about that colt."

"Here it is!" exclaimed Ezra joyously.

"What?"

"The deed to Forest Farm. There's a purchaser" — The young man dashed out of the house, leaving the desk in confusion, and ran to the barn.

Helen was tightening the saddle girths.

"What is this for?" she asked, catching the excitement in his face.

"It's the only chance! I can't talk!" he exclaimed. He kissed her, sprang on the colt's back, and galloped off.

"Helen, that boy is crazy!" cried Mrs. Burchard in distress, running out to meet her daughter. "You don't suppose he would dare to try to sell Forest Farm! He has carried the deed off."

"Trust Ezra," said Helen stoutly. "I do;" but her heart thumped, and she too felt more troubled than ever before in her life. Might Ezra really have brooded over his troubles until his mind had become unhinged?

Meanwhile the swift colt had met the squire on the road, and the rider had reined up.

Silently he handed down the deed, which the old man examined eagerly. "Just as I thought," he said curtly; "not recorded. Have you money? Not enough, perhaps, for everything. Here, take this."

Ezra accepted the bill, and the brief instructions which the lawyer went on to give him.

"Better tell the Burchards, I guess. They'll worry either way. Thank you, Squire Winslow." Fairfax swiftly bent and wrung his old friend's hand.

"God bless you!" returned the lawyer unsteadily.

It would take too long to describe the details of

that ride. The road was a "short cut" compared to the roundabout way by rail from Edgecomb to Lowell. The brave colt did his best, rolling an eye around toward his rider occasionally as if to ask why, when so many steep hills had been traveled, he was still urged on; but when, jaded and worn, the two finally reached Lowell, the Registry of Deeds was closed. Ezra's voice was unsteady as he asked concerning the arrival of .the last train from Edgecomb. He found that it was in, but it too had arrived after registry hours. His chance still remained.

He saw to his horse's comfort; but for himself there was no sleep that night. Too much hung in the balance.

With the first rays of dawn he was walking about the streets, waiting for the appointed hour.

He turned his steps toward the best hotel in the place, and lounged near at breakfast time, but he did not see the face he sought among the guests. Suppose the stranger's deed had already been recorded before that experimental visit to Edgecomb! Ezra set his teeth.

But nine o'clock drew on. He dared linger no longer near the hotel, and moved away toward the court-house. As he approached the long brick building the hour sounded from a steeple. The bell electrified him and he hurried on; but suddenly a sight more moving still crossed his view. A well-dressed man, whom Fairfax recognized only too certainly, had just ascended the steps and was entering the Registry office. For an instant things turned black before the tired man; then he nerved himself, slouched his hat over his eyes, sprang up the steps after the gentleman, shouldered him aside, and edging through the room ahead of him, reached the desk first and offered his shaking paper.

"Where are your manners, young feller?" asked the registrar, glancing back at the somewhat annoyed and surprised look on the other man's face.

Ezra's cold lips stammered something about hurrying.

"There 's time enough in this world for folks to be civil. You 've got the day before you, have n't you?" said the clerk, looking, to Fairfax's acute apprehension, as if he might be going to order him aside in favor of the personage he had jostled.

The young man's excitement leaped from his eyes, but the slouched hat hid them. It was none of the registrar's business if this clumsy fellow's lips were ashy. He still grumbled as he reached for his rubber stamp.

The dull thud with which it struck the paper sounded above the ringing in Ezra's ears. Then the clerk glanced at the clock and proceeded to write in its place, in legal form, the moment of registration. Ezra's hungry eyes followed the carelessly moving hand which unconsciously held his fate.

"Nine hours and two minutes."

The words were written. Fairfax's unsteady fingers dropped a silver dollar with a clash on the desk. He staggered as he moved aside to let the portly gentleman take his turn.

The registrar with a casual remark pulled the second deed toward him, stamped it, then took up the pen and wrote: —

"Nine hours and three minutes."

Ezra held on by a corner of the desk, for the clock, the prints, and the maps on the walls were chasing one another madly around the room.

'Forest Farm was saved! And Helen?

Mr. Burchard returned home to find his strong, quiet "hired man" the hero of the village. Squire Winslow, delighted not a little with his own presence of mind in the affair, had exploited Ezra's victory far and wide.

"You know you always said, father, that Forest Farm was to go with me," remarked Helen demurely, " so, logically, I go with the farm — and the farm is really Ezra's."

She opened her eyes at her parent innocently and slipped her hand into her lover's, which was close by.

Mr. Burchard, still confounded by the risk his own carelessness had entailed, stared at them helplessly and yielded to the inevitable.

"Queer doings," he said to himself, and blinked his eyes. "Queer doings!"

"Just Nell's luck!" said her sisters, with good-natured envy — or, if that is a paradox, then we will say that acute wistfulness breathed in their tones.

Certain it is that they both wished they might be invited to visit at Mrs. Larrabee's country house on a ridge of Orange Mountain, to vibrate between the joys of New York and the loveliness of spring in that locality, where a large income is required to live near enough to nature's heart to see her wild beauty in the time of birds and blossoms.

The name of Larrabee had always stood to the Morton girls as representative of high life in all its fascinating ramifications. Their mother had been a fast friend of Mrs. Larrabee in girlhood, and Uncle Sam's postal system had preserved this friendship in spite, or perhaps because, of the distance across which the two widows' letters had traveled for many a year.

Every gala frock the Morton girls had ever possessed had been made over from some garment sent their mother by Mrs. Larrabee. This high-placed friend's Christmas money bought their muffs and skates. The photographs of the exterior and interior of her home were gazed upon by them with reverent awe. Indeed, were it not for the picture of their benefactress in Mrs. Morton's possession, the children would probably have grown up with an idea that Mrs. Larrabee floated above an inferior world on angelic pinions. As it was, her thin features inspired them with a fixed belief that flesh was undesirable, and her superiority to all the vulgar necessities of life went without saying.

Now a letter had arrived bearing an invitation to the eldest of the Morton girls to visit her. As in the case of royalty, an invitation from this quarter was equivalent to a command, especially when the request improved upon that of royalty and included a check for traveling expenses.

"I ask for Helen," wrote Mrs. Larrabee, "not only because she is the eldest, but because her picture looks so much more like her mother than the others'."

"Just Nell's luck!" said the others, upon this.

"Helen, if you please," corrected that young lady superbly. "Miss Helen Morton is going to visit Mrs. Larrabee, of Crest View. New York papers please take notice."

Upon this Miss Morton executed an astonishing pirouette, ending in a deep courtesy, which elicited a melancholy laugh from the Cinderellas she was leaving. It was bad enough that they were not bidden to see the glories of Crest View; but it was worse yet to exist a whole month without Nell.

So, though Gertrude and Lucy thought it would have been much more sensible in their mother's friend to have cheered her spacious mansion with the whole family of Morton, Helen alone set forth one morning, in the midst of warm embraces, much advice, and a few tears and flowers.

Harry Forsyth furnished the flowers, and had some difficulty in not adding to the tears. In his opinion, Mrs. Larrabee, if she belonged to the superhuman species at all, was an angel of darkness; and he returned Helen's parting gladsome smile with a gaze full of Byronic gloom. •

Miss Morton took out her fountain pen as soon as the train started and began a letter home. She knew what a gap her absence would make in certain quarters.

" Be good to Harry," she wrote. " Did you see the look with which he cheered the traveler on her way? It ought to have touched me, but I feel as if I had one of those red toy balloons inside me to-day in place of a heart; I feel so elated and inflated; and it would take more than a look from Harry Forsyth to puncture it and let the rapture out. But be good to him. He will like the one best who talks most about me, and I will bequeath him to either of you with pleasure. Seriously, I feel that I must do a lot of thinking, and make up my mind about H. by the time I come home. If

either of you would save me the trouble, I should
be so glad."

When Helen had changed cars in New York,
taken the suburban train, and reached the mountain station, she found her hostess waiting for her.

A footman in light-colored livery spoke her name
and took her bag. Mrs. Larrabee put forth her
hand from the glistening carriage which Helen entered, and, silver chains jingling and bay horses
prancing, they drove off with much state and cir-
cumstance.

Mrs. Larrabee bestowed upon her guest what
Helen decided was a spirituelle kiss, and they exchanged a gaze, on one side curiosity, on the other
eagerness and gratitude.

" Dear me! You 're not nearly so much like
your mother as I expected! "

The disappointed voice was like a dash of cold
water, but Helen replied gayly: " Then sometimes
photographic fidelity is n't faithful. I 'm sorry,
for we all like to look like mother."

" She was a nice girl." Mrs. Larrabee looked
away absently. There were two little worried lines
in her forehead, and they deepened as one of the
horses reared restively.

" Slowly, James," she called querulously. Helen
had been with her hostess but two minutes, and
yet she perceived already that Mrs. Larrabee not
only was not the angel of her transfiguring childish
dreams — she was not even a happy woman.

A little chill crept along her spine. " A month ! " thought the girl, and the loving warmth of her homely home-circle seemed very far away.

The satin touch of the elegant carriage-lining seemed to repel her as something alien. Her spirits rose. She was here because she had been urged to come. She could go away when she chose.

The horses pursued an ascending, winding road, a turn in which brought them to the gates of Crest View. A vast stretch of country suddenly unrolled itself far below.

" Oh, how fine ! " exclaimed the girl in delight.

" The view is very much admired," said Mrs. Larrabee dispassionately.

" And what splendid trees you have ! "

" Yes, vegetation flourishes in New Jersey."

" And what large greenhouses ! How I shall enjoy seeing them ! "

" The gardener is very proud of them."

" Does that fountain ever play ? " The enthusiastic girl looked eagerly toward the marble cherubs and dolphins grouped above an empty basin.

" Oh, yes," with cold listlessness, " if anybody cares."

" Well, some one has come who does care very much," said Helen smiling. " I like falling water as well as I do an orchestra."

Mrs. Larrabee regarded her curiously. "We have n't an orchestra just now," she remarked dryly.

The carriage stopped beneath the porte cochère, which Helen had often viewed with reverence in a photograph.

"Susannah will show you to your room, and the dinner-bell will ring in an hour," were the hostess's parting words.

Helen looked around upon her room with mingled emotions when the maid had left her. It was perfect in every appointment. After her ablutions she sat down at the dainty desk and continued the letter to her family begun on the cars.

"I have taken the plunge, — a cold plunge, I assure you. Imagine the sap all squeezed out of a poplar-tree, or picture an attenuated iceberg, and you have my hostess. I 'm going down to dinner in a minute. What will it be like? I suspect nobody but a professional sword-swallower could make a meal here. I anticipate pokers with mayonnaise, or yardsticks in cream!"

But it was a good dinner — indeed, a delicious dinner — that Helen found in the great dining-room with its inspiring views. Only the colorless hostess criticised the dishes and did not look out of the windows.

She glanced up at Helen during the salad course. "Can't you eat this either?" she asked in a vexed tone. "It has n't enough salt."

Helen winked the water away from her eyes and smiled in an embarrassed fashion. " It is very good, and I am hungry ; but when I chance to glance out there it is so beautiful that I choke up and can't swallow."

" Dear me! " said Mrs. Larrabee. " You are n't at all like your mother. I don't remember that she was imaginative."

The visitor bit her lip, but she answered bravely : —

" I 've only been sent on approval ; you can return me if I don't suit. I 'm afraid, though," — here her voice faltered slightly, but she was proud all night of the fact that she commanded it and did n't cry, — " I 'm only afraid that we can't refund the money."

" What are you talking about, child? I 'm glad you 're here. I don't like to feel that there 's nobody in the house I can speak to. But I 'm sorry you can't see my cousin, Rebecca Harding. She is the most agreeable woman I ever knew."

Curiosity surged up in Helen's brain to know what traits Mrs. Larrabee would recommend so highly. " I suppose Mrs. Harding enjoys this beautiful place," she said tentatively.

" She thinks it is very exposed, and so it is."

" But in warm weather? "

" Oh, we spend the summer at the seashore, although the dampness there aggravates Rebecca's neuralgia."

Miss Morton hurriedly put a piece of shrimp in her mouth. The picture of the two pampered women chasing discomfort through the changing seasons made her feel the necessity of something to bite on, lest she astonish her hostess and disgrace herself.

Two little homesick tears paid tribute to the situation about midnight, when the guest had for a long time been vainly wooing sleep in her luxurious bed; but when they had once been dried she knew nothing more until morning, and then her elastic spirits rebounded with delight at the beauty about her.

"I wish my eyes were telescopes," she said to Mrs. Larrabee at breakfast, where that lady appeared thinner, paler, more introspective than at evening.

"Oh, the views," she replied in a tone that plainly implied that there was no accounting for tastes. "There are some field-glasses about. Susannah shall get them for you after breakfast."

"And you will come out with me and tell me what things are, won't you?" said the girl recklessly.

Mrs. Larrabee looked at her in astonishment. "The grass will be wet for an hour!" she announced.

But Helen felt unquenchable. Her cheeks were glowing and her eyes sparkling with life. "I do think you ought to be the happiest woman in the world!" she said. "With such a home as this and such power to do good! Why, do you know, we girls at home have always considered you as nothing less than a patron saint!"

"Humph! I'm afraid a near view will be disillusioning," was Mrs. Larrabee's reply. Nevertheless her face looked as if a tiny drop of the oil of gladness had softened it.

"I do wish," said Helen timidly, "that you felt strong enough to enjoy your surroundings more."

"That is what Raymond says."

"Oh, I remember. Your son's name is Raymond. Mother has a picture of him in a velvet suit."

"Yes. He has gone West on business. He and Rebecca left me at the same time. I hope you can put up for a while with an invalid who has very little to offer you beside scenery."

Helen's generous heart experienced a quick revulsion of feeling. She determined not to send the letter that lay unfinished upstairs in the drawer of her writing-desk. "If I could give you my eyes for a while you would know how happy I shall be," she said warmly.

And just as hostess and guest had come at last to what seemed a pleasant understanding the disturbing cause made his appearance on the scene.

A flute-like whistle, the barking of dogs, a laugh and shout, suddenly made confusion outside the spacious windows.

Mrs. Larrabee looked up sharply. " What, Simpson ? " she said, addressing the butler.

And before the servant could reply a broad-shouldered, plain-featured, square-jawed man of twenty-five strode into the room with an air of tardily suppressing laughter and strength to the prescribed limits of the place.

" The bad penny, mother," he said, advancing and kissing her cheek carefully.

" Raymond, you give me palpitation ! " she declared, her hand on her heart.

" I 'm sorry," he answered mechanically; for whether he had played football, or broken a colt, or raced a yacht, or only admired a new girl, he had always been giving his mother palpitation. " I considered a telegram, but concluded that seeing me in a condition of rude health would be less of a shock. At the last minute it was decided that I should n't go West; that 's all."

Meanwhile the speaker had glanced at his mother's guest, and Mrs. Larrabee introduced him.

" You remember hearing about the Morton girls, Raymond, — the children of my old schoolmate."

There was more of warning than of enthusiasm in the mother's tone, but Raymond did not notice it, and Helen only vaguely perceived that just as her hostess ignored the beauties of nature and art about her so she failed to revel in this wealth of youth and vitality which seemed to invest the splendid home with its rightful soul.

Susannah was not obliged to search for the field-glasses. No longer did the guest lack a response to her enthusiasm, while as for Raymond Larrabee the good comradeship of this fearless girl was a surprise and pleasure whose novelty did not wear away with the weeks.

"It seems to me your business hours are shortening," said Mrs. Larrabee to him tartly one day when he came in early from the city. Helen had been reading aloud, and here laid down the book. "I sent for Helen to be company for me in my loneliness. If you are going to begin to spend most of your time at home, I need not have troubled her."

"It is such awfully nice weather for a ride, mother; but we'll drive if you would rather go with us."

"Thank you. I think I will accept your considerate offer," was the dignified reply.

So Raymond swallowed his disappointment. The saddle-horses were left in the stables, and Mrs. Larrabee held a silken wrap against her cheek to keep the wind from an offending tooth, and kept Helen beside her on the back seat of the carriage, while Raymond yawned and drove the horses at the unexciting pace she exacted.

That evening Helen remained in her room with plenty of food for thought. She was trying to subdue the indignation in her heart that had finally arisen as the slow conviction of Mrs. Larrabee's oft-displayed fears took possession of her.

She had fulfilled her part of their unwritten contract to the letter. No paid companion could be more attentive and devoted than she had been. Helen's conscience acquitted her. To go home before the time was come would be to own herself worsted. But one week was left. She would brave it out.

The next morning she and Raymond took the gallop which was their regular appetizer for the late breakfast Mrs. Larrabee preferred. The sun fell dazzlingly on the dewy grass. A bluebird called to the folded buds. As they cantered homeward in the full spring-tide of life, of year, of day, Helen reined in her horse.

" Ray," she began, the lashes shading her sparkling eyes, " before we reach the house I want to say something disagreeable."

He glanced at her, obvious admiration on his plain features. " You could n't.   Don't try."

She laughed. " How funny — for you to pay compliments ! "

" Not funny at all. I think that was rather neat."

" Well, I 'm glad you are in that mood, for what I have to ask of you demands a great deal of chivalry."

" What 's up, now ? "

" Why — oh, it 's not at all easy, you know," Helen stammered and blushed, notwithstanding the business-like tone in which she contrived to frame her sentence. " I want you to be — so awfully good as to — to let me — refuse you."

Raymond looked slowly at her and flicked his riding-boot with his whip. "Oh! is that all? Well, you would be the first girl to have the chance."

" And you know," she returned ingratiatingly, and rather short of breath, "there must be a first."

" You think so?" with a short laugh. " Thank you."

" No, no! That is n't what I meant! I 'm confused, and you must forgive me; but the point is that your mother is evidently afraid that you — that I — yes, she thinks — and I have to stay here a week longer" — oh, how hard he made it, staring at her so gravely! — "and we 've been such good friends, it would make it so much pleasanter for us all if you could just tell her that I did n't — but " — suddenly, and crimson with blushes — " I see you 're not willing. It 's no matter ; I can stand it "— She suddenly struck her horse with her whip.

The creature bounded forward, but Raymond was too quick. He seized its bridle, and simultaneously threw his other arm around her waist to preserve her from the shock.

" I nearly fell! " she exclaimed reproachfully.

" No, you did n't," he answered, and quieting the horses, he continued : —

"Of course, I've noticed what you refer to; and what you say leads up to what is on my mind. I've wanted to ask your advice about something myself — or not so much your advice as your sympathy and coöperation. Mother has always been jealous when she even suspected there was a girl in the case. Now I want to confess to you that I am in love; not passingly and superficially, but with a feeling that will only deepen all my life. Mother has not consented. She won't listen to me. I want to show you this woman. She meets me sometimes in the grounds here. She is coming to-night. I want you to be at our meeting-place, if you will." Raymond's lips, Helen noted, had grown pale, and his words came with difficulty. " Now, where do you think filial duty should cease and a man's own life-happiness should begin to be considered ? "

Helen, too, had lost color in her surprise. "I don't know the woman, remember. It is too much responsibility to take! Don't ask me."

"Yes, I ask you to come and see her. If she is all I believe her to be, have I not the right to claim my own? Don't refuse me this! At the head of the ravine at ten o'clock to-night. I claim it in the name of our friendship."

Helen gazed between her horse's ears.

" I will come," she said at last. Then in silence the two cantered homeward.

Helen sat long before her desk that morning,

meditating over her home-letter; but at last she wrote:—

"I have made up my mind about Harry Forsyth. What I am afraid he wants can never be. But I am so homesick! It seems to me the coming week will never pass. I shall count the hours and minutes; and rest assured you will never get rid of me again!"

All day her mood was so strangely quiet that Mrs. Larrabee was especially kind. Raymond made a long afternoon in town, and at dinner was abstracted. His mother made up her mind that the young people had had a misunderstanding, and she devoutly hoped it would last until Helen was safely started on her homeward journey.

In the evening Raymond went to make a call, and Helen read aloud to her hostess. The latter always retired early, out of respect to her invalidism, and a little before ten the girl went to the window, hoping that some sign of weather would release her from her promise. The full golden moon returned her gaze calmly. The tall trees beckoned in the hush of night.

Helen turned resolutely to her dressing-table. Without a glance at her own pale face, she threw a wrap about her head and shoulders and hurried out. Softly leaving the house, she ran across the smooth lawn in and out of shadows until she reached the adjacent ravine, whose steep depth was musical with a narrow tumbling brook.

A man stepped into the moonlight.

"Thank you, Helen!" he said warmly, holding out his hand. She was arranging the lace about her head and did not meet his movement.

"Are we early? It is ten, isn't it?" she asked.

"Perhaps; but while we wait, won't you answer my question of this morning? I think a great deal of your opinion. You know mother, and you know me. How long should I continue to pay regard to her in this matter? I beg for your sympathy and coöperation."

He looked so big and sturdy standing there, so masterful and able to conduct his own affairs, Helen felt a thrill at the idea of his depending upon her in any degree.

"What are you afraid of?" she asked, with a hardness and dryness that shocked herself. "Afraid that your mother might have heart-failure if you persisted, or that she would cut you off with a shilling?"

The man's eyes shone with eagerness as he tried to read her face, but her back was to the soft moonlight.

"You have changed to me, Helen! Why?"

"Nothing — except that our life was play, and now it is earnest. Answer if I am to help you."

"It is very likely that mother would cut me off with a shilling."

"And that restrains you?"

He could feel her scorn if he could not see it. "Should it not, for the girl's sake? This is a nice place."

"What is a *place* worth? Are n't you a strong man? You can be as kind to your mother as ever — kinder than ever; but she should n't control you in this — especially since you have made this girl — love you."

"I have hoped sometimes that I have; but how can I be sure?"

"Sure? Does n't she meet you here at night?" The acute voice changed to one that faltered. "I wish she would hurry. I am cold."

Raymond advanced a step and enfolded her in his arms.

She fluttered. "What are you doing?"

"Warming you. Lean your head against me, Helen; that is the sympathy I want. Give me your lips; that is the coöperation I long for. You must love me, for I love every inch of you, every thought of you, every look of you. Do you remember what you asked me this morning? Now, then, refuse me if you dare!"

His cheek was pressed against her hair, and she was trembling and clinging to him.

"Oh, Raymond!" she whispered, after a long pause. "Let us sit up all night. We may never have another!"

"Why, sweetheart, where has all that courage flown?"

“ Oh — we could n’t hurt her feelings ! ”

“ Could n’t ? I only hope she can’t hurt ours.”

“ Why — she can’t,” said Helen softly.

And, sure enough, Mrs. Larrabee could n’t, though she tried to conscientiously.

The lovers appeared before her in the morning, her son announced cheerfully his desire to be disinherited, and her visitor declared her willingness to return home immediately in punishment for having stolen her hostess’s most valuable possession.

In short, they so completely took the wind out of the outraged mother’s sails that there was little left her to do but press both hands upon her heart and have palpitation unlimited, while she glared upon them speechless for a minute.

“ You are both of you selfish and ungrateful,” she announced at last.

“ Please don’t call me ungrateful ! ” pleaded Helen, throwing herself suddenly on her knees beside the indignant woman. “ I ’ve always been grateful to you over and over again all my life ; and did n’t you send for me and make me stay here, and throw temptation in my way ? And how could I help loving him ? And I never knew it at all till yesterday, and now I ’m going home ” —

“ Indeed you are n’t ! Not until Rebecca Harding comes ! Don’t say another word about it ! ”

“ And shall I send Mr. Bingham out to see

about changing your will?" asked Raymond dutifully.

"Thank you. I am able to attend to my own business. You had better go into New York and begin to work in earnest."

"Yes, I'm going, mother." He stooped and kissed her, and in so doing drew Helen into the same embrace, so that Mrs. Larrabee was not only in a tight place, but a loving one.

She bore it for a stiff instant, and then she began to cry.

Raymond signaled eagerly across her bowed head to his fiancée: "It's all right."

And Helen nodded back through bright tears: "It's all right."

Gertrude Morton, when she heard of it, said again: "Just Nell's luck!" Then added: "Poor Harry Forsyth!"

Her sister Lucy smiled complacently and patted her fluffy hair. "Oh, I don't know," she remarked.